Parrots Prove Deadly

Books by Clea Simon

The Pru Marlowe Pet Noir Series
Dogs Don't Lie
Cats Can't Shoot
Parrots Prove Deadly

The Theda Krakow Series
Mew Is for Murder
Cattery Row
Cries and Whiskers
Probable Claws

The Dulcie Schwartz Series
Shades of Grey
Grey Matters
Grey Zone
Grey Expectations

Nonfiction
Mad House:
Growing Up in the Shadow of Mentally Ill Siblings
Fatherless Women:
How We Change After We Lose Our Dads
The Feline Mystique:
On the Mysterious Connection Between Women and Cats

Parrots Prove Deadly

A Pru Marlowe Pet Noir

Clea Simon

Poisoned Pen Press

Library of Congress Catalog Card Number: 2012910496

ISBN: 9781464201028   Hardcover
        9781464201042   Trade Paperback

Poisoned Pen Press
6962 E. First Ave., Ste. 103
Scottsdale, AZ 85251
www.poisonedpenpress.com
info@poisonedpenpress.com

Printed in the United States of America

For Jon

Chapter One

Polly didn't want a cracker. Polly didn't want much of anything anymore. Polly Larkin, aka "Room 203," had been dead several hours when her aide came to wake her, early on the morning of September third, and her days of haranguing the staff were done.

Nobody was surprised much by Polly's demise, least of all the aide. That she'd toppled to the floor at some point in the night, knocking over her walker, was unfortunate, but not shocking. Polly had been sickly for as long as anyone could remember—sickly and stubborn, refusing requests that she stay in bed until her aide or a night nurse could be summoned—and at 84, nobody expected her to last much longer. But even an anticipated death sets off repercussions in the world of the living, and while the assisted living staff was handling the arrangements, I had to deal with the parrot.

Randolph Jones, that was the parrot's name, and whether that was the deceased's idea of a joke or a handle the old lady had inherited when she adopted the bird was not shared with me. What I did get was an urgent phone call from the daughter, begging me to call her back on a matter of utmost importance.

"Please." The voice on the message gasped. "I need your help. It's life or death."

◇◇◇

I was making coffee when I heard the message, and I confess it didn't make me pause. I didn't know at that point that the old lady had passed three days before, but I've been in this business long enough to know that "life or death" rarely is. I'm an animal behaviorist, or almost, not a cardiologist or brain surgeon, which means I work with people's pets rather than anything they really care about. Used to be, I'd spend my time trying to understand why domesticated animals did what they did. If Spot's pooping on the floor, you know he's got a reason, same as you would. What the clients pay me for, though, isn't an explanation, it's behavior modification. They want the behavior changed, and my job is to change it.

I've gotten used to that. Hey, it beats watching Spot taken to the pound. Or worse, "released" by the roadside miles out of town, as they still do in my semi-rural burg. I've developed a repertoire of training tricks, reeducation if you will, to help everyone adjust. My refusal to pick up the phone before nine a.m. is an attempt to use the same techniques on the owners. It rarely works, but it's the principle as much as anything. Besides, I knew I'd be no good before I had my caffeine. In addition, while I was grinding the beans, Wallis had come into the room, and serving her breakfast trumps everything. And so while the coffee was brewing, I cracked open two eggs and scrambled them in butter. She kneaded the floor in anticipation, and so I didn't even wait for them to cool before scooping them onto a plate and placing them on the floor.

Wallis may be a cat—a mature tabby who has shared the last twelve years of her life with me—but she has more sense than most humans. If I had to talk down some hysterical would-be client, I wanted her in the room—and in the mood to consult. Besides, I cared about her happiness. The caller? Well, we'd see about that.

"Jane? Jane Larkin? This is Pru Marlowe, returning your call." I'd taken my mug over to the big farmhouse table that serves as a general workspace. "You said you had a problem?"

From the stuttering on the other end, I thought she'd forgotten me already. That was fine. I didn't need another client, especially not one who indulged in histrionics.

"Oh, Miss Marlowe, thank you." She had someone else in the room, I realized. I raised my eyebrows to Wallis, who started to bathe. "Things are just so crazy here."

I looked at the clock. Five past nine, late enough for me to begin my morning rounds. "I can call you back later."

"No, please. Can you come over today? The vet at the county animal hospital said you were a miracle worker, and I need... well, could you just come over?" I heard a deep sigh. "I've got a real problem with a very aggravated parrot."

I still hadn't heard how an angry bird translated to life or death, but I agreed to head over once I was done with my regular visits. She'd given me an address on the new side of Beauville, in the complex called LiveWell. Even I knew that euphemistic tag meant it was for old people, so I was rather surprised to find the array of activities listed in the beige and pink front lobby: movie nights, field trips. What have you. All on a billboard crowned with a stylized LW that would do minor royalty proud. And I was even more shocked when—once I'd smiled and nodded my way past the similarly colored receptionist—the door marked 203, along with that same logo, opened.

"Jane?" The woman in front of me couldn't have been more than fifty. A very tired fifty.

Before she could respond, I heard a voice yell out behind her. "Who the hell is it?" The woman at the door winced.

"I'm sorry," the woman whispered. "You can hear why I called." She led me in.

"Mind your own damned business!" The room was over-heated and dark, heavy shades covering the big picture window. I remembered how distracted she'd been that morning and dreaded meeting her companion. "Bugger off!"

"I just got here," my host said, walking to the window. When she pulled back the drape, I saw that the room was close for a reason. Small to start with, the studio was overstuffed. Boxes, some taped shut, were stacked against empty book shelves and more lay, waiting to be assembled, on what looked like a hospital bed. Photos had been taken down, showing lighter spots against the deep cream wall. Some were piled on top of the mini fridge, and more lay on a small table top, threatening to tumble.

"Your own damned business!" The woman winced again, and I turned toward the voice. In the corner, suspended from a frame, hung a birdcage. Inside the cage a large gray bird shuffled on his perch, turned his head, and seemed to appraise me with one cool eye. An African gray, known for their skills at mimicry and their longevity. In some circles, they're also known for their intelligence.

"And who the hell are you?" He asked me, punctuating his question with a squawk. "The cleaning lady?"

Chapter Two

"This, I take it, is the problem parrot?" I was addressing the woman who'd let me in, but I was looking at the bird. Large as a football, though a little more slim, he had a coat of rippled gray, like sea foam on the edge of wave. Behind him, I could see the distinctive red tail feathers of the breed. When I looked up, I saw the parrot considering me, the black iris sharp in that round yellow eye. Parrots have only limited binocular vision, it's true. But I couldn't escape the feeling the bird was looking at me askance, especially as he tilted his head to scan me from head to foot. "Are you the owner?"

"Oh, no!" I heard my host rustling around behind me, but I didn't turn. I'm not crazy about birds; they tend to be hyper-manic. Nervous. Parrots, though, can be different. Just by virtue of the fact that they live so long—seventy, eighty years—some of them have a little more gravitas than their feathered fellows. If there was anything here, I needed to get it.

"Squaw!" The bird turned to size me up with his other eye: a second opinion. I didn't know if I was being stonewalled. The woman in the room wasn't going to let me find out.

"Randolph—that's the parrot—he's my mother's." She interrupted my concentration with a voice only a little less annoying than the parrot's. "*Was* my mother's, I mean." I nodded and murmured something I hope sounded like sympathy. So that explained the boxes, as well as the worn look my hostess was wearing. "She passed away three days ago."

I turned then, bumping into a folding walker. This didn't look like three days' worth of packing, and as I well knew, the first duties after death don't usually involve bookcases.

Something must have shown on my face.

"This all…it's something to do." Jane looked around as if surprised by all the boxes. "I need to clean this all out. Sort through everything…."

I nodded, as if that explained everything. Maybe it did. I'd nursed my mother through her last illness less than two years earlier. She'd died at home, though, and the hospice worker had cleared away the hospital bed and IV set-up almost without me noticing. Still, by the last weeks, I was doing laundry voluntarily and had even cleaned out the fireplace. Anything rather than sit, listening to those labored breaths.

"And the parrot?" I turned back to the bird, looking harder. Something was off: the cascading pattern on the parrot's breast had been disrupted. There were pink spots showing through, bare skin that shouldn't have been visible. Birds tend to overgroom when they're upset. The death of a longtime caretaker could do that, as could the noise and disruption of packing—and of grief.

"Well, you've heard him." The parrot cocked his smooth head, listening. "I've left him here, where he's comfortable, hoping he'd settle down. But I can't take him; my apartment is strictly 'no pets.' And my brother won't. Not while he—"

"Bugger off, fruitcake!" The big beak moved. "Bah!"

Jane paused. The bird and I continued to eye each other, my two to his one. "Not while he keeps doing that. I need you to retrain him."

"Your own damned business," the bird muttered, and then whistled low and long. "Ignorant slut."

In any other situation, this might have been funny. Someone had taught this bird a litany of insults, and from the way the woman behind me had winced, I gathered she'd been hearing them for a while now. For me, the bird posed a larger problem, not one I could share with this potential client.

For starters, I'm not really a behaviorist. Not yet, and although I'm only a few credits and a thesis short of being certified, it's enough so that I tend to fly under the radar. She'd gotten my name from Dr. Sharpe, the vet at the county shelter, so I was probably good for the job. But if she started asking experts, they'd have questions for me, too. The real problem, though, was a little more involved.

You see, I'm not only an expert on animal behavior; I'm also an animal psychic. Not the kind who advertises in the back of pet magazines, the kind who tells you that, yes, Fluffy is happy over the Rainbow Bridge, and, no, Goldie doesn't blame you for flushing her. What I have is more like sensitivity. I don't hear messages per se. Animals don't function that way. I hear how animals are responding to their environment—and to us. That usually means some combination of fear, hunger, or lust. Aggression, too, but that's secondary. Unlike in our own species, what we would call anger is invariably linked to one of the other primary motivations: *My mate! My nest! My kill!*

Except in this case. I wasn't a specialist in birds. Didn't know much about them beyond what I'd learned back in class. But as I stood there, trying to make contact with those round little eyes, I could swear this parrot was seething with rage and something else. I would almost call it guilt.

"To hell with you," the bird said, with a squawk and a dismissive whistle. That whistle was the most animal-like sound he had made yet. Almost, it made me think the bird didn't mean every word. "Bugger off."

With a shrug that I meant as half apology, half acquiescence, I turned back to the woman. Up close, she looked younger than I'd thought. Younger, and a lot more tired. Grief could do that to you, I knew. But there was something worn down about her. The gray in her dirty blonde hair hadn't been washed out, but most of the color in her cheeks had. And from the chapped and bleeding look of her lips, she'd been biting back something for an awfully long time.

"So you are—you were—your mother's caregiver?" I wanted to tread carefully here. The rage I'd felt came from the parrot, but it could have been picked up from the deceased—or her daughter.

"No, no." Jane's lanky hair barely moved as she shook her head. "Jeanie was her aide for the last few months."

"Full time?" I didn't know what LiveWell charged its inmates, but I was betting one-on-one care cost extra.

Another shake. That hair looked dirty. "Days. My mother needed help getting out of bed, showering, getting dressed. And the management here said that if she was going to stay...."

I nodded. I'd briefly looked into places like this for my own mother. They're great if you can function, but once you really start showing your age the rules change. "She helping with all this?" I nodded toward the books, but I was thinking about the bird. Odds are, the woman who had spent her days here would be more likely to have some insight into the animal. Maybe she'd even want to adopt it. "Is she around?"

"Oh, no." She bit down on the words. "I couldn't afford to keep paying her." I could see how those lips got so chapped. I could also begin to imagine where the rage came from. Someone had lost a paying gig rather abruptly.

As if to bring me back to the topic at hand, the parrot whistled. Loudly. I walked back to the cage. The bird—Randolph—shuffled on his perch and turned again, keeping me in sight.

"I didn't know they let the—ah—residents keep birds." Somehow, I'd had the idea that old people's homes—and that's what it was, despite the fancy color scheme—had strict rules about pets, if not profanity.

"Small animals, including birds, are allowed, provided the resident can maintain sanitary conditions." Jane sounded like she was quoting. "And companion animals, of course."

"And mental hygiene?" I realized I was smiling.

"Letter of the law," Jane shrugged. "And my mother was not one who could be easily deprived of her rights."

"I'll bet." I said, under my breath. Randolph whistled once again.

◇◇◇

As much as I was enjoying the visit, I needed to get down to brass tacks. I told Jane my rates. When she agreed, I wondered how much the aide had charged. Then again, the worst I'd have to do was change the paper in the cage. With the big bird looking on, I asked some basic questions about the age, care, and health of the bird, and ended up getting a little more info on his late owner as well. None of it seemed out of the ordinary. Then again, none of it looked very helpful, either. By the time I'd gotten around to the parrot's routine, I could see that my human client was fidgeting. She, at least, was ready to fly.

A good part of training is knowing how to read an animal's cues. I could have used more information, but it was time to wrap things up.

"I'd like to leave him—it—Randolph," I caught myself, "here, for the time being." This bird had already been through enough change, and there was no way I was taking him home to Wallis. "Birds are very sensitive to shock."

"Oh." Jane was probably not the most articulate, even at the best of times. For a moment, I wondered if my explanation had sparked an idea. A dead bird would be convenient, I suspected. One more possession sorted—and discarded.

"These birds can be quite valuable." I covered quickly. I wasn't going to be party to an avicide of convenience.

"Mother loved Randolph." That wasn't an answer, but I took it. "Only, well, how long do you think this will take?"

"A few weeks, probably." I was winging it, so to speak. I'd never reeducated a parrot. The look of shock on her face brought me back to earth. The rent, of course. "Don't you have till the end of the month?"

"I'm trying to have everything cleaned out by the fifteenth. They've promised me a rebate…"

I nodded. "That gives us almost two weeks. Let's see what we can do." If Jane was that hard up, I wanted my money up front. "Should I bill you? Or is there someone handling the estate?"

"My brother, Marc." She looked around like her sibling might suddenly pop out of a box. "Only he—let me write you a check."

Curiouser and curiouser, I thought, as she retrieved a beat-up bag from the corner and fished a plastic-covered checkbook from its recesses. I took the check, though. I don't get paid enough to handle family dramas.

"When can you start?" She stood up straighter. Hiring some-one can do that. Transfers dominance. We're all animals.

"This afternoon. Now, even." It was past two, and I'd done my jobs for the day. "Will I be in your way?" The apartment wasn't that big, but maybe I could take the bird into the corner.

"No, I should go." She looked around at the mess and her shoulders sagged. I'd been right about the fidgeting, not that she was happy about whatever awaited. "Marc's meeting me. He's really busy, and we're supposed to talk about some things." She didn't look thrilled. "Do you want to meet him?"

I shrugged. Anyone who knew the bird might help me understand him. "Couldn't hurt."

"Maybe you could convince him to, you know, take Randolph?"

"Mind your own business, you ignorant slut." The voice—loud, harsh, and strangely asexual—interrupted whatever vague answer I'd been planning to give. African grays are talented mimics, and I could only guess at whom Randolph was doing now. Jane winced, but she didn't follow up when I smiled rather than give her an answer. Just as well, I was distracted. The parrot's voice had gotten louder, and something about his cool glance made me wonder if our exchange had prompted his words. "Bugger off!"

So she did, heading off to meet with her brother and leav-ing me in the close apartment with Randolph the angry parrot. Every surface outside the bird's cage was covered with books or knickknacks, so I wandered over to the windowsill and leaned back, the better to study my new charge.

"So, Randolph—" I paused. "Is that your name?" Now that we were alone, I needed to make some kind of connection with this creature. Often the first step to doing that is to acknowledge the animal's sense of himself—what he calls himself. This bird, however, was silent. A little shuffling on the perch with those scaly feet was all.

"Okay, then, how are you doing?" I was speaking out loud. More important, I was reaching out with my thoughts, trying to see the room as the bird might see it. "Do you miss your person, Polly?" With the light behind me, the parrot's ruffled breast feathers were obvious, as were the spots he'd picked bare. Animals experience grief, just as we do. Even when there is no affection, the habit of another's presence can become part of our lives—it's a habit that can be hard to break.

Nothing. Then it hit me. Randolph had lived—I checked my notes—for seven years with Polly Larkin. She had died here. Not in her bed, as I'd first imagined, but on the floor, after taking a nighttime tumble. I thought about the aide—and about Jane. Even if there had been money for twenty-four hour care, aides have been known to snooze—and the impulse to get up in order to go to the bathroom dies hard. I looked around the room again. It was small enough that the bed and both doors—to the bathroom as well as the hallway—would be visible from the cage. Small enough so that one old lady, with her walker by her bed, probably thought she could make it. She'd been wrong though. Such an event could easily leave an animal traumatized. I would have to get at that, work through the shock, before we could move on.

"Did you witness Polly's death?" I wasn't sure how to phrase it. "Your person?" I looked at the walker and down at the floor. I didn't know how far she'd gotten.

"Squawk!" The yelp—and something else—made me jump. For a moment, I had felt something. Pain? Panic? My words, or maybe my focus on the walker, had hit a nerve.

"Polly?" I moved over to the walker. Tried to imagine an old lady, small and frail, positioned behind its curved metal frame.

It was light. Hollow, but supposedly strong enough. I leaned on its rubber grip.

"Put that down, put that down. Stop. That's mine." I resisted the impulse to pull back. The bird wasn't talking to me, not like other animals do. This was a parrot. It was mimicking someone—the eerie voice had gone higher and scratchy. An old lady's irritation showing through. Either the walker, or my movement, had triggered this, and I needed to let the parrot roll. Anything could be useful for getting inside that sleek gray head.

"Stop! What are you doing? Stop it! What? Waah!"

The next sound made me fear the bird was choking, and I bolted for the cage, banging my shin against one of the boxes. It went over with a thud, landing up against the walker, and I ignored it, trying to remember anything I could about avian first aid.

That wasn't much, and I had only time to open the cage before the big bird faced me and barked out something that sounded like "Ka-duh-klump"—a sound that was echoed a split second later as, behind me, the walker tumbled to the carpet in a jumble of metal tubing. The sequence confused me, for a moment, and I turned from the bird to the walker and back again. The parrot was still now, standing and breathing normally. Still, something was off.

"Randolph," I addressed the bird. I didn't really see an option. "What did you say?"

"Ka-duh-KLUMP!" The bird repeated, louder this time. Sounding for all the world like a walker, holding up the infinitesimal weight of a frail old lady, as it tumbled first against a table, and then to the floor.

Chapter Three

I'm not insane. No matter what some of my clients would say, were they to know how I really got the dirt on Flower's biting habit or Pinky's litter problems. I do have a rudimentary knowledge of animal behavior.

Parrots are smart—for birds. Some studies suggest they have the intellect of a human toddler, with a similar ability to string words together for simple—very simple—sentences, and that they do have a sense of what they say—the meaning of words. But they don't usually pick things up immediately. Certainly not after one hearing. So just because I had heard something that could have been an aural recreation of Polly Larkin's death—a death apparently brought about by an interaction with an intruder—didn't mean that was actually what Randolph the parrot was reproducing for me.

Still, when the door opened behind me, I jumped.

"Who the hell are you?" A man, short, dark, and stocky, stood bull-like just inside the door. "And what the hell are you doing here?"

"I'm Pru Marlowe, the behaviorist." I reached for the knife I always carry. The bullish little man wasn't moving toward me, but I wasn't going to take any chances. Sure enough, the knife was in my pocket, its handle cool to the touch. "And you are?"

"Oh, huh." His already limited vocabulary seemingly exhausted, the man relaxed. "Sorry."

I waited.

"Marc! There you are." Jane appeared behind him, in the doorway. "Miss Marlowe, this is my brother? Marc?"

I looked from my client to her sibling, unable to see any resemblance between her pale hesitation and his florid bulk. "Charmed." I put an extra dollop of acid in it. Hey, he'd startled me.

He had the good grace to blush, his olive cheeks turning red as he raised one hand to brush over his close-cropped hair. "I'm sorry, Miss. It's just, well, we've had some problems."

"I understand." I wouldn't have phrased the death of a parent that way, but we all experience grief in our own way. "I'm sorry for your loss."

"No, that's not it. I mean, thanks." The blush was deeper now. "I didn't mean my mother. Since, well, before really, there've been some problems with things going missing. Some important family things. The aides, you know."

"Ah." What had the parrot said? *Put that down. That's mine.* A dozen questions sprang to mind.

"But what are you doing *here?*" Jane stepped between us before I could phrase any of them. "If I hadn't seen you—you said Tupenny's."

I remembered that she had left in a hurry. The self-consciously cozy tea house was on the other end of Beauville's main drag.

"Did I? Gee, sis, you sure?" Jane was blocking my view of the little man, so I stepped to the side. His color had faded back to normal as far as I could see. "Now that you're here, though, maybe we can get some things settled."

He looked at me as he said that, and I didn't like it. I get paid to work with animals. Families, that's a whole different species of trouble.

"I mean, Jane and me." He was still looking at me. I know I'm easy on the eye, even with my long hair tied back and my curves camouflaged in denim. Something else was going on here, though. Something between this man and his sister—something I had fallen into. "We've got some things to discuss."

"Do you want me to go?" Behind me, the bird was quiet. I wished I too could just listen in here.

"No," said Jane. "Yeah," said Marc. I looked at Jane. She was the one paying me.

"I want her to work with Randolph." She was standing straighter and was clearly taller than her brother. "That's what Mother would have wanted. And you said, if the bird didn't curse so much…"

"So *much*? I have kids, Jane." This sounded like well-worn territory, and I waited for her response. "You don't have anything else to take care of."

"You know my landlord won't allow pets." She sagged visibly. Usually I reserve my sympathy for animals. They're the ones who can't defend themselves in our world, but this was too much. I could be wrong, but I was betting that Jane had done the lion's share of caring for their mother—the lioness', actually—and was now in charge of cleaning up.

"If you'll excuse me." From the look I got, I almost thought they'd forgotten me. "I think I may be able to retrain the parrot. They're very intelligent birds, you know." A faint chirp behind me made me feel the compliment was appreciated. "If not, I can help you find some options."

"Mother wouldn't want Randolph to go to strangers." There was a prissy tone in her voice that I knew would have gotten to me.

"I'm not exposing my kids to that kind of language." Then again, he wasn't much better. "They're *kids*, for Christ's sake."

I raised my hands for quiet before the parrot could chime in, too. "Please, we have this room till the end of the month, right." Jane started to interrupt, and I remembered. "Until the fifteenth, I mean. Let me see what I can do."

They both nodded, Marc only after his sister glared at him, and I saw the dynamic: she was the elder, the one who ultimately managed everything. The responsible one, despite what Marc had said about her getting their meeting place wrong. He was the one who had gotten away—and gotten a life.

"I'll need your contact info, Marc." I reached for my note-book, looking up only when he squawked, parrot-like.

"Why?" His face grew dark again. Suspicious.

"You're a family member. Randolph here has some experience with you. And if the plan is for Randolph to live with you, it may help for him to learn a different set of reactions to your presence." It was all true, but it wasn't the only reason I wanted this man's information. I handed him my notebook and watched as he took my pen to scribble down some numbers. Keeping as quiet as I could, I waited to see if he was going to turn back the page, look at what his sister had told me about his mother's decline and death. He didn't, but I got the feeling he wasn't happy—either at giving me his contact info or at finding me here in the first place.

Jane might see him as her naughty baby brother. The one who wouldn't help out.

Me, I was thinking about what the parrot had said. I was wondering why he'd misled his sister about their meeting place and tried to sneak into his mother's empty apartment. I was wondering, too, why he couldn't meet her eye.

Chapter Four

"A bird." Wallis was washing her face. I knew that each time she swiped her white paw over her whiskers, however, it was really to avoid facing me. *"She's listening to a bird now."*

I didn't answer her, even though I could. Wallis and I have something special. With most animals, I hear their thoughts. It's like I'm eavesdropping usually, and as my brief time with the parrot had reminded me, the give-and-take is pretty iffy. Wallis and I can have actual conversations, although I usually speak out loud and her voice is only in my head. I suspect that this two-way communication is because we've lived together for so long. She's sure it's because she's a cat.

What I did know was that her feline nature lent her a certain attitude toward other, smaller animals. And while a day before I might have agreed with her about avian authority, at this point, I just couldn't be sure. Those sounds—that virtual reenactment—had been a little chilling for my taste.

None of which I could explain to my tabby housemate. I'd hit the Internet as soon as I had gotten home and only after a couple of articles had I related my day's experience. And then the chime of the doorbell, followed by a hard rat-a-tat-tat rap on the door, had interrupted us.

It was the police. One officer, actually, and he squinted back at me as I eyed him, door opened part way.

"Evening, ma'am." With that angular face and the short hair, he looked like a boy scout, all grown up. "We've had reports of a disturbance."

"No disturbance here, Officer." I leaned on the doorframe. I could feel Wallis around my ankles, but I tuned her out. I was focused on the cop's blue eyes. They didn't blink. Neither did I.

"You're not in need of assistance then?" For a moment, he glanced down, and I could feel Wallis tensing ever so slightly.

"Assistance?" I let my gaze slide over his body. Slim, muscular. Definite boy scout. Definitely grown up. "No."

"Well, how about pizza then?" He proffered a flat box. It smelled of anchovies. Delicious, but I wasn't hungry for pizza.

"Maybe later," I said, letting my voice soften. He took my cue, setting the pizza box down to take me in his arms as Wallis trotted away.

Twenty minutes later, I was getting dressed. That was supposed to be a hint. Jim Creighton—Detective James Creighton—and I had been seeing each other regularly enough that his showing up unannounced wasn't totally out of place. But he was pushing, and as much as I enjoyed interludes like the one we'd just had on my sofa, I didn't want him to get too comfortable. I had a lot on my mind, and the one colleague I wanted to discuss it all with was tiger-striped.

"You hungry?" He reached over to where the pizza box had been abandoned on the coffee table. "It's still warm, and I know Wallis wants some."

I looked down. Sure enough, my tabby had returned to the living room, and now sat on the rug, tail neatly curled around her front feet and a look of devotion on her face.

"Well, mozzarella wouldn't melt in your mouth," I said to her as I accepted a slice. Wallis brushed against Jim's shin as he stood and reached for his pants, and I wondered what both of them were playing at. It wasn't all about the cheese.

I was right. "I want to ask you something, Pru." I'd started toward the kitchen, but I could hear fine. "And I don't want you to take offense."

I returned with a six-pack. That was better than a verbal response.

"It's about your old friends." He opened two beers and handed one to me. I took it, and waited. "Really old friends."

Wallis had jumped up on the sofa by then, and I sat beside her. With both of us focusing on him, Creighton would have had to be made of something harder than stone if he didn't crack.

"I'm not saying anyone you know is involved. I'm just—" He waved one hand in the air, nearly knocking over his drink. "I'm kind of at my wit's end with this one, Pru."

"So, tell." I had some pity and took a swig of beer.

It broke the tension. "We're seeing a flood of drugs in town. Drugs we haven't seen before. Prescription drugs, for the most part. Oxycodone, Oxycontin, and a new synthetic opiate that's even more powerful." He waited, and I nodded. I read the news occasionally. "The usual route is from Canada. There have been some big busts in Albany."

Another nod. I'd heard.

"This is something different. It's more powerful, and the money involved seems to be much bigger, as a result. I wasn't sure if you were still talking to Mack—"

"Whoa!" This was too much. My sort of ex might not be the straightest arrow, but I didn't see him as a dealer. Even if he was, I didn't know if I'd rat him out to my current beau. And if Creighton thought I was still seeing them both…"Off limits."

"I'm not saying he's involved." I glowered. Beside me, I could feel Wallis' fur begin to rise. "Honest! I was just wondering if he'd heard anything."

"Heard?" He wasn't getting off that easily. "So this wasn't just a booty call."

"Look, it's going out to schools, okay, Pru? It's serious." He looked at his beer. I noticed he didn't drink. "This new drug, it's brutal. Two kids ended up in Berkshire General over the weekend. One didn't make it."

"I'm sorry." I was. Some things might just be more important than my loyalty to an old flame. Besides, I'd been the one to set the terms on our relationship; Creighton's only innovation was the pizza. "Look, I'll ask around, but that's not—that was never Mack's thing."

"I know." The pressure off, Creighton looked years younger. "I'm just clutching at straws here. And what happens between us…" He paused. He knew if he continued, I'd shut him down.

"Understood," I let him off, as Wallis flopped on her side. "Now, are you going to eat that, or let it get cold?"

A half hour later, we'd finished most of the pie, and I'd filled my guest in on my unusual new client. Since he was here, I shared some of my suspicions, too. "Something's wrong with that family," I'd concluded. "Something besides grief."

That was when Wallis had broken in: *"A bird. What's next? A dung beetle?"*

It was her tone as much as the words, and I'd had to catch myself before responding out loud. To Creighton—to anyone really—she probably appeared to be just another dumb animal, grooming her neat tiger-striped fur after a special treat of cheese. I knew better.

I also knew that Creighton had some suspicions about me, about my gift. He'd picked up enough—and given me some funny looks. I didn't want to go there. Instead, I pressed my point. "I think something happened with the old lady. Something besides an accident."

"Haven't you had enough of murder?" His voice was soft. The look I gave him wasn't. I'd been involved with some bad types recently. It wasn't an experience I'd choose to repeat.

"I know you're busy, Jim." I held his gaze. "I'm not asking you to do anything. I just wanted to—" I paused. What did I want? "I wanted to talk this over with someone beside Wallis." Let him think that was a joke. "And I'm not imagining this. You know me."

"I do, Pru, I do. It's just that I really don't know if you should give much credence to what you hear from a parrot," Creighton said, echoing Wallis so closely that the tabby and I both paused and turned toward him. "I mean, they make noises, right? They repeat what they hear."

"That's the thing." I started picking pepperoni rounds off the last slice. Wallis isn't as young as she thinks she is. "Usually, parrots learn by repetition. They mimic what they hear often, which is useful in training." Every now and then, I throw that in, just to remind Jim that I have a rational reason for my "hunches." "But I've been doing some reading. There are some new studies that suggest they may also pick up sounds that make an impression—sounds that are loud, scary, or stressful, for example. That they're not just mimics."

I'd already told him about Alex, the famous parrot who seemed to be able to form simple sentences. "There's evidence they understand what they're saying."

"You're seriously saying that this parrot witnessed a murder?" Creighton reached for his beer, but he kept his eyes on mine.

"I'm saying there's something off. That someone broke in—or the old lady thought someone was there—and that's why she fell." I didn't say what I really felt, that she was pushed. The basic principle of any training regimen is to go one step at a time.

"And you think this because the parrot told you so." Creighton was fully dressed again, but he wasn't drinking. He was watching me.

"The parrot would have no reason to link those particular sounds without reason."

"Pru, this is a bird we're talking about." He took a drink finally. A long one. "A *bird*."

"*Told you so.*" Next to me on the sofa, Wallis began to purr.

A tactical retreat was in order. "How do you explain what it did keep repeating, then?" I'd stopped stacking the pepperoni, and Wallis leaned forward to sniff at it, and I put my hand on her back to restrain her. The purring stopped. "I mean, 'stop,' 'what are you doing?,' 'that's mine'? That all sounds pretty suspicious to me. Besides," I reached for my knife—my dinner knife—as

I made my point. "The son said they'd had some problems with theft."

"Maybe they did. Maybe they didn't." Creighton had collapsed back into the sofa, beer in hand. "For all we know, the old lady was dotty. Maybe she misplaced things—and then assumed they'd been stolen. You know what old people can be like."

I nodded. "But it was the son who told me."

"Sounds like the daughter was the one who was around more." He had a point, and he knew it. That was probably why he offered me a bone. "But look, why don't you speak to the aide? Maybe she, ah, knew something."

Like that the old lady was paranoid. Or that her job was time-limited, and she had to feather her own nest. "She might be able to help me with the retraining." I gave him that. "She was there long enough, she could probably tell me about the bird's routine." I began scraping the cheese off the slice.

"And the daughter's." Wallis looked up, eyes glinting. I nodded back. Exactly.

"You're trying to make more work for me, aren't you?" Creighton was joking, but I could hear the edge in his voice. He knew there was something going on that he wasn't party to. He's a smart guy. "You want it to be a murder."

"That's pushing it, Jim." I scooped the cheese onto my plate, and pushed the plate toward Wallis. "I didn't know the lady. I have no reason for wanting her death to be anything, natural or otherwise."

"I didn't mean it like that, Pru. I'm just wondering if, well, if you've gotten caught up in the idea of solving crime. If, maybe, what you're doing—you know, the animal training and, well the rest of it—" He was too polite to say dog walking—"isn't enough to occupy your mind these days."

I didn't respond, and he stumbled to fill the silence. "I mean, you're too smart to spend your days talking to animals. And, hey, are you really going to give all that cheese to Wallis?" We both looked up at that. "I mean, isn't she kind of stout already?"

"Down, girl!" I heard the voice in my head. *"Isn't it time for you to leave?"* I swear, I didn't know which of us was talking.

Chapter Five

Finding the aide was simple. I called LiveWell first thing in the morning and found out that Jean Sherry was working with other residents. Apparently, the aide was a longtime employee of the center, which spoke well for both her honesty and for a lack of financial duress. Not that I assumed "senior care aides," as the receptionist had called her, were that well paid. If LiveWell was placing her with private clients, LiveWell was taking a cut. Still, it made it more likely that the aide hadn't fled the state with the Larkin silver, and that I'd be able to find her when I went over for my afternoon session with Randolph.

Before then, I had my regular clients: two dogs and one confused dogcatcher. Okay, in truth Albert was more than a dogcatcher. As I pushed through the glass doors of our town pound, I had to remind myself that the bearded lug behind the desk wasn't some homeless guy or—considering our semi-rural surroundings—a lost mountain man who had stumbled into civilization. The flannel-clad man-lump seated behind the desk was the animal control officer for the town of Beauville. Not that he seemed to know it.

"Hey, Albert." The beard bounced off this year's plaid, and I realized he'd been sleeping. "Too early for you?"

"What? No." He sat up straighter and blinked. "I was cogitating."

"Cogitating, huh?" The pound was quiet at this hour, and I pulled up the guest chair to sit down. I was hoping to spy a glimpse of Frank, Albert's pet ferret. "Hope you don't hurt yourself."

"Uh, I don't think so." He sputtered. "I mean…"

I smiled. Frank liked to collect shiny things, too. Only his command of the things he found was better. And I was pressed for time. "Never mind, Al. You called about a consult?"

"Yeah, yeah, I did." He shuffled some of the papers on his desk, as if looking for notes. "It's about a raccoon. A problem over at Evergreen Whatsits?"

"Evergreen Hills." I knew it. A condo development carved out of the woods. Longtime residents wouldn't have called Albert about a raccoon problem. They'd trap it themselves. Or shoot it, I realized. Maybe having Albert here had some benefits. "Young male, right?"

"Seems so." He gave up with the papers. I doubted he had legible notes anyway. "They were calling it ah, um—a 'home invasion,' I think."

I rolled my eyes. Autumn and the young animals leave the nest. As the weather gets colder, they start looking for new places to stay. And as we encroach on their territory, they return the favor. "Got into the attic, huh?"

Albert nodded, his beard bouncing on his chest. "I used the box thing and got it out." Humane trap, raccoon, I translated. "The peanut butter really worked." He chewed his lip at the memory, and I wondered how much had made it into the trap as bait. Enough apparently. "Thanks."

"And where did you release the animal?" I don't know why I bothered asking.

"Mile away." He paused. "At least."

He'd let it go around the corner. "And it came back?"

He nodded. Of course it did. To a young animal out on his own for the first time, those showy dormers looked as good as they did to the city folk. "The manager called. Again," he said, his voice low. Someone had been angry.

I sighed. A local would have been easier to reason with: if animals get into your house, you find out how—and block the entrance. Some of these new people didn't get that. They just wanted the problem fixed. At least it wasn't nesting season. I wasn't as easily cowed as Albert, but I wouldn't want to explain to some irate vacationer that Mama Coon got to stay while her kits were growing.

"You want me to remove the animal?" I didn't get paid to do Albert's job, but I'd help him out. Hell, I'd be helping the animal, too. At some point the manager would probably poison it if it came back. I pushed out of the chair. "Traps in the back?"

He scurried to follow me. "Actually, Pru, the raccoon is back there. I went back and got him."

That manager must have been furious. That said, I wasn't sure why Albert had called me in. He bit his lip again, and I waited.

"They say it might have rabies." He paused. I didn't know what he was thinking. My gift doesn't work with people. I knew I was getting angry. Yes, rabies in raccoons is epizootic—the animal equivalent of an epidemic—and zoonotic, which means it can be transmitted to people. But sick animals act like sick animals—they charge at you. They look like hell. From everything I've heard, this poor creature was only trying to find a safe place to spend the winter. "I had to take it."

That was that, then. "Did you send in a sample?" Our little pound doesn't have the facilities for medical testing.

"A sample?" Albert blinked up at me. The idea of him at a microscope almost made me smile.

"Of the brain matter." Another blink. "You know, the animal's head?"

"Oh, no." He looked over his shoulder. "I was hoping you'd handle it."

I closed my eyes. It wasn't that I *wouldn't* be paid for this; it was that I couldn't be paid enough to do it. "I'm not killing a healthy animal, Albert."

"Killing?" For a big man, his voice sure could squeak.

"That's how they do the test." My curiosity was aroused. "So, when you said you 'took it…'"

"I mean, I took it in the trap. It's in the back." He motioned toward the pound area, and when I opened the door he made to follow me. "Alive."

"Albert." I turned and he raised his hands in surrender.

"Sorry. I just…" He had no excuse, and I felt for him.

"Look, the animal is probably freaked out as it is. The fewer people who go back there, the better."

He nodded and returned to his desk. As he did, he pulled open a drawer and a familiar masked face popped out.

"Frank!" I did my best to keep my excitement out of my voice. "I didn't know you were here today."

"*Cave, cage, locked in…*" The ferret was not happy at being confined.

"I was going to start cleaning the cages when you came in," Albert fumbled for an excuse. "I wanted him to be safe."

"Uh huh." He'd been napping and didn't want his companion eating his lunch, more likely.

"*I ate the pistachios already.*" Frank stood, his nose twitching. The little mustelid had more need of food than his person. "*Half the donut, too.*"

I couldn't help smiling. Frank, at least, could take care of himself. That raccoon, though—he might be in trouble. Still, while I was here…

"How's the cute little boy?" I spoke out loud to explain why I was bending over Albert's desk, reaching my hand out for the ferret to sniff. I had barely touched the parrot during my visit, unable to find an excuse to take him out of his cage. And I had showered this morning, so even any lingering traces would be gone. Still, it was the only way I had of cluing the ferret in. Help me, I was saying. I need your expertise, your particular animal skill. Silently, I was visualizing the parrot. The gray smooth back, the roughed-up belly feathers. The cursing.

"*Nest—birds. Big bird means big nest.*" I held my breath. The children, I'd known something was hinky with them from the start. "*Big nest means…big eggs!*"

"Sorry, Frank." I swallowed, my own mouth suddenly full of saliva. "No treats for you today." So much for that idea.

Chapter Six

Twenty minutes later, I was on my way. Beauville—deep in the Berkshires—was in peak color, the maples sugar red, the birches gold, but even though the scene was gorgeous and my car, a vintage Pontiac GTO, was purring like a kitten, I couldn't focus on foliage.

For starters, I'd promised Albert I'd help him with the raccoon. The animal certainly couldn't help himself. A young male, as I suspected, he'd seemed as healthy as I was. And although that's no guarantee of anything, there were so many other reasons for the young animal's behavior that I couldn't see euthanizing him just to make sure.

When I'd gone back to see him, pacing back and forth in one of the pound's large dog cages, I got the complete disorientation of an adolescent out on his own. He'd left home for the first time only a month before. After a few weeks of wandering—and some scrapes with other young males—he'd found what seemed to be the perfect burrow. Warm, high up, and dry, the attic was everything a raccoon could want, and this little creature was smart enough to know it—and to find his way back after being relocated once. What he couldn't understand was his removal. He hadn't even had to fight anyone to get in there. The space was empty; it should have been his.

In a just world, it would've been. I didn't want the poor guy to get in any more trouble, though. The condo residents might be city folk, but at some point they'd contact a local—someone other than Albert—who would rid them permanently of the raccoon. I knew the type. Those city folks wouldn't want to see what was done, but they'd be happy the "problem" was "resolved."

As I turned onto the highway, pulling directly into the fast lane to avoid the leaf peepers, I decided on a plan of action. I'd drive over to Evergreen Hills later, talk to the property manager. I figured if I showed him the point of entry—despite the animal's dazed state, I had a good visual image of a missing shingle under an eave—I could make a case for sealing it off. Then I could release the raccoon—I was sure Albert wouldn't rat me out, especially if I was helping him out of a jam. As long as he stopped "invading" their space, there was little chance the residents would recognize the young male.

I was thinking about communicating with the raccoon as I drove over to LiveWell. I hadn't had much luck during my brief visit, when I'd stood and watched the poor animal pace. Back and forth, back and forth in what is usually a dog enclosure in the locked rooms behind Albert's office, he'd been too anxious to relax. Which might be why I'd only gotten the little bit I had: just a few jumbled images that gave me the beast's history, leading up to his current predicament. Other than that, it was all just a sense of a fit, young animal, confused by life. Of course, I could have been projecting. That's the kind of thing I have to be on the lookout for, but what I hadn't gotten was the usual jolt of comprehension—a voice, a sound, a *feeling* that let me know I was tuned in to the real thing.

That may have been me. I hadn't tried my usual method for jumpstarting communication: reaching out for the kind of physical connection that can sometimes share a shock of knowledge. Partly, I didn't want to disturb the freaked-out animal any further. A wild animal—even a raccoon—was not going to find human touch comforting. Partly, I'll admit, I didn't want to get bit. I really did not want to kill him in order to test him for rabies. But I don't believe in taking stupid risks, either.

In truth, I didn't know how much I could get from wild animals, those not socialized in our terms. Birds, I heard. They're usually direct—they want to broadcast their message to everyone within earshot. And they could be noisy, especially out here in the woods. The occasional squeal of fear reached me when I was outside, too; prey animals reacting to the cruel realities of their world.

More often, though, I found myself talking to domestic animals, usually the ones I came into contact with through my work. It gave me a leg up, helped me understand why they were acting as they did. And I'd told myself it also provided some insight into the animal brain. Maybe I was flattering myself, though. Maybe I could "hear" these animals because they were so attuned to humans, to how we communicate. Even birds, after all, know something about us. Maybe a raccoon was simply so foreign I didn't know how to relate, not unless and until he wanted to.

That, I decided, was a problem for a different time. For now, I'd settle for getting that hole closed up. First, I told myself as I turned into the LiveWell lot, I needed to focus on my latest paying gig. My car—baby blue and built to get the most out of its 450 cc engine—stood out among the Toyotas and Volvos scattered through the visitors lot anyway, so I took my cue from the one oversized SUV and pulled in at an angle, taking up two spaces. I'd only recently had her painted, and I didn't want any dings. I could take some abuse from a crazy relative or two. My GTO? No way.

"Nice! Nice!" I picked it up as I walked away and smiled. No, it wasn't a compliment about my car. Or for me, for that matter. Someone had lined a den with soft down. Someone else was appreciative.

It's always good to be loved. It doesn't always happen. No relatives were in evidence when I walked into the LiveWell lobby. Despite its almost-chic color scheme, the place was deserted. Well, not entirely: I could hear someone calling bingo from a nearby room, and two women—at least one of them evidently deaf—were loudly discussing an upcoming daytrip to one of the casinos over the border. But the family members who were supposed to be appeased by the fancy decor were missing. The only person in sight under the age of sixty was the receptionist. She looked like the one I'd checked in with yesterday. Young and blonde, with a little too much eye makeup for the setting, she nodded at me as I walked in, and then turned back to the magazine she had opened on the calendar blotter. I didn't know if she remembered me, or if I looked benign. Considering my suspicions, I thought a little more caution might be advisable.

Not that I wouldn't take advantage of the situation. "Hi," I approached the desk with a big smile. "I'm looking for Jean Cherry?" I could see the clumps in her mascara as she blinked. "I believe she's working with Rose Danziger this morning?"

"Oh, yeah, Jeannie." She nodded again. "Rose's aide."

I stood corrected as she consulted a clipboard decorated with the LiveWell logo.

"They should be in Rose's room, 204."

I thanked her and headed for the elevator with a little extra spring in my step. I wasn't crazy about interrogating the aide. I remembered my mother's last days all too well and suspected what she'd been through. Plus, I had been hired by her last client's relatives, which would add to any natural reticence the aide might feel about talking with me. However, the room number was promising. As Polly's neighbor, Rose might have seen something.

I was in luck: 204 was right across the hall from the late Polly Larkin's apartment, the numbers set in that overdone logo.

"Coming!" The voice sounded about the right age, and I was encouraged by its vigor. "One moment!"

But any hope I had of Rose Danziger having seen something was dashed, as the door swung back to reveal a pale and tiny figure in dark wrap-around glasses, holding onto the harness of a guide dog.

"Rose Danziger?" I addressed the woman. The dog held its place by her side, but I could sense the animal—a dark shepherd-mix by the look of the long, intelligent face—sniffing me, sizing me up. *"Cat, person, dog, dog…raccoon?"* This canine companion had a good nose.

"The one and only." The woman by the dog's side looked up at me as if she could see me, a big smile on her dried-apple face. "And who might you be?"

"Pru, Pru Marlowe." I held out my hand and felt, as much as saw, the dog go on alert. So I turned it, palm up, for him to sniff. He craned his neck, but didn't take so much as a step from his person's side. The ears, they were pure German shepherd, large and sensitive. So was the focus. The size was a little off, a little short in the body, and I put that down to the crossbreeding, but he reminded me of Cousteau, my neighbor's dog back in New York.

Cousteau hadn't been a happy pup. I'd finally convinced his macho owner to have him neutered. Even with his lusts contained, though, he was bored. These are work dogs, happiest when they have a task that they can accomplish. Right now, this dog was occupied judging my role in his person's life to determine if I was a threat. While he made his mental calculations, I made a few of my own. I'd get to the aide. First, I wanted to talk to the neighbor. Blind or not, she seemed quite alert. "I've been hired by Jane, Polly Larkin's daughter, to help with the parrot."

"Oh, Jane. Jane and Randolph. What a fakakta cock-up!" She turned with a gesture that seemed to dismiss the whole family. The dog made a larger circle around her so as not to trip her up. I got a sense of herding, of sheep, as if Rose were a young ewe rather than a white-haired human. Cousteau would have loved this gig. "Come in."

"You know her?" I followed the little woman into a room that would have almost mirrored the one across the hall, if it had been filled with boxes. This one looked a little smaller, but felt more spacious, one end made into a neat little parlor with a short cream loveseat and two off-white chairs. Rose settled into one, the dog lying by her feet, a sense of deep contentment coming off him like warmth from his fur. I admired his training.

I wasn't even getting any sense that he was tempted to jump up on the remaining chair. "Jane Larkin?"

"Of course I knew Jane. Polly and I were friends." The old lady turned and called into an alcove. "Jeannie, did I know Jane?"

A young woman, very tall and ebony skinned, stepped into the living room, holding a small tray with a teapot and a plate of cookies on it. "I don't recall you ever calling her by her right name, Rose." She ducked back into the kitchenette and returned with three mugs. "Not in my hearing."

I was trying to place her accent as she sat in the remaining chair. No mistress-servant relationship here, then. Not with the aide, at least; the dog didn't even look up as she passed the plate of cookies, and when I tried to reach out with my thoughts I was rebuffed. *"We are sitting."* Yes, I figured that much.

"Oh?" I figured the women would be a better bet, and primed the pump as the aide handed me a mug. Chamomile from the smell of it. Well, I'd survive.

The old lady and the young turned toward each other silently, as if to share a look, and then the aide burst out laughing. The dog remained silent.

"Jeannie thinks I'm an old bitch." Rose leaned forward with a conspiratorial air. The dog shuffled slightly. Taking in her movement, that was all. "She knows what I'm talking about, though."

I nodded and turned toward the aide. "So you must be Jeannie Cherry."

She nodded, her mouth full of cookie. Rose, however, corrected me. "It's *Genie*"—she softened the word, changed the accent—"not 'Jeannie.' It's short for Eugénie, as in Napoleon's empress." She reached for a cookie and motioned for me to take on. "And her last name's Cherie. Like the drink, if you can't speak French."

"My apologies." Haitian, of course. That slight lilt was Creole. I wondered how many other residents here would respect the young woman's heritage. "Genie. But dare I ask?"

I raised my eyebrows and left the question open, taking a bite of cookie. These two seemed ready to gossip, and the cookie was surprisingly good—a crisp lemon wafer dusted with confectioner's sugar.

Genie looked over at Rose, and I wondered if I'd gone too far. It's one thing to correct a third party about a mispronunciation. Another thing entirely to badmouth a client's family—even a former client.

"Rose believes that Jane is a—a milksop," Genie said, after a brief pause, obviously making an effort to use different language than Rose favored. "No family of her own. No independent life." The aide shot a look at her charge. "I think she was a good daughter, doing what she could."

"She used her mother as a tired-ass excuse." Rose gestured with her mug, coming just short of spilling the hot tea. "Polly didn't need that much care. Not till the end. And even then that washed-out overgrown girl didn't do anything that you weren't capable of doing much more efficiently."

Genie sighed and nodded. This wasn't the first time they'd had this discussion, I'd have bet. No wonder the dog remained so calm. "But she wanted to do it, Rose." The emphasis was gentle. "Polly was her mother. It's different when it's your family."

"Genie doesn't want to say how clumsy that girl was. She made Genie's job harder. I know, I heard it all."

"Bathing Polly. Getting her dressed. It wasn't what the girl was used to." Genie gave her that. "She was there every day," she said to me. "She wanted to be of use."

"Everyday?" I looked from the aide's unlined mahogany face to Rose's white-on-white wrinkles. It was easy to forget that eye contact didn't matter with the old lady. "She didn't have a job?"

"She quit her job when—" Genie didn't get a chance to finish.

"She was fired again, the stupid cow. Like what happened the last time." Rose took another cookie and turned as if to stare at me. "That girl had no life, and taking care of her mother was her excuse for not having one. Not like her brother, Marc."

Genie was shaking her head, and Rose turned. For an uncanny moment, I wondered if she was faking her blindness.

"You know what I'm saying, Genie. I could see it. Hell and damnation, even Buster here could see it."

She reached down and gently patted the dog by her side. It was the first time she'd acknowledged the dog, a fact I put aside for later. For now, I looked at Genie, but she only continued shaking her head. I waited for her to say anything, but the moment passed, and I didn't want to break up the collegial mood.

"I met Marc yesterday," I ventured finally. Rose beamed, but I saw Genie's lips grow tighter as if she were physically holding words back. I remembered Marc's accusations and wondered how much he had expressed. Clearly he hadn't been able to prove anything, or Genie wouldn't be working at LiveWell. Still, it couldn't be pleasant to be accused of theft. "He seemed, well, a bit on edge."

"Being with that useless sister drives him batty, that ignorant slut. He's a doll." I was beginning to see where the parrot got his language. But I'd get back to the bird. For now I turned to Genie, waiting for her response. When none came, I smiled, as if that might disarm her. "You're not crazy about him, are you?"

"She thinks Marc was just after Polly's money." Rose broke in before Genie could respond. "She thinks he tried to have her fired, even though I keep telling her otherwise."

I looked at Genie, but her face had gone as blank as the dog's.

"She thinks Marc wanted his mother dead." The old lady broke one of the cookies in half and reached down to offer it to the dog. "She thinks Marc murdered my old friend and that he's going to get away with it." With an audible snap, the dog grabbed the cookie, and we sat there, the only sound the wet munch of Buster, enjoying his treat.

Chapter Seven

I'd have loved to grill the old lady further. Despite her blind-ness—and questionable judgment about her friend's son—she was an observant old coot, and I trusted her memory, especially when it pertained to her late friend. Unfortunately, Genie had her own ideas. No sooner had we all caught our breath than the aide jumped up and began to hustle her charge out the door.

"Look at the time!" Genie consulted her watch, which might have been a bit of pantomime for my benefit. "Rose? We have to go."

"The casino trip?" I had an image of the blind woman at a card table. It made me smile.

"Oh, no." I could have sworn the old lady had read my mind. "I don't do that silliness. That's all—"

"Rose?" Genie interrupted her before she could say more. "We can't keep Dr. Wachtell waiting."

Buster stood, his senses alerted by Genie's actions, if not by her words, and watched as Genie hurriedly stacked the cups and returned the tray to the kitchen area. Looking down at the dog's bright black eyes, I realized I'd missed an opportunity. The shepherd mix had an extremely narrow focus—a necessity for the job, I figured—but if his mistress had strong feelings about what was going on across the hall, he would have picked up on something.

"May I help?" I was stalling, trying to think of an excuse to tag along and continue the conversation.

"No thanks. The doctor's office is in the complex." Rose reached for my arm and once again looked up at my face as if she could see me. "I would take my sweater, though." She made to get up—this was her home base, after all—but the aide was quicker.

"I've got it." Genie strode over to a closet, moving fast enough so that I almost believed they were late for an appointment.

Rose sighed, but waited, still hanging onto my arm. "You should come again." Her grip was firm. "We can talk about Randolph—and about Polly."

"Rose?" Genie had the sweater over her shoulders and was gently pushing.

"I will." I nodded to the old lady, not caring that she couldn't tell. "Thanks for the tea and cookies." This I directed to Genie. "And the conversation."

Genie lifted her eyebrows at that, and continued to hurry her tiny client toward the door.

"I'll be by tomorrow." I called after them.

"Rowf." Buster barked once, softly. *"Plans,"* I translated. *"Don't distract us."* But Rose had invited me back, and no matter what Buster or Genie thought, Rose was still the boss in that apartment.

◇◇◇

I watched them head down the hallway and waited while they got into the elevator. Chasing after them was pointless, but I was curious to see how they interacted. Genie's interruption certainly seemed timed to shut Rose up when the old lady wanted to say more, and I had to wonder what she was on about. The old woman clearly liked her—hell, I had too—so why didn't Genie want Rose to talk to me?

It could have been anything. Genie knew I was working for Jane Larkin. Maybe she was afraid I'd carry word of gossip across the hall. Maybe she was afraid I'd piss off the mourning daughter. Maybe the Larkin family still owed her money. The fact that Genie's services seemed to have been arranged through

LiveWell made it unlikely that she'd be invoicing separately, and I didn't get the sense that Jane Larkin was one to welch on a bill. Marc, well, maybe he did think his mother's care was costing too much. I remember thinking something similar when I got the itemized expenses for the home hospice care. Didn't mean I'd killed anyone over it, or even shirked on my bills.

I was in the hallway for so long that the voice behind me made me jump.

"Oh! You are there!" It was Jane Larkin. I checked my watch. Sure enough I was ten minutes late for our appointment. "I was wondering if you'd gotten delayed."

"I'm sorry." I put on my best contrite smile. "I ran into someone. I didn't mean to keep you waiting."

"That's okay." She turned and led me back into her mother's apartment. Now that I'd seen another unit, I realized that Polly Larkin must have one of the larger studios. Not that this apartment was what you'd call spacious, crammed as it was with boxes and furniture. It did make me wonder just how much LiveWell cost—and how tight money was for the Larkins. I couldn't exactly ask the faded woman, who was now bent over assembling a box.

"I'm going to start with the parrot now," I said instead. "Will you be staying?" I couldn't think of a nicer way of asking, and scrambled for an excuse to get her out of here. "I usually work with the animals alone." I paused. "I mean, in private."

She looked up, her pale face lined with worry. "I'll be quiet, I promise. It's just, well, I really need to finish the packing. Besides, Randolph is used to me."

A low whistle from the cage said it all.

"That's the problem." I was grasping at straws. "I need to break him of habits. Get him thinking in a new way. And it's too cold for me to take him outside."

"Oh." She put down the tape dispenser. "I didn't—"

What she didn't do was finish her sentence. I wasn't going to make it easy for her and stood there, hovering. Inside his cage, Randolph muttered. "Crap. Crap in your hat."

I tried not to smile, but the colorful expression did the trick. "Wait here."

I hoped she'd come back from the closet with her coat on. Instead, she held a key.

"You can take Randolph across the hall. Mother and her neighbor were friends, and Mrs. Danziger always took Randolph in when the cleaning crew was here. She won't mind."

I opened my mouth to object. To explain. Anything—and shut it before Jane could notice. She didn't need to know I'd already met Rose. The blind old lady was out at her appointment.

"She'll probably be grateful for the company," Jane's confided, her voice lower. "She's almost ninety and blind as a bat, and I think the lack of mobility is making her a bit nuts."

"She's the woman with the seeing-eye dog." It seemed sensible to establish that I knew *of* the neighbor. "German shepherd mix."

"Oh, of course." She looked at me as if I'd said something witty. "Of course you'd notice that. But don't worry, the dog isn't dangerous."

I didn't know whether she honestly thought a trained service dog would threaten a person, or if she was referring to Randolph. But I took the cage down from its hanger as she asked and followed her across the hall. She was knocking, and I went through the charade of waiting for an introduction, all the while keeping my eye on the elevator at the end of the hall.

"She must be out. No matter." Jane tried the door. It wasn't locked. "She and Mother were in and out of each other's places all the time," she said, pocketing the key. "There, now you can have some peace and quiet."

Not knowing what else to do, I stepped back into the parlor I'd vacated only a few minutes before. Jane headed for the door, pausing only to call back. "Don't worry if she comes back while you're here, Pru. She's a little past it, if you know what I mean. But she won't freak out on you. There are people in and out of the units all the time, here. They don't even allow you to have a deadbolt put on, just in case there's, you know, an emergency?"

With that she closed the door behind her, and I took a seat. She was my client, and I was supposedly booked for the next hour to work with Randolph, who was still muttering various scatological phrases, his big beak working as he turned his head side to side, taking in his surroundings with those strange yellow eyes. I wasn't thinking about the bird's dirty mouth, though. What I was realizing was that security in this pricey community was virtually nonexistent. If someone were stealing from Polly, the pool of potential suspects was building-wide. More, even, if you counted all the outside contractors who must come in each day with only a smile to the receptionist. And while Jane had confirmed her mother's friendship with the elderly neighbor, she had also cast doubt on her perception. Not to mention her sanity—and, possibly, her motives.

"What do you say, Randolph?" I was looking at the bird, but I was really talking to myself. Call me biased. I didn't think the avian brain was up to the situation.

"Some piece o' cake, huh?" The parrot barked out what sounded like a laugh. "Stupid cow."

"And just who are you talking about?" He was repeating words. He had to be, I wasn't getting the usual feeling of connection—of translation or psychic contact, and yet…. "The neighbor Rose? The daughter?"

"Daughter, daughter. Dishwater!" With a loud squawk, he flapped his wings and succeeded in fluttering above his perch. Nothing else; no mental messages. Still, I felt for him. This cage was too small for a grown bird. Then again, Polly's apartment had been too small for a grown woman, even an old one. I looked up and saw he had trained one cool eye on me, as if expecting a response. I reached out with my thoughts: *What are you trying to tell me? Is it about Jane?*

"Dishwater!" The hoarse voice could almost have been laughing, but there was nothing more.

"I think we agree on that one." I said finally. "What I want to know is who said that?" I didn't really expect an answer. We were in Rose's apartment. Randolph had been here before, Jane had said. It was likely that he'd picked up Rose's words, maybe because they rhymed, and it made sense that being back here would spur him to repeat them.

"No talking. Shut up. Shut up. Skwah?" Randolph shifted on his perch, stopping only to groom his breast. He plucked out a bit of down, enlarging the bald spot. This was anxious behavior, the avian equivalent of biting your nails until they bled. This was the problem I should be addressing, not some crime that may or may not have ever happened. I shook my head. I was being worse than foolish, I was being neglectful. Whatever else was going on, this was an animal in distress, and I had been hired to help him.

"Crap!" He said, loud and clear.

I had to laugh. Okay, I hadn't been hired to help the bird except indirectly. I'd been hired to clean up his language, which would allow him to find another home. The fact of his distress, or his loss of his longtime companion, might be relevant, however. I thought of the comfort he must find in repeating phrases that he either heard from the old lady or that had amused her and shook my head. Yeah, my clients were the people who paid me. Times like this, I really wished I could just avoid that part of the transaction entirely.

"Randolph, let's talk." One yellow eye focused on me, and for a moment I wondered. I didn't think he understood me. I wasn't getting any of that connection I would have with a cat or even with a focused work dog like Buster. Still, that cool sideways gaze made me wonder. What the hell, I thought. The sound of my voice might reassure him—might serve as a point of contact. "Would you like to talk?" The eye looked me up and down. "About Polly?"

The bird whistled and shuffled down his perch, his gaze moving on to the apartment around him. There was no connection here; my first instincts had been correct. Randolph was still, however, an animal in crisis. I looked around. I'd love to let him out, let him stretch what looked like considerable wings. However, we weren't in his home apartment, and I didn't want push the bounds of neighborly privilege. Parrots aren't usually litter trained.

"It's fine, sweet cheeks. Caw!" The gray head tilted and suddenly the parrot was sizing me up again. This time, I did the same. Those little eyes were cold, but just then, I'd have sworn there was something in them—some spark.

"You know, I think you can understand me. At least sometimes." I waited, trying to blank out my mind of anything except the bird. Then I let in other images—the apartment we had just left. Jane.

Another low whistle, and the bird took a dump.

"Was that an editorial comment?" I asked, unable to stifle a chuckle. He didn't respond. In truth, I was lost here. I wanted the bird to be happy. I wanted him to quit pulling out his own plumage. That meant finding him a home. To do that, I needed to retrain him—and fast. "Okay, forget that. Let's start with the basics."

I put my face close to the cage and waited until the bird looked at me again. "Nice birdy," I said, enunciating each syllable. "Nice, nice birdy."

I felt like a fool. The parrot's silence felt like scorn. But what choice did I have? In the absence of a single, strong stimulus, parrots learn by repetition. Tomorrow, I'd remember to bring some treats; positive reinforcement works for anyone. The key, though, was to replace those offensive phrases with something more benign.

"Nice, nice birdie. Bird-eee."

A little flutter, an understated coo. "Birdy?" I was trying.

"Bitch." Another squawk followed, but I'd heard him loud and clear. The bird was getting to me. I could see why Marc didn't want him. I wondered whom else he'd pissed off. "Stupid bitch." I would have dismissed it, too, except that I got a flutter—I couldn't call it more than that—of something underneath the human-sounding words.

Bad. Bad bird. Then again, out loud: "Bitch."

"Randolph?" A squawk. "You're not—you aren't calling me a bitch, are you?"

Nothing. Nothing from the parrot, anyway—and it hit me. The kick I gave myself could have knocked me down. How stupid could I be? Just about the first thing I'd learned with my gift was to ask an animal its name. Wallis had told me that, once I'd stopped freaking out. She'd been called Mrs. Ruffles before, a stupid name, but the one she'd had at the shelter where I found her. Turned out, she hated it more than I did.

Now I turned to the parrot once more. "I'm sorry. I started to ask you yesterday, but we got interrupted." I didn't know if any of that would translate. Still, it couldn't hurt to be polite. "I'm Pru, Pru Marlowe. Would you tell me your name?"

"Skwah!" Another shuffle. "Crap!" More obsessive grooming, so painful to watch. "Bitch!"

I wasn't getting anywhere. The parrot didn't want to talk, only to curse. There had been something though—the briefest of thoughts: *"Bad bird."* The words echoed in my head.

Where had that come from? Well, Marc was one obvious source. I remembered, I'd been thinking of the old lady's son when the bird had started talking again. Marc had probably said as much, maybe worse, to his sister—or to his mother—in the bird's hearing. And the rest? Would Randolph call Marc a bitch? I didn't know enough about avian comprehension. For that matter, I didn't even know if the words Randolph repeated back to me were connected with anything he meant. They might just be sounds. Noises that got him attention and, just maybe, kept him from finding a new home.

Marc didn't like the parrot, that was clear. If Jane couldn't take him, though, he was the obvious one to give him a home. He'd mentioned kids. Maybe one of them would take to this lonesome parrot, teach him new words and let him fly around a room. If I could get the bird to where Marc would let him into the house.

"Bad bird." There it was again, gone as soon as they appeared. Randolph was peering around, his little head craning this way

and that. Marc might not be on his Top 10 list, but there was something else going on.

As if to emphasize the point, the parrot reached down and pulled out more silver down. I watched the slight, curled feather drift out of the cage and to the floor. This apartment held bad memories for the bird. I thought of Rose. She seemed innocuous, charming even in her gruff way. To a captive animal, she might seem quite different—and she did have strong feelings about her former friend, and all those who were close to her. Then again, Genie, the aide, had been here, too.

I needed to go back to my old notes. I couldn't remember much about parrots—how they learned or the way their memory worked. They had excellent vision, I recalled, better than most mammals. There was something else—something about having more cones, more sensors, in their eyes. As I mused over this, more came back to me: some theory that said parrots had the gift of filling in the blanks, of seeing what *should* be there, as well as what shouldn't—a gift that would be crucial to survival in their native jungle habitat. Was there anything in this room that would have, *should* have been a visual clue to the parrot? Something that would remind him of Genie? Or of Polly?

I was stretching. I knew that, but with little else to go on, I looked around the little living room. Neater than her across-the-hall neighbor's, but not as spare as I'd originally thought. I saw photos, a lot of them, framed on the wall and along the long windowsill, easily visible from the parrot's perch. Would a photo register to a parrot?

"Aw-wah!" I turned as Randolph—or whatever his name was—gave a strange-sounding call. He was biting at the bar of his cage, his hooked beak gnawing on it.

"You okay?" He stepped back, head bobbing, and I considered how he'd been standing. Head bent, sideways, he'd have been staring at the floor. At a large rawhide chew toy. Buster's no doubt. That didn't mean—

"Bitch!"

Of course. The service dog would always have been here, in this room. That's what Randolph was looking for, what he didn't see.

"Bitch!" The parrot was louder this time, and it hit me. I hadn't examined Buster, simply assumed he was an altered male. He was small for a shepherd, but I'd assumed that was a result of whatever cross had given him that glossy dark coat.

"Buster?" I did my best to look the parrot in the eye, one eye at a time. The result was disconcerting.

"Aw." The parrot clicked with his tongue, his disappointment clear. I had not only not seen the obvious, I had been a fool. Buster was a female, a bitch. And my suspicions had once again come to nothing.

Chapter Eight

"It's hopeless. I really am the sad sack Creighton thinks I am." An hour later, I was home again, trying to unwind with a beer and my cat. "I can't even get the basics about a damned guide dog right."

"Well, those animals have no life." Wallis gave the feline equivalent of a shrug, flexing and settling her long white whiskers. *"No sense of self. No sense of* fun." Wallis may be neutered; she'd been spayed in the shelter where I found her. She liked to let on about a wild past, however.

"It's worse than that, Wallis." I joined her at the windowsill. The view from my mother's kitchen took in a stand of birches, already golden against the bright red of the sugar maples. "I'm imagining murders now, too." I told my feline companion. "When all I've really got is gossip, an overworked daughter, and maybe some interspecies tension."

I confess, I was looking for more than sympathy. Beyond support, I was hoping for confirmation of what I'd suspected, and I did what I could to relax my defenses. If she could see what I saw, sense what I had experienced, maybe she'd have another take on it—another way in. Maybe I wasn't making this all up.

"You are bored, aren't you?" Wallis' eyes closed slightly as she stared at me, taking it all in.

"Maybe a little." I had to give her that.

Her whiskers flattened out against her face in satisfaction. Our move back to Beauville had been my decision, made unilaterally. As much as she enjoyed the view of the woods, I knew she would never let me forget our panicked flight from the city—from everything she had ever known.

"Little town, little life." She turned toward the window and, with a moment of calibration, leaped to the sill. *"What fun is it without the chase?"*

I didn't answer that. I did, however, think of Creighton. He thought I was amusing myself. Maybe not consciously, but at some level—looking for a bigger mystery than the one I was really supposed to be solving. Meanwhile, he had real problems on his hand. And if he was asking me for help, he was stuck without a clue.

I took in the vista outside. For all its problems, until now this little town had managed to escape the drug scourge that had swept through so many other former industrial towns. We had tourism. Those maples, the ones turning red, were worth their weight in gold. And we were small enough, our industrial past far enough behind us, that our troubles tended to be small too.

Without thinking, I reached to stroke Wallis' back. I hadn't had a friend like her when I was growing up. Maybe if I had, I could've held a little steadier. Instead, I'd gone as wild as was possible. In those days, that meant drinking too much. Smoking pot and driving wild. The low point for me had been a scary night in an earlier incarnation of the cop shop Creighton now occupied, pulled over in a stolen car one of my buddies had jacked for a joyride. When my mother had bailed me out, she'd sat me at the table that still stood beside me. Read me the riot act. And I'd made up my mind to get out—as soon and as far as I could.

Wallis' fur was a lot warmer than any of those memories. Still, it made me sad to think of those days. Not that I'd come back, but that my town had grown so much harder and more dangerous.

"Tell me about the bird."

I looked down into Wallis' green eyes. Was my cat trying to distract me?

"*I find birds…amusing.*"

"You find the hunt amusing." She didn't deny it. However, it was useful to catalog what I knew.

The bird's repeating things it heard, I "told" her, letting the memories sift through my head. Not even necessarily what it had picked up from Polly. I thought of Rose and her foul language. Maybe the two old friends had spent more time together than apart; maybe they'd cracked each other up teaching the bird insults. I knew I should find out more about their relationship. Maybe Genie would know. Or the resident doctor.

It was pointless. Maybe the parrot had come to Polly cursing. Maybe he'd spent decades living with an actual sailor. There was no way I could tell who he was mimicking, or when he'd picked up whatever he repeated to me now. Not unless he let me in, and I was beginning to believe the bird's limited mental capabilities would make that impossible.

"*Now, now, don't underestimate the undersized chicken.*" Wallis had begun using metaphor more. I didn't know if this was something she was picking up from me, or if I was just hearing her in a new way. "*I told you, it's a skill that you have to work at.*" That came through loud and clear. "*Funny, isn't it? When prey animals do it so naturally?*"

"What was that, Wallis?"

"*Listening.*" She looked up at me as if I were a kitten. "*They have to understand, or they're what you call toast.*"

"So you think that parrot understands me?" I tried to get my mind around this. "Even if I can't understand him?"

"*From what you've told me, ahem…*" A little hiccup that could have been a hairball, but was more likely her way of accenting that I 'told' her more unconsciously than with words. "*He's got a few years on you.*"

Great. I was being played by a parrot.

"*Not necessarily.*" Wallis wasn't the type to humor me, so I paid attention. "*He may be waiting, testing you. Especially considering all he's been through recently.*"

She had a point there.

"*Besides, they hear what they need to hear—but they don't neces-sarily get the larger picture. There's a reason they call them feather brains. Juicy, though.*" I waited, trying to ignore the way my own belly had started rumbling in sympathy. "*But for noticing the little things? Well, they can do that.*"

A wave of disappointment came off Wallis, and I had the distinct desire to turn around and check to see if a twitching tail had given me away.

Chapter Nine

I wanted to go back to that parrot. To talk to him, see if I could break through his bird-like reserve. Not that I trusted Wallis' words entirely. Like everyone, she had her angle. But for her to credit a bird with anything—besides flavor? I had to give it some credence.

I'd made a promise, though. A spoken one to Albert, and a silent one to that caged raccoon, pacing in his cage, and so before it got too late, I headed out again. The tourists had disappeared as the shadows lengthened, making the drive more fun. Besides, I'd figured my visit with the Evergreen Hills manager would be the easy part of the day. Animal expert making a house call, suggesting an easy fix to keep the residents happy; what's not to like? I was even careful about parking, pulling neatly into a space marked for visitors before I went searching for the man in charge. I didn't expect it to be difficult: Evergreen Hills—"Your Place in the Pines"—seemed to believe in obvious signage, with placards pointing the way to the sports center and the manager's office in a green and yellow combination not found in nature.

"Mr. Gaffney?" When I found the office locked, despite the acid-yellow sign saying "open," I began to poke about the grounds. The sign said someone would be on duty until five, and an hour seemed a reasonable time to settle this mess. The birds were all settling in, quiet coos of nesting and nighty-nights as the shadows lengthened. They kept earlier hours than most humans, however. "Hello?"

"Pru!" I turned to find a heavy-set man who looked surprisingly like my father, what I remembered of him anyway, complete with the gin-blossom nose and the jowls of a hound. "I thought it was you."

"Jerry?" Jerry Gaffney had been part of my crowd in high school. We hadn't had much in common besides drinking and cars. Still, seeing him shook me. He didn't look good. "Good to see you." I fixed a smile on my face and submitted to a hug. He held me a little longer than necessary. Then again, from the smell of him, he probably hadn't had much of an opportunity to get close to a woman recently.

"God, you look great." He practically licked his beefy lips. "I'd heard you were back in town. Couldn't stay away, huh?"

I smiled in reply. I was used to this. People in Beauville were either surprised I'd come back or pleased, and not in a good way. It didn't say much about the town that returning was rated a failure, but there it was. "So, you're the manager here?" Albert had told me his title. It was a fancy term for "custodian" or "groundskeeper," which made me wonder who was really in charge. I needed Jerry on my side, however. As I've said, a little positive reinforcement works for everyone.

"Yeah," He puffed his chest out so it extended over his belly. "I keep the yuppies in line."

"Great." This was what I wanted to hear: he'd be easier to handle than a professional property manager—or a dozen screaming condo owners. "I think I've figured out your raccoon problem for you."

"That's right. You're the animal lady, now." He smiled. I didn't like his smile. "We have a lot to catch up on."

Not if I could help it. I remembered him from high school. I hadn't wanted anything from him then, so things had been easier. For now, I smiled back. "Sure do, but I've got to file a report on this one, so—"

"I've got it all under control." He was moving in. I sensed I was being herded back to the office. Or worse, his truck, where there was less chance of meeting anyone else. I'm not a big believer in aversive training, or I would have smacked his snout. Instead, I fell back on conditioning. What did he want? My attention. Which would be denied until he learned to behave properly.

I stepped aside, away from the outer wall of the building, and turned away. Just like any hound, he sensed the distance and suddenly became solicitous. "You came all the way out here, though…" He left it open-ended. I waited for more. "You had something to tell me?" Even his voice had grown softer.

"More what I wanted to show you," I said, using my firm "command" voice, and walked him over to the corner of the property. Sure enough, up under the too-bright eaves and beside a nicely branching maple, I could see a hole. Not big, but big enough—just as the raccoon had remembered it. "There," I pointed. "That's your problem. That's where raccoons and other animals are getting in."

I made a point of using the plural. I didn't want this lug having it in for any particular raccoon—and I wanted to make him a little nervous. "Other animals" could be anything. Squirrels. Rats.

"Oh, yeah. I knew about that." He was bluffing. I began to relax. "I'm going to have the guys fix that when they do the gutters next month."

"Why wait?" I didn't want to hold that raccoon longer than I had to. "We removed one animal, but another will find it soon enough."

"And will he get a surprise." Jerry chuckled, his belly bouncing. "I know you people use the Hav-a-Hearts, but I got some of the other kind of traps from my cousin. You remember Jimmy?"

I did. He was a creep even back in high school.

"He got me some of them. The permanent kind. Let's see how they like that."

I had to think fast, and I had to hide the fury that was building inside me. Luckily, Jerry's own body betrayed him. The chuckle had turned to hiccups, and soon he was bent over coughing. I patted him on the back, possibly harder than was necessary.

"You okay?" I was calculating. If he keeled over, I could walk away. I didn't think anyone had seen me come back here.

He stood up, face red. "Yeah. I, uh, I've got to lay off the butts."

And the booze and the burgers, I didn't say. However, he'd given me my answer. "Maybe you should get those gutter guys in sooner," I said, trying to look like my concern was for him. "I mean, trapped, dead animals—you're going have to be up and down to that attic everyday, twice a day. Otherwise, you're going to start getting complaints about the smell. Flies...."

The blank look on his face made it clear he hadn't thought that far ahead. "Hell, you're right." Then it faded into a smile. "That don't matter, though. Joey's been looking for a gig. You remember my other cousin, Joey, don't you?" I didn't, but I wasn't surprised that there was another one. "He can check the traps. Every day, twice a day."

"Have you spoken to Albert about this?" Albert was a town official. I wasn't. He also wasn't particularly threatening.

"Oh, Al. He's all right," the big man said. "What? You squeamish?"

Jerry started grinning then, the kind of grin that was halfway to a leer. One that made me want to punch him in that gut of his. He'd seen my distaste for his methods and read it as sentiment. I opened my mouth to cut him down—and stopped. Maybe this could work for me.

"Well, I do work with animals, you know." I couldn't bat my eyes at him. Just couldn't. "And raccoons are actually very intelligent. Cute, too."

"You want me to spare the little guys, don't you?" It was working. I smiled. Positive reinforcement.

"Yeah." I tossed my hair, extending my neck as I did so. It felt like Nature Channel 101, but if it worked..."That would be great."

"Wish I could, doll." He stepped closer, hooking his thumbs in his belt loops in a way that dragged his jeans dangerously low.

I saw my error. He had taken my signals as cues to act in a way he considered masculine—now that he saw me as submissive. "Wish I could."

"You do know using 'kill' traps—leg traps, crush traps, and the like—for raccoons is illegal." I switched back to business mode so fast, I could see the recoil on his face. "And that raccoons, while they may be deemed a nuisance, are protected."

"Protected by who?" He put his chin up in defiance. "Albert?"

"The state." I met his stare and held it. "Department of fish and game."

"You gonna tell them?" He looked me up and down again. This time, it was meant to intimidate.

It only got me mad. "If I have to."

"Pru Marlowe." His big face was brick red. "You used to be so much fun."

I didn't respond. I'd had that reputation, but he and I? Only in his dreams.

"Good thing Joey's got some other tricks up his sleeve. Some fun powders," Jerry said. "Maybe you should start watching out, too."

So much for that simple fix. I drove away replaying the interaction, wondering if there was something I could have done to keep it from turning into Mutual of Omaha's Wild Kingdom. I knew I had a temper. I didn't need Creighton—or Wallis—to point it out to me. But Jerry Gaffney seemed like a loser. A loser with just enough power to threaten a harmless animal. If he did any research at all, he'd find out it would be legal to hunt raccoons—to shoot them, that is—as soon as October started. I didn't think he'd bother. That didn't make him any less dangerous.

I stepped on the gas and enjoyed the surge of power as my car responded. The sun was setting, the half-light making the reds and golds glow. It was such a beautiful scene, I nearly missed the obvious point.

Jerry Gaffney wasn't merely a danger to any raccoon that came by. Unless I had missed something, he had threatened me as well.

Chapter Ten

Routine has its benefits, and not only in training. I'd been a little shaken by the time I got home. Blame it on some mishaps I'd had recently. While my car had been fixed up, my nerves were maybe not quite as resilient as they'd been a year earlier.

I'd been hoping for some companionship. Wallis hadn't been around when I got home again, though, and so I poured myself a bourbon and built a fire. I could have called Jim, I knew, but that would make two nights in a row—and I had too much on my mind. Besides, I wasn't sure if he was a habit I wanted to encourage, for either of us. Things were good now, as they were. I'd take my comforts as I could find them, and try to let everything else slide.

I sipped my whiskey and tried not to listen for sounds in the house. It didn't pay to worry. I didn't like to think of Wallis going out—in addition to her thirteen-plus years, she was far from the biggest predator in the woods. Considering our relationship, however, I didn't feel like I could restrain her. Besides, I suspected that more often than not, she was simply enjoying a nap in some quiet corner of our big, old house. Making me worry was good for her mystique.

I tried to focus on that, not on fat guys with poison. And before I knew it, the whiskey was gone and I'd pulled the afghan off the back of the sofa. Some nights take care of themselves.

When Wallis didn't show for breakfast, however, I did find myself wondering, the unfamiliar anxiety giving an unpleasant edge to my caffeine.

"Wallis?" I'd made her egg. Usually the smell was enough to lure her. "You there?"

The creaks and groans were only from the wind, and so after a few minutes of poking around I grabbed my keys and headed for the car.

Routine, as I've said, can be useful, and I found my nerves settling as I drove to my first client. A year before, I'd have laughed at the idea that I'd feel this good, going to walk this particular dog. But Growler—I just couldn't think of him by his human-given name "Bitsy"—had become an ally, if not exactly a friend. A tough, often resentful bichon frise, Growler had a pronounced antipathy to females of any species. I'd met his human, the walking horror known as Tracy Horlick, so I knew why. I did what I could to alleviate a borderline abusive situation, and in return he trusted me—as much as he could trust anyone. In return, I found myself putting my faith in the little white puffball—more than in most humans. More than most animals, to be honest. His keen nose and acute observations had gotten me out of jams before. Much as I love Wallis, she's got her predispositions. At times its good to look at things from a radically different—a canine—perspective, and a walk with Growler could often clear my head.

My brief search for Wallis had made me a little late. As I pulled up to the curb by the Horlick house, I saw his mistress in the doorway, waiting for me. Dressed in her usual housecoat, still in last night's makeup at nine a.m., she resembled nothing so much as the gossips of my childhood. Women like Tracy Horlick had made my mother's life miserable, after my father left. All hate and wrinkles, she wouldn't have been one of the females who'd lured him from hearth and home, but she could have been one of many who blamed my mother for losing him. As if husbands could be misplaced through carelessness or some other moral failing.

"Good morning, Mrs. Horlick." I knew better than to ask my client how she was. Instead, I hoped to make a quick exit, with the dog. "Lovely weather today."

"If you like fall." She flicked an ash from her cigarette. I watched it fade on the concrete walk and kept coming. "And things dying."

"Nonsense." I'd learned to affect a certain deafness in regard to Growler's human. "Lovely out." I stepped up as if to enter the house, but she blocked the way. "Is Bitsy ready?" I even managed a smile.

"I hear you're mixed up with the dead again." One thing Tracy Horlick did have going for her was the finest tuned ear for gossip in all of Beauville. Somehow, between her bridge club, the beauty salon that lacquered her hair every week, and the convenience store where she bought her cigarettes by the case, she managed to know everybody's business. Even, to my dismay, a good deal of mine. "Over at that new place?"

I nodded, hoping to make this quick. "LiveWell," I acknowledged.

She snorted, smoke coming out of her nostrils. "What a ripoff. You know what they want for a place there?"

I didn't, though it was mildly interesting that she'd looked into it.

"Four grand. A month!" She waggled her cigarette for emphasis. "For a studio!"

"Well, that probably includes nursing care, meals, and such." Good thing she'd never moved to the city. This house was in one of the older developments. Not as spacious as my mother's place—or as expensive to heat, I'd bet—but old enough so that her late husband, or, hell, maybe her parents, had probably paid off the mortgage years before.

"Someone's making money off that place." She paused to pick a piece of tobacco from her tongue. Behind her, a muffled bark rang out.

"Sounds like Bitsy is ready for his walkies!" I put my best effort into it, and got a sour look in return. "Look, I don't know anything about the economics of LiveWell," I reverted to my normal voice. "I'm just helping retrain a parrot."

"Huh." Tracy Horlick wasn't mollified, but she must have figured that she wouldn't get anything else out of me because she turned and went inside. I reached in the door for the lead and a moment later Growler came bounding out of the basement. Snapping the lead onto his collar, I nodded toward the house and we hit the road.

"She lock you in there all night?" During the summer, I knew Growler had been left in the tiny backyard. I wasn't sure this was an improvement.

"It's dry." With a grunt, the bichon let me know he wasn't in the mood for pity. *"And there's prey."* He added. I looked down and as those button eyes stared up, I got a sense of mice burrowing in. Looking for a safe place to spend the winter...

"Huh!" He turned and pulled me toward a small elm. I got a whiff of Lars, an overweight beagle, and something else—something golden and brown. *"Roberto."* Growler filled in the name. *"And you're getting off the topic, walker lady."*

He was right. The image of the mice, their whiskered faces staring up at me, had sparked something. The raccoon—of course! I would have to deal with Jerry, though I wasn't sure yet how. In the meantime, I thought about poison. Tracy Horlick wasn't ever going to win prizes for her humane treatment of animals, and I needed to warn Growler of the consequences of eating anything he caught.

"Got it." The ease with which the small dog read my mind jolted me. I'd thought I had to direct my thoughts to be understood. *"No, not really."* His gruff voice answered my unspoken question. *"Thanks, though."*

It was unnerving, and as I tried to shake it off I let the little dog wander. *"Hmm... Gus, that kidney problem is getting bad..."* The idea that the bichon was letting me eavesdrop as a way to apologize for listening in on my thoughts was making me a little crazy. I needed to get ahead of it.

"Look, Growler?" I didn't stop walking. That would have been rude. I did, however, speak out loud. "Can we try to keep our communication conversational? You know, like we ask each other things? Not just listen in?"

"*Huh!*" I tried to take the dog's brisk chuff and not the fact that he stopped to urinate on a tree as my answer. A moment later, he gave me more. "*So, are you going to ask me?*"

He'd caught me off guard. I'd been looking forward to consulting with the wise little dog about a number of things: the parrot, mostly. But I'd thought Growler might also have some insight into the raccoon situation, particularly after that revelation about the basement. Maybe, even, he could give me a clue about communicating with that sphinx of a guide dog.

"*Stupid bitch...*" I knew he meant in a technical way. Growler is not fond of any females. He'd picked up that "Buster" was female, but that didn't surprise me. Wallis had already taught me that animals get clues from us that we aren't aware of. They have to; for them, more often than not, knowing who and what you're dealing with can mean survival.

"Speaking of that raccoon..." Might as well start with the problem uppermost in my mind.

"*Mating season?*" Growler's ears stood up.

"What? No." That would be in the winter. Then I heard what he'd responded to: a car, much newer than my own, pulling around the corner.

"Hey, Pru." Creighton rolled down the window of his cruiser. "Got a minute?"

I looked down at Growler. He looked up at me, silently. "Thanks for the warning," I muttered as I walked us both over to the curb.

"How'd you find me?" I leaned in. This felt wrong somehow. I like to keep the day and night parts of my life as separate as possible.

My nighttime buddy only smiled. "Good morning to you, too."

Okay, so I was being about as pleasant as Tracy Horlick. I nodded, waiting.

"Look, I know Mrs. Horlick is one of your regulars, and when I drove by, I saw your car there." He looked back at the corner. It was true; Growler was a little dog and our walks didn't usually take us too far. "I wanted to ask you something."

"I'm here." I was also getting intense waves of interest from the dog by my side. Interest in our discussion—or in Jim Creighton. I didn't know which. Creighton is a sexy man.

"You went out to that new condo complex late yesterday. Evergreen Hills, the one right by the town line." It wasn't a question, so I didn't respond. "I was wondering what brought you there."

"And you care, why?" Creighton had startled me, showing up in the wrong context like this. I heard the snarl in my voice, though, and decided I should give him something. "It's an animal issue, Jim. I'm helping Albert."

"Albert, huh." He nodded, and I wondered what I had just confirmed. "You know Joey Gaffney?"

"Sort of. I mean, I remember him from high school." He'd been a troublemaker then. From what his cousin, Jerry, had said, he wasn't doing much better now. Though it sounded like he was at least trying his hand at honest employment. "I gather he's doing some work up there?"

"You talk to him?" Creighton was asking the questions, not answering them. No matter what Growler might think, I do have my own internal sensors, and they were on alert.

"I talked to his cousin, Jerry." I waited. Nothing. "On an animal matter." I repeated. "For Albert."

"Uh huh, good." He nodded again, in confirmation of I knew not what. "Good to hear it, Pru." He put the car in gear.

"Wait." I kept my hands on the door. "What is this about?"

"Timing, Pru. That's all." He looked up, those baby blues cool and innocent. "And for once, maybe it really is better off that you don't know anymore."

Jim Creighton knew me. He drove off before I could work up a comeback, leaving me openmouthed. A slight pressure on the side of my leg, and I looked down at Growler.

"What?" I didn't mean it to come out that way. "Seriously, you have any thoughts?"

He tilted his fluffy little head. If I'd been anyone else, I would have been overwhelmed by his cuteness. Instead, I waited.

"Didn't get much," he said finally. *"Car was too cold for good scenting. There was something though. Something besides mating."*

He was having trouble, I could see it in the way his whole body trembled. Tension, not fear, was what I was picking up from the little dog, but I wasn't sharp enough to get at the root of it.

"Fear, that's it," Growler said finally. I started to correct him, to explain that he was picking up on my perception. He barked once, short and sharp, to cut me off. *"It's the poison, isn't it?"* The little head tilted up toward me, the button eyes holding me in their stare. *"There's some danger around the poison, and car man is thinking you're involved."*

Chapter Eleven

Creighton—and Growler—were right. I was involved. And although I wasn't afraid of Jerry Gaffney, I wasn't enough of a fool to take him on alone. For once, the law was on my side, and if I had to get a court order to stop Jerry and his numbskull cousin from slaughtering wildlife, so be it.

I'd kept Growler out longer than usual by then, so I walked him back to the Horlick house, my other questions still ringing in my head. Knowing now that the bichon's perception was sharper than I'd thought, I tossed some of these at him as we walked.

"That parrot—is he telling me something, or just repeating words and sounds he's heard?" That was the big one, and I thought the little dog had paused as he considered it. That he'd paused by a particularly well-used hydrant brought me back to reality. This was Growler's one outing of the day. He had his own needs, his own social agenda to fill.

"*Huh.*" The chuff again, as he sniffed open-mouthed at the hydrant. "*That's a fight waiting to happen. Someone's going to the vet again.*" I didn't want to interrupt as he catalogued the various scents. I did hope, however, that the object of Growler's interest wasn't another of my clients. "*No trusting that one. Not him.*"

"You are talking about another dog, aren't you, Growler?" Something about the vehemence worried me. That on top of Creighton's cop-like reticence made me curious. "Or are you talking about 'car man'?"

He lifted his leg and then with a sigh that carried a wave of resignation, he plowed ahead toward his inhospitable home. *"Women."* That I got, loud and clear. *"Don't see what's right in front of them."*

"What, Growler?" I stopped, and since I held the other end of the leash, he had to, as well. He turned and eyed me, his button eyes cold.

"The guide dog—the one you call 'Buster'?" He broke his silence. *"She's more concerned with her person than with anyone else—and with good reason. People die there. She smells it, and I can smell it on her."*

I nodded, grateful for that damp black nose. He was gleaning things from my memories that went beneath my radar. We continued walking, and I mulled over that last statement. Yes, people died at LiveWell. It was an old folks' home, no matter what anyone called it. Death's waiting room. Did he—or did Buster—mean there were suspicious deaths? Deaths that shouldn't have happened—what the coroner would call misadventure? Or even murder?

"Watch what happens to that bird," Growler said, barking once as we came up to his door. *"Nobody likes a blabbermouth."*

Chapter Twelve

If I hadn't been concerned about Randolph, I was now. Yes, he was a nuisance, and, yes, he was going to be hard to place, given his vocabulary. But would someone besides me take his rantings seriously? Had the big bird repeated—the word "confided" didn't seem right—his demonstration to anyone else?

I rushed through my next few jobs—a regular claw clipping for a Persian who was a lot more accepting than Wallis would have been and a dachshund whose back necessitated physical therapy—and then raced over to LiveWell. I was early, but, hey, Jane had said she was always there these days, hadn't she?

The woman who answered my knock was even more of a mess than the day before. Eyes swollen, nose red, Jane had been crying. Bawling was more like it, if the little hiccups that had her head bobbing as she let me in were any indication.

"Are you okay?" I didn't want to get involved. Humans can care for themselves. However, this human had already given me a hefty deposit. "You know, I lost my mother about two years ago."

She turned and I followed her into the apartment. The box level looked pretty much the same as it had the day before, though the fast food wrappers were new. The parrot, however, looked worse. That bald spot on his chest was worried and angry. I nodded at him, trying to catch his eye. Before I could say anything, the woman who'd let me in coughed out a sob that had me looking for a box of tissues. She was ahead of me, though, and grabbed a bunch before turning to face me again.

"It's not that." Her nose still looked sore, but the hiccups had subsided. "It's—the hospital."

I waited while she grabbed another bunch of tissues. Those final bills can pack a wallop, but not enough to provoke tears, I figured. A lost wedding ring, maybe. It seemed unlikely they'd lose a body. "Didn't she—" I caught myself in time. "I thought she passed here, in her home."

Jane shook her head and dabbed at her nose. "No, well, she did, it turned out. But they took her to the hospital anyway. She'd been there—Berkshire General—just a few weeks before, so officially she was under their care—as well as Doctor Wachtell's. I don't understand the arrangement."

"Wachtell is the gerontologist on duty here?" She nodded. Sweet arrangement: all your clients in one place. "He probably has an affiliation with Berkshire, so he can admit patients." My mother had died at home, with hospice care. Still, I'd ended up learning about so-called institutional end-of-life treatment. "Care" had little place in the routine of tests and procedures. "He was probably her doctor of record."

Jane just shook her head. "I wish he'd been the one. He's the best, really. At least, she was beyond hurting by that point."

But not beyond a couple of grand's worth of procedures, I'd bet. Still, I didn't see how all this had led to tears—and I wanted to get to work. "Is it—the thought of her being there?" I'm no good at this. Behind me, the parrot shuffled and muttered. "Damn it all." I tried not to smile.

"They had a meeting." She bit down on the last word. "Mortality and—morbidity?"

"Yeah, that sounds right." Too many memories.

"They're saying that the death was not natural." She had to pause there and reach for more tissues. I turned toward the parrot. Randolph tilted his head. "That someone was 'at fault.'"

I whipped back to Jane. "At fault?" God, I was sounding like a parrot.

"Her care. *My* care." Ah, that was why the tight mouth.

"Are they going to do an autopsy?" How many days had the old woman been dead—five? No, six. "Can they?"

A sharp, quick shake of the head. "They'd asked that morning, when she—when she—but I said no. I didn't think…"

I'd made the same decision. The offer seemed so pointless, the exact cause of death after so many months of suffering a useless bit of knowledge. Under the circumstances, though…

Jane was still talking. "—saying she should not have been left unsupervised, because of the level of medication. The number of prescriptions she had."

My look asked the question. "Painkillers," Jane said. I thought of the voice I had heard. Maybe that hadn't been recent. Maybe Polly Larkin hadn't been able to speak at the end. Keeping my own memories in mind, I tried to phrase my next query gently.

"Was she in a great deal of pain?" Listening to my own voice, I could imagine how Wallis would scoff. Humans, as she well knew, were wimps.

Jane was toughening up, though. "It was her back. Something with the cartilage in her disks—it had worn away. That was why she had the walker."

Another shake of her head, as she reached for some books. "But they didn't know her. They didn't know how tough she was. The amount of drugs she'd had, the strength of some of them, she shouldn't have been able to get out of bed at all, they said." She shoved the books into a box as if they were to blame and reached for more. "The doctor on the phone told me that his committee was going to discuss starting some kind of inquiry."

"Well, that's good, right?"

In response, she grabbed more books. Anger came off her like heat, replacing the earlier sadness and shock. What I didn't understand was why.

"Pain meds." More books. At least she was getting the packing done. "Their fancy new 'miracle drug.' None of it was working."

"Damn it all!" Randolph startled us both. "What are you doing? What are you doing?" He'd spread his wings—the cage gave him just enough room—and was flapping them as he shrieked. "Put that down!"

"What?" Jane looked up confused.

"He's agitated. Your voice." I went over to the cage. "Is there a cover? It might calm him down."

She handed me a light-resistant cover that I wrapped around the cage, fixing the Velcro shut. "Damn it all!"

I shared the sentiment. "Look, maybe you should take a break. Go get a cup of tea or something." I looked around at the hamburger wrappings, the Styrofoam cups. "Have something proper to eat. I'll take care of Randolph."

Jane stopped packing. "Thanks."

As she reached for her coat, I had another thought. "When was the last time you let Randolph fly around?"

"Fly around?" She turned back toward me, clearly clueless.

I tried not to sigh audibly. "A bird that size, especially in a cage that size, should have some time to fly every day. Surely, your mother…" I paused. I really didn't want her to start crying again.

"She—I always thought that was a filthy habit. The bird is," she bit her lip, "not trained."

"No, they aren't. Still…" Even under his cage cover, we could hear Randolph fluttering, jumping from perch to perch. "Look, I'll keep an eye on him and clean up if he poops anywhere." I forced a smile. "You deserve a break."

Now that her anger had dissipated, the wan blonde did look exhausted. And so with one more nod, she let me escort her out the door. The moment it closed behind her, I fetched the canister of treats I'd packed for training purposes and hurried back to the cage.

"Randolph?" I opened the cover tentatively. If the bird had fallen asleep, I'd let him be.

"What the hell do you want?" It was as clear an answer as any I'd heard, but it wasn't accompanied by frantic flapping. So I pulled the cover back and found myself once more eye to eye with the big, gray bird.

"Would you like some fly time?" I had no idea what Polly had called it. Clearly, her daughter didn't. "Fly time?" I offered a treat. "Fly?" I still had no bond with this bird. Without that, I didn't stand a chance.

"Waah," the bird took the treat, then looked down and pecked at a large scaly claw. "Couldn't hurt."

"Okay, then." I opened the door and stepped back. Parrots can be aggressive, and this one was large and agitated. Plus, I'd realized, his favorite perch put us at eye level. I didn't know how much this bird understood. I did know I didn't need to get into a dominance contest with a client. "Go wild."

"Waah! Go wild."

"Very good." Randolph stepped onto the door frame and accepted a second treat with his massive beak. "Go wild," I tried again.

"Wild." He peered around the room. I didn't think he was looking for Polly. The mess, I figured. Things must seem strange. Still, he spread his wings and took off. I stepped back and still felt the breeze from his wings. He was a big bird, and once again I wondered how old he was. How much he must have seen.

I walked over to the wall to get out of his way. To lean back, I needed to move some of those boxes. "That's mine. Stop it!" He squawked, landing on the windowsill. "Get your grimy hands off."

"Sorry." I couldn't help but smile. Polly must have been a little paranoid at the end. That was a much more logical explanation than an intruder. Than murder.

"Waah!" Randolph accented his comment by letting loose some droppings. Well, the sill would be easy to clean. "Filthy animal."

"She said that to you?" He was perched below my eye level, and I had the uncanny feeling this was intentional. Randolph didn't want me worrying about dominance, either. "Or are you repeating someone else's words?"

Rose, maybe. Or more likely Genie—though from what I'd witnessed, either Jane or her brother might have made comments if they'd visited and found the bird flying free.

"Waah." Randolph started to groom, working his thick beak through the feathers on his left wing. It must have felt good to stretch out, I thought. Being cage-bound was almost as bad as being bedridden. I shook the treats canister to get his attention, and then stopped myself. Thinking back over what Jane had said, what the doctors had said, was making me cautious. Parrots bond, and Randolph probably missed Polly. Still, this bird's stress issues might have dated from long before Polly's death. I didn't want to push him.

"Crap!" The bird stopped grooming and angled his head to stare at me. "Shit on a shingle!"

"Okay," I spoke carefully. "Maybe it's not the same." Did this bird understand me? My morning with Growler had alerted me to possibilities I wouldn't have considered only a day or two before.

"Bullshit." The bird elongated the first syllable in a manner that would have been comical under other circumstances.

"What are you trying to tell me, Randolph? If Randolph is indeed your name?" This wasn't what I'd been planning. Still, both Wallis and Growler had put me on alert.

"Full of crap, that one. Put that down! What are you doing? What are you doing? That's mine! Aaah!" And with something that sounded eerily like a human shriek, the gray bird took off again, circling the room one more time before returning to his cage once more.

I stood up in alarm: too quickly for the cluttered room. One box teetered, and I caught it. That walker though, it crashed forward with a familiar sound. In his cage, Randolph was watching me, the black pupil alert in the bright yellow iris. "Ka-da-klump," he said. "Oh, my."

Chapter Thirteen

"You do know what you're saying, don't you?" I stood facing the open cage door. "You're saying that Polly, your person, was murdered."

"I am?" The bird tilted his head at a quizzical angle. With his wide-set eyes, I couldn't tell if he was still staring at me—or if he was focusing on the cuttlefish bone wired to the side of the cage.

"You know you are." I caught myself. Pru Marlowe: interrogating a bird. "At least, I think you do."

"Know what I'm saying. Aww." Either this bird was toying with me, or he was an extremely fast learner.

"Hello?" A different voice, much softer, caused me to whirl around. Rose, with Buster and Genie in tow, was sticking her head through the door. "Anyone home?"

"It's me." I started toward them and paused. The bird, the dog—Buster was well trained, but still. I reached back and closed the cage.

"Crap," said Randolph.

"I found something!" Rose walked into the room slowly. Buster leading her between the boxes—and leaning back against her ever so slightly before she could bump into one of Jane's piles. "Genie?"

The aide stepped around them and held out a book to me. It was huge and hardbound, and I could see why the little neighbor had recruited the aide to carry it. "Sophie's Choice," I read the cover. "Large-print."

"Genie was reading it to me," Rose gestured in the direction of the aide. "But I thought Jane might want it."

As a doorstop? I shot her a look before I once again realized that she couldn't see it, and put the book on one of the more stable piles. "I'm sure she'll appreciate your thoughtfulness." All the clichés from my mother's final days were coming back.

"Someone's been busy." She looked around as if she could see, and I wondered how total her disability was—and how well her other senses compensated.

"That's Jane. I've just been working with Randolph." I became aware of a movement behind me. Genie had seen the bird dropping and gone to the kitchenette for a paper towel. "I'm sorry, I meant to clean that up."

"No trouble." Her voice was flat, and I kicked myself. Another white lady making work. "That bird…"

"It's healthy for him to fly free a little. And this is an enclosed space." The expression on her face let me know what she thought of my priorities. Then she smiled and shook her head. "Polly really did love that bird."

"So I gather." I smiled back, and Genie went to toss the towel.

"She doesn't like the parrot," Rose lowered her voice just enough to not be audible in the kitchenette. Genie, already returning, pretended not to hear, so I didn't respond either.

"Put that down! That's mine!" I turned, but not before seeing the surprise on both Rose and Genie's face.

"He's been doing that," I said, as a thought hit me. They were both watching the bird, and I could study them. "And more."

"Stop it! Stop it! Ka-da-klump!" The crashing noise was eerily accurate, and I saw Rose wince. Genie simply looked stunned. "Aaaah…" Randolph finished his recital.

"Interesting, isn't it?" I said, after a moment's silence.

"Disgusting, that's what it is." A new voice. Marc Larkin was standing inside the opened door. Behind him, his mouth ajar, stood a tall stranger, blinking, the blood drained from what should have been a well-maintained tan. "Dr. Wachtell wanted my mother to get rid of that bird."

"Indeed I did," said the tall stranger, regaining his composure—and his color. "It was never a healthy pet for a woman in her condition."

Chapter Fourteen

"Excuse me?" I don't like being startled. I really don't like amateurs judging other people's pets.

"Hey, Pru." Jane's brother lumbered in. "It's Pru, isn't it? This is Dr. Wachtell."

I turned toward the stranger—and saw Rose push by him, led by Buster. "'Scuse us," Genie said, taking up the rear. Wachtell had turned to open one of the kitchenette's cabinets and didn't respond. I made to stop them, but Marc put his hand on my arm.

"Let her go," he said, nodding toward their backs. "I don't like her hanging around here anyway. Never did."

"Which one?" I turned and looked down at the short man. I was pretty sure he meant Rose. Old women may not count for much with his type, but black women probably counted less.

"That old hag from across the hall." Marc walked over to one of the boxes and began picking through it. "She was always hanging on my mother. Bothering her."

"I thought they were friends." I didn't want to get caught up in this. My job was the parrot. Still, I liked the blind woman. More than I liked Marc, at any rate. "She came by to return a book."

Marc was leaning so far into a box that it muffled what I supposed was a laugh. "Right," I thought he said. "A book."

I looked over at the big, battered hardcover. It was true, it had seemed a minor thing, but I'd taken the gesture at face value.

"It was a prop," he said, as he sat back. "She wanted to nose around. I've got to get that key back."

"Rose has a key?" Jane had a key to her place, I recalled. But Marc shook his head. "That aide. She's another one."

Suddenly aware of the third person in the room, I bit back what I might have said and turned instead to the doctor.

"I'm Pru, Pru Marlowe." I held out my hand. "Jane Larkin hired me to work with the parrot. I'm an animal behaviorist." I wasn't, not quite, but doctors respect degrees.

He turned from the open cabinet, but hesitated before taking my hand. "George, George Wachtell." We shook, and I waited. Usually men were eager to make my acquaintance. Then again, I'd pretty much forced him into giving me his full name. Whatever the reason, he wasn't talking.

"So, George." He wasn't *my* doctor, and I saw no reason to offer him the respect I'd give to Doc Sharpe, the vet at County. "What do you make of all this?" I looked up at the tall newcomer. With that tan now fully restored and a touch of gray at his temples he could have been from Central Casting.

"We try to encourage varied socialization at LiveWell. It is true, however, that not all the relationships that form are of the healthiest variety." He could have been reciting from a script. "Patients confide in me," he added.

"Yeah, but what do *you* think?" I crossed my arms.

A dimple appeared in one cheek. "For the most part, I try to remove myself from the squabbles and rivalries that spring up in such close living conditions."

He might be amused. I was curious. Unlike the good doctor, Genie hadn't been in any position to hold herself aloof from the residents. That might be partly the difference in rank and income, I thought, as I watched Marc pulling books and knick-knacks out of the boxes that Jane had worked so hard to fill.

It also might have been something else. The aide had been hurrying after her charge, but I'd seen how she averted her eyes from the newcomers. Wachtell—George—was a bigwig here. If not her boss, then certainly *a* boss in the LiveWell hierarchy. Along those lines, Marc might have had more direct contact with the Haitian aide. I wondered who had paid her last bills, and if any kind of severance—not to mention a gratuity—had been included. I also wondered what he was after.

"Ignorant slut!" Randolph's barking voice startled me. I'd almost forgotten him. "Bugger off."

"Great job you're doing." Marc looked up from another box.

"It's been three days." I hate being put on the defensive. "And you're not exactly giving me time alone with the bird. I was working with him when you and George here came in."

"Working, huh?" He stood and puffed out his chest. I had at least four inches over him, but he wanted me to know that he was a man. It was a pose Growler would have understood.

I stood, too, and crossed my arms. The same principle I'd considered with the parrot—that the one whose head was higher had dominance—was at play here. "Trying to," I said, as pointedly as possible. "What are you looking for anyway?"

"You wouldn't—" He was interrupted by the return of Jane.

"Marc! I spent all morning packing those." In addition to the books, her brother had unwrapped a little figurine from its protective bubble wrap. "What the hell?"

"What the hell!" Randolph chimed in.

"Sorry," I shrugged. "We were working on learning new words."

"They're gone, Jane. Aren't they?" Marc didn't seem to need height to dominate his sister.

"They're not—oh, Christ. What else have you been doing?" She was looking into the little kitchen area. Only now did I notice that the cabinets had been emptied in a haphazard fashion, cups piled on dishes on the tiny counter.

"I'm sorry," a deeper voice as George Wachtell emerged from the bathroom. "I'm afraid I've contributed to the general disruption."

Jane colored, just a little, but visible with her pale skin. I didn't think it was anger. "Doctor!"

He smiled, bringing that dimple back. "I've been lax, I know. I'm so sorry for your loss, Jane."

Marc was quiet. I didn't know if he was seeing what I was seeing—the grieving daughter in awe of the good doctor, a fact the medical man was well aware of—but he was watching something.

"Thank—thank you." She flushed more, and actually looked down. It didn't make me like either of them.

"So what were you doing, messing around in the cabinets?" I butted in. Jane was an adult and not my charge, but there was such a thing as sisterhood. "Looking for a cookie?"

"Looking for the late Mrs. Larkin's meds, actually." The smile disappeared, and I swear his voice got deeper. His doctor voice, I figured. "I ran into Marc in the lobby and realized I hadn't come by to collect her unused medications." He raised his hands. They were empty. "This is why. It appears I was already too late."

"I'm not surprised." Marc was trying to brush newsprint off his hands, using one of a stack of towels. "Jane, do you have anything besides books in those boxes?"

"What? No!" Jane rushed over. "Please, Marc. Those are clean. And, no, the sealed boxes are just books. What were you looking for, anyway?"

"The silver candlesticks." He said it like it was obvious. Like she should know. "The ones Nana gave her. They're gone."

"Oh." Jane put her hand to her mouth, thinking. "Honestly, Marc, I can't remember where I saw them last. Julie didn't take them for Thanksgiving?"

"My wife is not a thief." The little man leaned forward, his florid cheeks growing dark. "And if you hadn't given keys to every *helper*—"

"Now, wait a minute." It was partly his tone, but the little air quotes he'd made around that last word really bothered me. I'd heard the parrot mimicking Polly—or someone—in protest. *"That's mine! Get your hands off!"*

I also knew what category he'd put me in, before taping it shut. "You come in here, when your sister's been doing all the work—all the work that the paid aide hasn't done. You don't help pack. You don't clean. Ten minutes later, you're accusing the staff of—what?—of stealing the family heirlooms?"

That shut him up.

"Well, I'm not sure this is an appropriate conversation to be having. Not here." Wachtell stepped further into the room. Probably thought his gravitas—if not his charm—would work on me, too. It didn't. "And comparatively, the cost of some of those medications considerably overwhelms the—"

"You're not much better—" I had a head of steam going for me now. "Aren't you a little lax about drugs here? I mean, I know a cop who—"

"Just a minute!" Marc had caught his breath. "Just because my sister is getting all sentimental about that filthy bird, doesn't mean you have the—"

"Oh my God!" Jane, her voice raised above ours, interrupted everything. "What's wrong with Randolph?"

Inside his cage, the parrot was shaking, his wings extended slightly from his side, his feathers puffed up as if by the cold. I grabbed a towel and raced over to the cage. Before I could open its door, his little body jerked once, as the parrot vomited. And then Randolph fell off his perch.

"Do something!" Ever the big sister, in a crisis Jane took charge. In this case, that meant yelling at me as I scooped the bird out of his cage and wrapped him in the towel

"Doctor?" I looked up at Wachtell. I didn't have great hopes there, but any medical expert in a storm. He shook his head wordlessly, and I turned back to the siblings. "Did your mother have an avian first aid kit?"

They looked at each other. Jane shrugged. "It doesn't matter. There isn't much I could do." I'm not a trained vet tech, and I'm just not as up on my birds as I am on cats and dogs. Not that they had to know this. I looked down: Randolph was breathing and beginning to stir. "I'm going to take him to County. To the animal hospital."

They nodded—I was in charge now—and parted to let me through as I headed toward the door.

"What's wrong with Randy?" A woman in a wheelchair was waiting at the elevator. "Is he sick?"

"Seems to be," I said, cradling the bird, who had begun to move. I needed to keep him warm and still. I certainly didn't want him getting loose outside the apartment. "You go ahead." She motioned me in as the elevator arrived. "He's more important."

"Is Randolph sick?" I heard Rose's voice from down the hall. I didn't wait to hear the wheelchair-bound resident's answer. I was too busy thinking through the events of the last few hours. The treats had been sealed. Could they have been bad? I thought of the fast food wrappers. The empty coffee cups. The dust of packing. The missing meds. Hell, even something in the forced hot air that had made this building an overheated solarium. Any of these could have sickened Randolph. He'd been flying free moments before—

That did it. I went through the timeline in my head. When the door to the late Polly Larkin's apartment had opened. When it had closed. When Rose and Genie had come in, then Jane, Marc, Wachtell…All of them seemed to think nothing of going in and out of the unlocked apartment. All of them had been there when the parrot had done his macabre routine; odds were, they'd heard it before. It was a reach, but I had to consider the possibility. Any one of them could have ducked in at some point. Any one of them could have wanted Randolph to shut up. Any of them could have poisoned the parrot.

Chapter Fifteen

"Hang in there." It was a silly thing to say to a bird, especially such a still one, as he lay wrapped in a towel on my passenger seat. But as I peeled out of the LiveWell parking lot, I wasn't thinking of parrot vs. cat, or even animal vs. human. I was thinking that a creature in my care was ill, and that all I wanted to do was get to help as soon as possible.

The options weren't great. As the elevator descended, I'd raced through them. While there were private vets closer by, County—the combination shelter/animal hospital—still seemed like the best bet. The hospital part was well stocked, and Doc Sharpe, the director, was easily the most experienced vet around. Problem was, County was close to twenty minutes away, even as I drive. I didn't know if Randolph had it.

"Hang in there, Randolph." I didn't know where that came from, it just sounded right. And as I swerved around a minivan, I was gratified to hear an answering squawk.

"Help." The voice was soft but audible. "Get help."

"That's right, Randolph. We'll be there soon." Leaf peepers were everywhere, and I had to keep my eyes on the road. Still, the shuffle next to me sounded more like confused bird than convulsion. One more car passed, and I dared a glance. One bright eye stared back up at me, but the parrot was shivering.

"You warm enough?" I'd been afraid to blast the heat. Who knew what spores lived in my radiator? This bird was already in a weakened condition.

"Yah." It could have been an affirmative. It could have been a senseless squawk. Any sign of life was good. Cheering. "I'm sorry about the hasty exit." I found myself just this side of babbling. "And the towel. Wallis would hate that, I know. So undignified. She's a cat. Does anyone at LiveWell have a cat? Maybe not. "

"She's—" Silence. I glanced over, and the little eyes still seemed bright.

"She's a cat." I repeated. It wasn't a useful phrase. However, if Randolph was still interested in mimicking me, he wasn't that far gone. And by then we didn't have that far to go. I was driving faster than even my usual, I realized as I careened around a hesitant Volvo onto the exit. We'd be at County in less than a minute. "A cat."

The only response was a soft whistle, weak and low. We were on small streets now, and at this speed I couldn't take my eyes off the road, but I needed to check. I reached over. Yes, I felt movement.

"She's a cat," I repeated, as much for myself as for Randolph. County. I heard my tires screech as I pulled into the lot.

"She's—" I slammed on the brakes, reaching for the bird before he could tumble to the floor.

"Hang on, Randolph." Clutching him to me like a football, I charged from the car. Rammed through the door. "Doc Sharpe?"

"Not—" I thought I heard from the towel-wrapped bird. Could have been "Doc." Who knew? "She's not—" At least the bird was still alive.

"Doc?" I pushed past Pammy, the vet's ditsy assistant, and into the back hallway. "Doc Sharpe?" I didn't have time to check each examining room and his office. Randolph didn't have time.

A bald head looked out, eyes wide behind wire-rimmed glasses.

"Doc, I've got a sick parrot here. I'm not sure if he inhaled something. Might have eaten something. Might have been—" I paused, catching my breath and holding the parrot in front of me. "Poisoned."

"Poison." Randolph's hoarse voice was loud and clear. "She's not—" Then the wrapped bird gave strange avian cough and went limp.

◇◇◇

"Exam room A." Doc Sharpe ushered me down the hall. I placed the parrot on the table and stood back. The vet was washing his hands, and Randolph wasn't flying anywhere. "History?"

"The bird seemed fine until about forty-five minutes ago." Had it been that fast? "Maybe thirty. I'd been letting him fly around the apartment. There were numerous small objects and possible sources of toxicity." I tried to recall Polly's room as I'd last seen it, and began listing the dangers. "Possibility of onions, caffeine. Small non-food objects. Also, the heat was on." Doc Sharpe would understand.

"Okay, then." I washed up as he opened Randolph's beak. The vocalizations were a good sign that his airway wasn't blocked, but I knew he'd be looking for other clues—irritated throat or other mucus membranes—that might give us an indication of what had happened. "No prior issues?"

"No." I stopped myself. "Some over grooming, but the bird's owner has recently died and his routine has been changed."

"Ah, the Larkin bird. I remember." He was unwrapping the bird and palpating his belly. Now that the towel was off, I could see how pink and exposed his skin was, the beautiful pattern of his plumage interrupted. "Should have insisted on a physical." I didn't know if he was talking to me or to himself, so I kept my mouth shut. "Seizures, you say?"

He was talking to me now, so I answered. "Yes, he fell off his perch. He may have vomited."

"Huh." Doc Sharpe is a man of few words under the best of circumstances. I waited. He ran a finger under the parrot's feet. "That's interesting."

He looked up again. "Come here, Pru. Learn something." I did. "See how the bird's feet are relaxed? Not clenched? That lessens the odds the bird has lead poisoning. That's good. Plus, the belly is firm, but not distended, and the bird seems alert now.

There are neutralizing compounds, if we knew what it may have ingested, and I was considering an IV—saline—but hydration has its own dangers. No." He stared at his diminutive patient. The parrot stared back. "I think not. I think rest and warmth and quiet may do the trick. We'll keep him here for observation."

I nodded, not trusting myself to answer. I'd seen this bird collapse. I'd wanted something done. I'm not the vet, though. Hell, I'm not even fully qualified as a behaviorist. "Keep him here?" I choked out.

"Overnight, at least. That way, if it was something from the ventilation system…" He took his hands off the bird, and we both watched, waiting as Randolph flapped his wings, then flipped over and stood up. Craning his head to take in his new surroundings, his sharp eye settled on me and his head bobbed. Or, I thought to myself, Randolph nodded. At this point, anything was possible.

"Okay, then." Who was I to argue? "I should call his owner."

"That's right. Isn't the son taking the bird?"

"That's the problem." I was too tired to explain. "I haven't had a chance to do much with the bird's vocabulary. Though he did start talking on the way over. 'She's not poison?'" I chuckled despite myself. "Maybe he was trying to clear the daughter's name." Or the aide, or the neighbor. It was too much to get into. "Help us identify the hitman."

Doc Sharpe turned a gimlet eye on me. "Hitman?"

"It's a long story." I held out my hand for Randolph to climb onto and rested my other hand gently on his back. This parrot needed rest. So, for that matter, did I. "It's just—I think there may have been something suspicious about Polly Larkin's death, and Randolph here keeps saying things that sound, well, incriminating."

"Pru." Doc Sharpe doesn't have a loud voice under any circumstances. Right now, though, it was particularly soft. "I know you lost your mother not long ago. Is going to LiveWell too much?"

"No, I'm sorry. I'm tired." I walked up to the door and waited while the good vet opened it, basically forcing him to lead me to the cage room. "It's just that some of the things that bird says are uncanny."

"African grays can be like that." He couldn't have been more noncommittal as he put down bedding and found a cuttlebone and water dish. "Their gift for mimicry is astounding."

"Yeah." I knew I should leave it at that. Doc Sharpe was not only an ally, he was the source of much of my income. "He just sounds so—"

"Doc? You there? Doc?" I was saved by a strawberry blonde interruption. Pammy had barged in with a whine loud enough to make dogs howl.

"What is it, Pammy?" The vet was either used to her or beginning to lose his hearing.

"The Lucknows have been waiting." Her emphasis on the last word made it clear that the scheduled clients weren't the ones most discomfited. "I don't know what to tell them."

Doc Sharpe was patience personified. "Tell them, we've had an emergency, Pammy. Tell them I'll be with them as soon as I'm able."

She clucked her disapproval, and I turned toward Randolph, waiting to hear it echoed back. He restrained himself.

"Tell them, I'm almost done. I should be out within five minutes." On that Pammy spun on her heel. I watched her go, wondering. In truth, I could have set Randolph up here.

"Doc, you want me to finish up?" Randolph was hopping around his cage now, but there was paperwork. Instead of looking relieved, however, the bald vet took my elbow to draw me close.

"I have to confess, I've been a tad worried about you, Pru." Doc Sharpe is old Yankee. They use words like tad. I knew I'd gone too far.

"Doc, really—it's just the situation—"

"No, Pru. There has been another situation that has been reported to me. Another, frankly, disturbing development."

I held my breath. Someone had heard me talking to Wallis. Or, worse, to Growler or Frank. I'd spent time in the psych ward—voluntarily, back when my gift had first manifested itself. I did not want to go back.

He looked down at the floor, then up at Randolph's cage. These were not good signs.

"I hear you've been keeping a wild animal caged. Over at the shelter."

I opened my mouth and then shut it. Doc Sharpe knew as well as I did that Albert ran the shelter. He also probably had a fair sense of how easy it was to run Albert.

"A raccoon," he finished.

"That's an odd situation." I fished for a way to explain it. "A young male, and he keeps on entering an attic over at the new condo complex. I thought if they'd just make their attic raccoon-proof…."

He was shaking his head. "I heard that they wanted it tested for rabies—"

"It's a healthy animal, Doc." I had no way of proving this. "I've been observing him."

"Pru, what you are doing is unethical and also unsafe. You need to destroy the animal and submit it for testing. Sentiment has no place with a viral infection, a zoonotic viral infection. You know the mortality rate in mammals." He leaned in and I saw the concern in his eyes. "All mammals, Pru."

That took the wind out of me, and he saw it.

"All right then?" He patted my elbow. "I'm sure you'll take care of everything." With a nod, he stepped out of the room, to wait on the impatient Lucknows. And I was left wondering what I was going to do with a healthy young animal when it hit me: Someone had dimed me. Either Albert or—more likely—Jerry Gaffney had wanted to put me on the spot.

I don't take kindly to being put in a corner. And I don't put healthy animals to sleep. There was a way through this, I simply had to find it.

"Go get 'em." The voice was a little softer than before, but recognizable. Randolph was back. "Nasty buggers!"

Chapter Sixteen

"What, no pizza?"

I'd gone home after leaving County, the better to figure out what my next step should be. Wallis had been waiting for me, tail neatly coiled around her white forepaws. I'd been thrilled to see her. The anxiety of the morning had come rushing back as I'd approached my own front door, but I knew better than to fuss. Instead, I'd started telling her about my day—and about my latest predicament. Wallis is a wily old soul, and while she's not keen on either birds or raccoons, she's also not one to back away from a fight. Before I could tell her everything, however, the doorbell rang. Creighton, looking as tired as I felt. And not, it appeared, here on a social call.

"Pru, can we talk?" Those big blue eyes melt me, usually. Tonight they made me pause. Had Gaffney sicced Creighton on me already? What would the charge be, exactly—harboring dangerous wildlife? Harassment by raccoon?

"Sure." I didn't see any way out of it, and so I let him in. He walked past me without even an attempt at a kiss and collapsed on my mother's old couch. Wallis, that fickle girl, jumped up right beside him. "Want a beer?"

"Sure." Okay, it couldn't be that bad. By the time I returned, two longnecks in hand, Wallis had flopped down beside Creighton, and he was stroking her tiger-striped fur. I took a seat opposite, so I could watch his face. Wallis looked over at me, her green eyes cool. I couldn't read either of them, not yet, and so I waited.

"You're still working with that parrot, right? Over at LiveWell?"

Jim knew this. "I only started a few days ago."

"This is the old lady who you think didn't die naturally?" I nodded again. "Pru, have you told anyone your suspicions? I mean, anyone besides me?"

I was suddenly glad my conversation with Doc Sharpe had been interrupted. "I told Wallis." I forced a smile. If he wanted to think I was making light of his question, so be it. "That's it."

"Hell." He ran his hand over his face. Took a long pull of the beer. "Well, you've made an enemy somehow. There's been a complaint."

"If this is about that raccoon, I have my own complaints—"

Creighton raised his hand to silence me. Since that hand had been petting Wallis, she looked up. I stopped talking. She placed one paw on his thigh.

"Please, Pru. This is my job. It seems some family heirlooms have gone missing. And I have been told that you have been left alone, more than once, in the late woman's apartment."

I could have slapped somebody. Not Creighton, though. He looked too drawn. "Look, Jim, I told you something was off with that family." I kept my voice even, aware that Wallis was watching me with interest. "That parrot is repeating things no bird should even know about. And I haven't said anything, but everyone in that family—and a few of the LiveWell staff, too—has heard him. It's eerie, Jim. Truly."

A deep sigh. "I'm not going to question a parrot, Pru."

"I wish you'd come by. At least listen—" Then it hit me. "The bird isn't even in LiveWell anymore. He's at County. He got sick. I think someone might have tried to poison him."

He didn't have to voice his skepticism.

"Seriously, Jim. What if I file a complaint? A suspicion of animal cruelty report? Wouldn't you have to investigate that?"

If it would work with the parrot, maybe I could use the same strategy for the raccoon. My mind was getting ahead of me.

He was shaking his head. "You know that's not my territory. That's Albert's area."

"Jim, animal cruelty is a criminal act." If I could just get him over to County...

"Bring me evidence, Pru, and I'll see about it." He finished his beer. "Same with the old lady's death. Until then, maybe you can make nice with these people?"

"Jim—" He was on his feet, shaking his head. I walked him to the door and stood there as he bent over to kiss me on the forehead.

"Proof, Pru."

"I heard you." It was that chaste kiss that did it. Either he was tired, or something was very, very wrong. I watched him drive off and replayed the brief visit. The consummate cop, he hadn't named the source of the complaint. Marc, I'd bet—but I couldn't be sure. Jane had been shaken—by her brother, by the doctor. By the parrot. Hell, maybe one or the other of the siblings had complained to LiveWell management, and someone in the upscale care facility had wanted to shift the blame from their residents—and their employees—onto me.

I stood there, looking at the empty drive and considering possibilities until I felt the soft brush of fur. Wallis, twining around my ankles.

"Aren't we the little housecat?" I was in no mood. She'd gotten more petting than I had. "Did you forget who feeds you?"

She sat back on her haunches and appraised me with those cool green eyes. Then she started washing, wiping one white mitten over her dark-tipped ear.

"You have your methods, I have mine." Her voice rang in my head, loud and clear. *"Don't you want to know what I found out?"*

Chapter Seventeen

One of the tricky things about my gift, I've learned, is that I cannot make any assumptions about priorities. One animal's treat is another's trash, and neither species is really capable of understanding the other's viewpoint. Therefore, I didn't get too excited as Wallis preened, fluffing up her snowy bibb in anticipation of enlightening me. As much as she and I have come to understand each other, I wouldn't have been utterly surprised to hear her tell me that Creighton had fish for dinner. Or another woman on the side.

"Huh," Wallis huffed. *"As if I cared about that."*

I looked at her, curious. Wallis is both spayed and unsentimental, but I had my suspicions. The round tabby had been openly critical of other men in my life, and I didn't think she'd only cozied up to Creighton to pick up clues.

"Well, do you want to hear what I found out, or not?"

"Sorry, Wallis." I returned to the living room and took a seat on the couch, waiting while she jumped up and kneaded the sofa cushion beside me to her satisfaction. Cats do like their drama.

"So?" I said finally. Wallis might have started off trying to build anticipation, but after a few minutes, I was pretty sure she was nodding off.

"Organizing my thoughts, rather." Those green eyes opened to stare at me. *"Something you could do more of. Especially in this case."*

I bit my lip, waiting.

"*To start with, he's worried about you.*" Wallis was watching me, so I nodded. I'd kind of figured this out. "*He doesn't think you know what you're getting involved in,*" she responded. "*Or not enough, anyway. There's a cage in there, somewhere, and it scares him.*"

That one startled me. Was this about the raccoon? We hadn't discussed it, and I hadn't thought he'd been aware. Then it hit me: "cage" didn't mean the same thing to Wallis as it did to me.

"Does he think I'm in danger of getting locked up?" He'd said there had been accusations. I didn't see how quickly one could follow on the other, but then again, he hadn't gone into detail.

"*Yes, that's it.*" Wallis started purring, an involuntary response. She liked being understood. "*Cages. But not...sticks? Fire sticks?*"

"Candlesticks." I tried to visualize a pair, tall and silver, to explain myself to Wallis. That had been what Marc Larkin had been talking about.

"*Not him.*" The purring stopped. "*Fat, bull man.*"

"He's not fat, just—solid." I was getting distracted, I knew. Still, I couldn't erase the image of the stocky little man from my mind, and Wallis turned away from me in disgust. "I'm sorry, Wallis. I know, you were telling me about Creighton. I was just—" I didn't know how to explain. "I think Creighton is worried because of Marc, the bull man."

"*Stupid people.*" Wallis tucked her nose under her tail, leaving me with a view of her tiger-striped back. "*Not fat man, not fire—not* candle*stick. Stupid.*"

"Wallis, I don't understand." She was pissed off, I could tell. What I didn't know was whether that was because she had been caught out not understanding something—or because I hadn't been wowed by her revelation. Either way, I had only moments before she drifted off to sleep. "Please, Wallis?"

I don't often beg. Neither of us is the type, and my plea—or maybe its novelty—caused her to open one green eye and peer over her shoulder at me.

"Please?" I tried to keep my mind blank and open.

"Nothing to do with the stupid sticks." Her voice, even in my head, was growing fuzzy, drifting toward slumber. *"It's the poison that worries him. The poison and the cage."*

With that she shuffled, the black line of fur down her spine rippling once as she readjusted, and fell asleep, leaving me to decipher not only her words but her intent.

Wallis is not a simple creature. I knew that, for her, appearing both intelligent and knowledgeable were as important as actually conveying information that could be useful to me. It's not that she didn't worry about me, it was more that she trusted me to take care of myself, or so I believed. Plus, I couldn't discount the fact that Wallis was getting on in years. I was grateful that she didn't go out to hunt much anymore. The woods around Beauville held much bigger predators than my little domestic tabby. She was sensitive about any comments about aging or diminished ability, however, and might jump on anything that showed her in a more complimentary light, as a player, if you would, in my own particular hunt.

Therefore, I had a couple of things to work out. First, had Wallis actually gotten anything from Creighton that I didn't know? If she had, was she correctly interpreting it as it pertained to me, or to our, affairs? Or was she stretching the little bit she already knew in order to make herself appear more important? And, really, how good a judge was my cynical tabby of the outside world?

The only way I could think of to approach it all was by looking at the details of what she'd said. *Poison.* I'd brought it up in connection with the parrot, but I didn't think I'd mentioned anything about Gaffney threatening the raccoon. Same with the cage, although Creighton certainly knew the setup at the shelter. Still, cages might appear an awful lot like traps to an animal who was working off a visual impression from someone's fleeting thoughts. Or Wallis could have been mistaken about those words, or misinterpreting. If "cages" could be "traps," then—

I stopped, amazed at my own stupidity. Here I was, assuming my cat had misread a sign, when I was falling into the same old snare myself. Poison: I shook my head. What had Creighton been warning me about, but drugs? The drug trade, and whether any of my old "buddies" from high school were looking to get me involved again. I didn't know whether my cop beau was having me followed, or simply had surveillance on Joey Gaffney, but clearly he'd gotten word that I'd been talking to Joey's cousin. He must have thought that I was investigating, that the raccoon was a front, an excuse for me to go down to the condo development looking for one of the Gaffneys and to ask some questions.

Unless—I swallowed, another interpretation sticking like a peach pit in my throat—unless he thought I'd gone to the condos for another reason. He'd warned me about the drug trade, and what had I done? I'd gone directly to find one of the most likely culprits, meanwhile making up some cock and bull story about a nuisance animal. Could Creighton think I was in league with some local dealers? Or seeking to warn an old friend that the law was on his trail? Creighton knew I was hard up for cash; walking people's dogs didn't really pay enough to heat this old house and winter was coming in fast. Still, he couldn't think that of me, could he?

"You've not given him much reason to trust you." I looked over. Wallis' face was still hidden deep in the black tuft of her tail. *"And you haven't been particularly welcoming recently."*

"I've been busy, Wallis." I swallowed again, to get rid of that lump. It was true that I hadn't let him stay the night for a while. It was also true that Creighton and I had fallen into a routine, and routines, after a while, make me itchy.

"Maybe that's the problem, Pru." My cat was drifting toward sleep again, her voice growing faint in my head. *"He knows you've been busy. He's afraid of finding out why."*

Chapter Eighteen

There's only so much a girl can do. I'd told him, when he'd asked, that I wasn't in touch with any of my former running buddies. And I'd told him, also, that I'd gone over to the new development because of a raccoon. If Jim Creighton didn't believe me, then it was out of my hands.

I knew I was being defensive. I don't like being suspected of things I didn't do. Stupid things, the kind that hurt others. I also knew that I had precious little say about who or what Creighton chose to believe. I'd been involved with a cop before, back in the city, in my wild days. Some cops are a law to themselves; all of them like to see themselves that way.

No amount of willpower could keep me from worrying about the situation, though, and I had a restless night. Wallis didn't help. Although I sensed her coming into the bedroom at some late hour, I wasn't awake enough to hash it out with her. And in the morning, she was absent again. I'd never gotten the chance to tell her about the latest with the parrot. And by the time I'd gotten her egg and my own coffee ready, I was late for my rounds.

Tracy Horlick is a nightmare on the best of days. This one had started off bad, with a headache from the whiskey I'd drunk to make myself stop thinking and the dreams that had followed, full of suspicion and doubt. The way she was leering—I couldn't call it a smile—as I started up her walk made me wonder if she had some psychic ability. Then again, maybe she was simply mean.

"Aren't we bright eyed and bushy tailed?" She punctuated her greeting with an exhalation of smoke, and immediately took another draw on the cigarette clutched between her stained fingers. "Late night?"

"I've got a lot of new clients." I mustered a smile. I couldn't afford to lose her, nor did I want to abandon Growler to his mean-spirited mistress. Still, I couldn't sacrifice all my dignity.

"So I hear." She stepped in front of the open door, crossing her arms. "Makes me wonder."

"Oh?" I tried to peer around her, but her faded housecoat was flapping in the breeze. "Is Growler ready for his walk?"

"*Growler?*" I kicked myself.

"Just having fun," I made the smile wider and blinked, for good measure. Standing in the doorway, three steps up, she was already taller than me, and I was damned if I was going to lie down, exposing my belly. "Bitsy is such a little toughie."

The dog would forgive me. He'd done a few submissive gestures in his day, too, in order to appease old Horlick. From somewhere deep in the house, I heard a bark.

"Huh." She threw her head back, blowing smoke out of her nostrils. The offering was accepted, and she turned. "You," she said, "wait here."

The sky was overcast, but the fresh breeze—smelling of rain— was preferable to her stale smoke, so I was happy to linger on the stoop as I heard a door open and the scurrying of small claws on old linoleum. Tracy Horlick reappeared, extending a claw-like hand. I took the lead from her as the little bichon bounded out from behind her ankles.

"See you later." I batted my eyes again for good measure as the old bag retreated. As we turned onto the sidewalk, I caught a glimpse of her watching us, but the curtain whisked back as I waved.

"*Come on, walker lady.*" Growler was all pent-up energy, and I knew our time would likely be his only chance to get outdoors all day. "*It's hopeless, you know.*"

"I'm sorry." I was. The spirited little dog deserved better.

"*Not* me." The white powderpuff stopped to sniff a tree and then to mark it. "*Where's Gus been?*" His black leather nose was working overtime.

"Is it something with Gus?" I only had a faint idea of who the German shepherd was, but I tried to get a picture, if only to allow Growler to express himself.

"*What? No.*" A short, sharp bark, and he pulled me forward. Not the ideal way for a dog to walk, and in another animal I would be trying to retrain him away from tugging at the leash. In Growler's case, however, I was willing to give him leeway. He had so little control over the rest of his life.

"*Like you do?*" The button eyes were looking up at me. "*Smiley eyes?*"

"I was trying to humor her." I didn't think I had to explain myself to the bichon. After all, he lived with Tracy Horlick. "She was in a worse mood than usual, and I'm—well, I'm tired."

"*Huh.*" Growler had moved on, digging briefly in a pile of new-fallen leaves. "*You'd do better humoring the other people.*" I waited as he moved on, sniffed and sprinkled again. "*The ones who are talking about you. She just laps up what they spill.*"

Once we got to the end of the block, I let Growler off his leash. Again, while this was not my official policy, it seemed the least I could do. Besides, I wanted to think over what he'd said. Tracy Horlick was a world-class gossip, inhaling rumor and innuendo like smoke. That someone had told her I wasn't to be trusted seemed likely. Coupled with her words—and the way she'd stood, guarding her front door—it seemed likely she'd heard about the thefts over at LiveWell.

I felt myself growing angry. It's one thing to talk to a cop. If valuables go missing, you have a right to pursue justice. It's another to cast aspersions. Add in that Jane Larkin had hired me—and that she and her brother were at odds—and I began to get really steamed. I didn't know if anyone really suspected me. In cases like this, other people get dragged in as proxies for the principles. I did know that I wanted to put a stop to it.

"You ready, walker lady?" The air had gotten colder, and here, down by the river, the dampness was palpable. I had lost sense of time. *"Not that long,"* said Growler.

"You *want* to go back?" I felt better. The fresh air and time to think had cleared my head—and given me the determination to set things straight.

"Ha!" Another short bark. *"As if."* I got it. Growler had made his connections—and relieved himself. He didn't want to aggravate his person. *"Not exactly."* I looked down at those button eyes, as the bichon waited for me to reattach the lead. *"I know you're on the trail, and I don't want you to lose the scent."*

Chapter Nineteen

If Creighton hadn't wanted me to get any more involved with the Gaffney clan, he was out of luck. Albert still had that raccoon in a holding pen in the back of the shelter. I'd told him I was dealing with it, and I would. The good news was that the flannel-clad animal control officer's natural reticence to do just about anything requiring exertion meant I still had more time. The accusation of theft, however, was another matter entirely. Much as I may dislike the idea, I'm in a service profession. Word gets out that I can't be trusted, and I'm screwed. And from Tracy Horlick's reaction this morning—the image of her standing there, arms crossed as if on guard—word already had. I needed to do some damage control, and fast.

As soon as I got through my other morning jobs, I made my way over to LiveWell. The morning's overcast had turned to a drizzle, and while that set off the foliage nicely it did very little for my mood. It also meant I was going to have to seek people out. On a day like this, nobody was going to be sitting on the benches out front.

The rain, or maybe the hour, also had kept the number of visitors down again. A little after eleven and I had my pick of parking spots. In all fairness, most of the family members who might be visiting would probably be working at that hour. Jane Larkin didn't have a job, but she had to be the exception. That reminded me to make a note of the prices here. Old Horlick might have had them right. I saw no evidence of a larger conspiracy, but it couldn't hurt to know what the incentives might be.

The same receptionist was at the front desk when I came in. She seemed young enough to be in school, but out here, this probably passed for a good job. So I introduced myself and was rewarded with her name: Nancy. And when I put on a grin and asked her for a brochure, she was friendly enough.

"Sure," Nancy smiled back before pulling open a drawer by her feet. "But I thought you were working here. For Miss Larkin?"

"I am." I waited while she retrieved the slick folder, grateful for a moment to put my thoughts together. Grateful, too, that she didn't seem to know about Randolph's removal to the animal hospital. "But I've got an aunt who's getting on, and I figured, while I'm here…" She handed me the folder, and I made my smile wider.

"Thanks." I meant it. She'd just given me two interesting pieces of information. The first was that, as vapid as she might look, she was taking note of who came in—and who did what. She might not know the details—like that the parrot had gotten sick—but she saw the faces and she knew where they went. The second thing she'd let me know was that the facility was expensive. Too expensive for the people who worked here, anyway. The brochure, I saw as I quickly flipped through it, was too genteel to mention actual prices.

I was dying to ask her about comings and goings, to see if anyone had suddenly showed up the night the old lady had died. I knew there were better ways to flush out prey. "Hey, I was wondering." I leaned in to make it seem like I had something to share. "Speaking of the Larkins, what's the story with the brother, Marc?"

Wallis might not have been that proud of me, but the line did its work: Nancy's eyebrows went up. Good, let her think I found him attractive. Girl talk was likely to get me more than a more specific inquiry.

"He is a cutie, isn't he?" She leaned forward, a light flush reviving some of the faded freckles on her cheeks. "He was on the football team with my brother, before he went to college."

She shrugged. "He was one of those guys, you think he'll go to the city and never come back."

I kept my mouth shut. I was one of those girls, once upon a time.

"But he did. With a wife." Another shrug, another one lost. "Good place to raise your kids, I guess."

"Moved back to the old homestead?" I needed to find out when Polly Larkin had been moved out of her house into LiveWell, and by whom. Houses out here can go for a lot, if they're properly fixed up.

"Oh, no." A little pout. "They're in that new development, over by the town line. Her old house wasn't big enough."

Funny how time changes things. I didn't know how many children Marc Larkin had, but Polly had raised two, presumably under one roof. Still, she'd given me an opening.

"So Polly must have already downsized, huh?" I was prying now, there was no getting around it, so I added some sweetener. "I'm trying to get an idea of how she lived before coming here. You know, so I can understand something about the parrot's training."

It paid off. "No, she lived in the same house she'd always had." Another shrug. "At least that's what Jane says. She says that these days, families want more indoor space. And all that land was just going to waste. It made more sense to sell the place, back when Polly first got sick. Besides, he was already out here by then. He handled the sale and everything, the business side, anyway. I think Jane did all the packing and moving."

That was a lot to digest. I did, however, have a real job here— and so I followed through. "And the parrot?"

"Oh, he came with her. A really cool-looking bird, don't you think?" Nancy looked up at me, blue eyes wide. "He didn't talk so much back then, though. At least, not with such bad language."

Chapter Twenty

Who had taught Randolph to curse? It wasn't the key question, but it did grab my imagination as I waited for the elevator. Rose Danziger seemed like the best bet, possibly with the collusion of old Polly herself. Everyone had commented on their friendship, and Marc's dislike for the blind neighbor could have been sparked by her salty tongue.

I rather liked the idea of the two old women, sitting around on an afternoon, teaching the parrot insults. It seemed so much jollier than my own mother's last days. Granted, I'd only returned to Beauville after she was sick, but I could guess. She'd been buttoned up so tight when I left that I don't think the word "fun" was in her vocabulary. Those last few months certainly hadn't been—her, sick as a dog, tight jawed even when the pain and the meds would have made anyone else giddy. Had there been more? I'd been gone for over ten years, tearing out of here after high school and only returning when I needed a place to hide. As the elevator took me up to Polly's floor, I tried to imagine her having a romance. A friend. Even a pet. I couldn't.

I was so caught up in my own memories that I nearly walked into Genie, the aide. Granted, I had the feeling that Genie—like most of the aides here—probably worked hard to make herself invisible. That was no excuse for bumping into her as the corridor turned. It was, however, an opportunity.

"I'm sorry. My head was elsewhere." I'd backed off, but kept a hand on her upper arm.

"It's no problem." She shook her head, and I saw how tired she was "I'm half asleep, too."

"Coffee?" I needed to talk to that parrot—and get him to talk to me. Any ammunition I could get might help. "Come on, my treat."

Genie checked her watch, a pretty silver number half hidden under the cuff of her pink sweater, and then nodded. "I could take a few minutes."

"Great." I stepped back. "Lead the way." It occurred to me, then, that the staff probably had its own break room. I had a brief vision of a basement cubicle, with three other aides and a custodian clustered around an old Coffee Master. That would be about as conducive to conversation as a prayer meeting. Luckily, when this complex had gone up, someone had thought to stick an overpriced coffeehouse around the corner. "Starbucks?" I asked.

Her raised eyebrows confirmed my suspicions, but she nodded and we took the elevator back down. As she waved briefly at Nancy, and we headed out, I pondered this. I realized that maybe Genie had her own reasons for wanting time alone with me. Then again, I thought, as I followed her lead, this was her turf. Eschewing the sidewalk, we hugged the building, its decorative edging almost shielding us from the rain that was still misting down, and ducked into the storefront coffee shop with a mutual sigh of relief.

"Vente latté, with a shot of almond, please." She ordered without looking at me. It was also possible that she simply liked Starbucks. I got my own cup—black, large—and by mutual consent we found a table in the farthest corner of the little storefront.

There we sat for a full minute. About halfway into that, she even stopped playing with her coffee. Before long, we were smiling at each other—a collegial game of chicken.

"So, you have questions?" She broke first, albeit in a noncommittal way. "About the bird? It is going to be okay?"

"It is." I watched her, wondering if that was good or bad news for her. "Something must have…disagreed with it." I'd get back to that later. "And, yes, I have questions. About the parrot—and about Polly." I took a sip. Starbucks pretty much burns their beans. I don't care. I like my coffee bitter. "About her whole family, come to think of it." Another sip. She was watching me, smiling softly to herself. "After all, they seem to have some questions about me."

That did it. "Don't," she shook her head, a little sad. "Don't let that get to you." She paused, and I didn't think it was just to sip at her milky drink. "It is always difficult when a family loses someone." When she came back, it was to recite from a script, doubtless passed down to all the aides. "People express sadness in different ways."

"That's not it." I wasn't buying it. "I understand grief. I've lost people, too. There's something odd going on here. Something with those kids. And I think you have some ideas about it. You're there; you cared for the old lady. You know that something is very wrong."

Genie looked from me down into her cup. She'd already added sugar and stirred, which left her nothing more to do than stare at the foam while she thought. I didn't push her. She worked at LiveWell. It couldn't be an easy job, and I didn't know what alternatives she had.

When she looked back up, some of the fatigue was gone. Replaced by curiosity, I thought. Or suspicion. "You are not just asking because of what happened to the bird are you?"

Her gentle accent gave her words a clipped, almost formal tone. Even if I hadn't wanted to share some of my suspicions with her, that tone—with its edge of schoolmarm—might have urged me on.

"I have some questions." I wasn't going to be a fool, though. If anything amiss had happened, Genie might be aware of it, whether or not she played a role—either with the parrot or Polly Larkin. "Are you fulltime at LiveWell?"

It wasn't the question either of us had expected. Once I asked it, though, I realized how important it was: An aide who relied on one facility, its staff and its clients, for her livelihood would be in a very different position from one who freelanced at various hospitals around the county.

"I am a contract worker." She smiled; she got it. "I am on the roster of LiveWell as one of their senior aides, so I am assigned to several of the residents. The contract entitles them to an hour of assistance daily. Because of my seniority, I am also recommended for those seeking additional, private care." She looked to see if I understood. "It is a good living. Better than when I worked for Berkshire General."

I nodded. The county medical center had a reputation as a warehouse. Working there, especially in the lower-status jobs, would not be fun.

"Then I'm glad you have it. And I'm glad you're working with Rose now." I was. The old lady was a firecracker, at least compared to my mother.

Genie looked up. I'd missed something. "You're not working with Rose?"

"No, I am, but…" She paused. Of course, I was asking her to break confidentiality.

"She's not a private client." I filled in the blank. Genie smiled and gave me a half-nod of confirmation, and I filed the information away. Genie wasn't making anything extra from Rose, though I was willing to bet she gave her more than the mandated hour of her time. "But you spent more time with Polly, because she was a private client?"

A shrug. Rose was lucky. I still had questions: "Let's put it this way: to help me with the parrot, to understand what Polly's pet has gone through, I think it might be useful to know about her last days. How was she, at the end?"

Genie took a long pull from her paper cup and then looked out the window. She might have been savoring her drink, but I didn't think so. She was weighing something, considering the costs of talking or not. All in all, it was promising, and I tried to contain my impatience by sipping at my own cup.

"She was bad, you know?" said the aide. I looked up into those dark eyes and waited to hear the worst. "But she wasn't that bad."

I waited to hear about whining or complaining, but Genie clarified. "The pain, I mean. Polly, she was a funny one. She liked to complain. It was fun for her, but she was jolly, too. And she would not have been cracking the jokes like she did if it had been that bad."

I nodded, wondering where this was leading.

"He was wrong, you know." Genie wasn't done. "About her."

It took me a moment. There were quite a few "he's" around. Then it hit me. "You mean, the doctor?" Something Jane had said surfaced. "Giving her all those pain medications?"

Those dark eyes latched onto mine, and she nodded. "I'm not saying Polly was tough. She was strong enough, sure, but she didn't have to be an iron lady. I'm saying she didn't need those drugs. They want Rose to take them. They push them on everyone now, but Polly? She didn't need them."

I nodded, trying to understand what she was saying. Yes, I could well believe that an overworked gerontologist would overmedicate his charges. It could be Medicare fraud. It could also be simple laziness. More pain meds would make the inmates at LiveWell more docile, and, really, if it hastened the end of a few, who would complain? Besides, most of them probably were in pain. My mother had been more stoic than most, and I still remembered her whimpering in the night.

Then again, "need" was a funny word. That doctor had said the drugs had gone missing. Did that mean someone else did "need" them?

◇◇◇

"She didn't need them," Genie repeated. "She didn't want them, and she didn't take them."

Someone did. I didn't need Wallis by my side to point out the obvious. Nor that repeating something can be a way to prove it to yourself. For example, if you can tell yourself that an old lady didn't really require medication, you might feel better about stealing it.

"There seem to be some differences of opinion going around." I tried to smile. I didn't want to suspect this woman. She was a working stiff, just like me. Then again, I also didn't want to miss anything.

"It's that son of hers." She nodded. Something had been confirmed. "He thinks I stole from her. From *them*."

I waited. The fact that I shared her low opinion of Marc Larkin didn't mean there wasn't some truth on both sides.

"He thinks I took those candlesticks." She looked up at me. "You do, too. That's what this is about." She raised her cup, and I felt myself begin to color.

"My job is to take care of the parrot. To retrain the bird so it can go to a new home." It wasn't a denial exactly. It was a clarification. It was also the truth.

"That bird." The acid was apparent now. "Flying around. Cursing. Messing everywhere. Not like Buster."

Of course, Genie worked with Rose, too. "You like dogs?"

"A dog serves a purpose." She paused, and I tried to keep my face blank. "That dog, anyway. I hope—"

She stopped so quickly, I looked over my shoulder to see who had come in. Nobody. The only sound was the rain on the front windows. Even the barrista seemed to have taken off.

"What?" It wasn't good policy, but my backward glance had already been awkward. "Is Rose going to lose Buster?" It seemed to me that a service dog would be allowed under any circumstance. And the dog was healthy and in her prime. Then again, if someone had it out for the parrot…"Do you know something, Genie?"

She shook her head, a look of pain crossing her face. "The dog is permitted, by law. It is all the little things. The food, the vet. Her contract covers my visits, up to an hour a day. As if that…" Another shake of the head. I was right: the aide spent more than that with the blind woman.

"So Rose is going broke." A guilty glance and a confirming nod. "Does she have any family?"

"I don't think so." Genie pushed back from the table. "And I should be getting back. On days like this, I take the dog out while she's at lunch."

I nodded and rose to walk back with her. "Would Rose want the parrot? If, well, if neither of the Larkin kids want him?" I was already planning on how we could do it. I bet I could get Doc Sharpe to help subsidize the bird's supplies.

"Lord, no." Genie waved me off and was out the door. "But good luck with all that."

She seemed intent on getting away, so I let her go, watching as she raced, hunched over, by the building. Anxious to get to work? Or to get away from me?

I was pushing my luck with Nancy. That was apparent from the moment I stepped back into the lobby, a little soggy and with a latté to go for her.

"Coffee?" I held out the cup. "We were just over at Starbucks."

"Thanks." She took it, but she wasn't smiling. "Are you going up to Polly Larkin's unit?"

"No, not now." I would have to talk to Jane and to her brother, but I wanted to gather more information first. "Though I was wondering if you could help me with some things."

The blonde paused, about to take a sip, and I could tell she was weighing the cost of the coffee.

"Nothing major." I smiled and leaned in.

Any hope I had of recapturing that girly-girl sympathy was gone, however. She drank, but she looked up at me as she did. "What do you want to know?"

"I'm trying to get a bead on Polly Larkin's parrot." It was true, more or less. "Trying to iron out its behavioral issues. And I thought it would help to know who else spent time with him. Who else might have been involved in the bird's care."

"I thought Genie would have been able to tell you that." The receptionist did notice who walked by.

"She did, but there are things she doesn't know." I was winging it, about as well as a caged bird. "About the finances, basically. And whether, well, whether Polly left anything to her friend, Rose Danziger."

Nancy looked a little surprised at that. "I wouldn't think so," she said after a brief pause. "I don't think she had anything—that is, I believe her estate was tied up in her care."

I nodded. "And her estate was administered by?"

"You'll really have to talk to the family about that." Nancy shut me off. It didn't matter. She'd already answered several of my questions. One, that Polly had money, at least enough so that a few extra—and unnecessary—prescriptions wouldn't raise the alarm. And, two, that her children, which meant Marc, Jane had said, had control over it. And that anything that Rose would have to remember her friend by—or to help her out—would only be whatever Polly had given her before she died.

I took the elevator up to the second floor, wondering what, if anything, all this meant. Rose had my sympathy. She seemed to be managing in her little studio, and I couldn't see anyone letting her dog starve, but it couldn't be easy. No money for luxuries like the occasional field trip—and nothing extra for a private aide, not beyond what the facility provided. Still, that didn't mean she would steal, either the candlesticks that Marc had all but accused her of or the drugs that had gone missing.

I didn't see how any of it related to the parrot, either. For all I knew, Randolph had made himself sick. Bird physiology wasn't my strongest point, but the progression from overpreening to some kind of autoimmune collapse seemed reasonable, if pitiable.

What I did know was that there were discrepancies in what I heard. Rose seemed to consider Polly her dearest friend, and seemed quite friendly with her parrot, too. Marc clearly considered the blind neighbor a leech. And Genie, who seemed to genuinely like Rose, disliked the bird.

As I walked down the hallway yet again, a stray thought hit me. Could Genie be afraid *for* Rose? If the aide had heard

Randolph repeat something—something that would get her blind charge in trouble—she'd have motive to hurt the parrot. It was farfetched, I knew that, and as I knocked on the door of 203, I tried to think of a next step. Pinning Marc down about his accusations would be a start.

I was out of luck. There was no answer. Even Jane seemed to be taking a break from her constant packing. Unless she was lying there, too. Cold and unresponsive.

I knocked again, and started at a noise behind me. It was Rose, with Buster, and Genie taking up the rear.

"Pru! It's Pru, isn't it?" The dark shades turned up at me, and I was struck by that uncanny sense that she could see me. "Are you coming to lunch, dear?"

"No, Rose. I was just looking for Jane." Above her head, Genie gave me a more quizzical look.

"Oh, she won't be back till later, dear." Rose had already started down the hall, Buster moving her slowly but purposefully toward the elevator. "Something with the hospital," she called over her shoulder. "A meeting about poor Polly, I believe."

I turned and exchanged looks with Genie. Neither of us said anything, but she turned briefly and checked to make sure Rose's door was locked.

Chapter Twenty-one

When in doubt, listen to the animal. It's not just basic training in my profession, it's common sense. And since I had played all the cards I could think of at LiveWell, it was time to hit up Randolph again.

Maybe, I thought, as I walked by Nancy once again, the hospital stay would have loosened the bird up. Then again, as my cheery "bye" went unreturned, maybe he would have taken a turn for the worst, and my job would be over.

Thinking of this, I gunned the engine. Out on the highway, my car is my therapy. People, they can drive you crazy. And animals I care too much about. Wallis would have me see the world as she does: divided into predators and prey, with death and suffering a natural part of the rhythm of things. She thought me weak, I knew that, but it was more than weakness. Too much of that suffering, too much of that death, was caused by my kind, by humans. I had to do what I could to stop it. Which meant that only when I was driving could I find something like peace. Since the latest round of engine work, my old muscle car's engine purred like Wallis on a catnip high, and I felt the knot of tension in my back relaxing. Even the setting was perfect. The wet day had driven off some of the leaf peepers, even as it magnified the colors. I had the road to myself.

Or nearly. Out of nowhere, a pickup appeared, rocketing unseen from some feeder road. Its bright yellow sideboards flashed and swayed like a hazard sign, and I slammed on the brakes as the truck fishtailed from its own sharp turn. For a moment, things looked iffy—I was close enough to see a crease in the rear gate, where the paint had peeled off. But I slowed, and the truck took off. I could feel my car slide on the wet newly fallen leaves and eased off the brakes. A baby of this vintage, its better to let her find her own way, and she did, rocking a little as she settled out. Up ahead, the acid yellow truck was disappearing against the softer hues, and I cursed both the driver and my own complacence.

"Bastard." I'd been careless. But my mood was shattered, and the road had lost its allure.

Driving somewhat more slowly, I made my way to County. Whatever peace I had regained was lost as I walked into the waiting room. The uproar of barks, mews, and crying children was enough to disturb a normal human. For me, the cacophony was full of anguish. Bow-wow became "ow, ow, ow" as a puppy pulled as far away as he could from his owner's sadistic older brother. "Home! Home!" cried at least three cats, thrown into this unknown—and frankly terrifying—environment. It was all I could do to not cover my ears as I made my way to the front desk where Pammy, oblivious to everything but her gum, blinked up at me.

"Doc Sharpe around?"

She chewed and considered before nodding.

"Mind if I go back?" It was a formality, but with this many people in the waiting area, I assumed Pammy had locked the door to the examining rooms. From the way she nodded, however, I reappraised, and turned to go find the good vet.

"Pru," she called after me. A thought must have surfaced. "Pru, are you taking that bird? Doc says we need the space."

I nodded and kept walking. Well, that sounded like the parrot was in good shape. Unless, of course, the vet had stored a corpse. But when I went back into the first cage room, I saw what Pammy had meant. Every available cage was full. One wall held cats, the other dogs and what looked like an adult monitor lizard. On the table, three carriers with their pets still in them waited like their people outside.

The small-animal room was no better. Spring is supposed to be bunny season, with Easter gifts bearing surprises of their own, but from the number of rabbits I saw against one wall, I could only assume that house rabbits had become trendy again. I would need to brush up on leporidae issues—dental and digestive, as I recalled—if this kept up. In smaller cages, I saw a variety of rodents: hamsters, guinea pigs, an ancient gerbil. Some budgies occupied the upper row. The buzz in here was quiet, most of these animals were used to living in their personal space, and having the outer world change wasn't a big deal to them.

What I wasn't seeing was a parrot, and so I continued on in search of Randolph or someone who could explain where the bird had gone.

"Pru, good to see you." Doc Sharpe looked as harried as he ever does, his white hair fluffed up like a new chick's plumage. "We're a bit busy."

"I'll say." Like any good Yankee, the vet was prone to understatement. "Is this all because of the new condos?"

He ran a hand over his hair and only succeeded in messing it up more. "The condos and that new development over by Amherst. Plus, all the weekenders. Vacationitis, you know."

I nodded. People on vacation tend to forget that their pets do better with routine. Feed Rover too many treats or take a day off from changing Dolly's cage lining, and pretty soon you have a sick pet. Sometimes, of course, the animal is simply disoriented or scared by the change in behavior or setting, in which case, bringing him or her here did more harm than good. Try telling the human that, though, when Bailey won't stop barfing.

"Do you need me to lend a hand?" I didn't have time, not really. I was hoping to settle the raccoon issue today. Doc Sharpe is the source of most of my referrals, though, as well as a decent guy.

"No, no." Now it was the glasses that he was fussing with, taking them off to rub his eyes.

"Doc, is something wrong?" Like I said, I like the guy.

He put his glasses back on before answering. "I don't know, Pru. I feel that things are changing. Maybe I'm just getting too old." He looked up at me and smiled, as if caught by surprise by his own confession. "Nevermind me, Pru. I'm simply a bit tired. But there is one thing."

I waited. For the old vet to have revealed that much was a sign of a greater disturbance.

"I could really use the cage space back. That parrot, the Larkin bird? As far as I can see, he is fit as a fiddle."

I nodded, thinking. Doc Sharpe is a good vet, and I trust him. But birds are tricky, and Doc Sharpe was clearly distracted. Besides, I didn't know just how safe the Larkin unit would be for the big parrot. Randolph had gotten sick there, and whether that had been by chance, accident, or intent, I hadn't decided. Still, I didn't want to add to the vet's problems.

"May I leave him here a few more hours, Doc? I need to make some plans." Not that I knew what those were. "And, Doc, where is he?"

"Sure, sure. A few hours should be fine." He turned to walk away and then stopped. "Oh, he's in the dispensary," he said, fishing a ring of keys from his pocket. "I had him in my consulting room, but—ah—he was proving a bit disruptive."

"I bet." That got me a tired smile, as I took the keys and the old vet slumped off to see yet another patient.

County may be the biggest and best equipped animal hospital around, but its dispensary is basically a large closet. That doesn't mean it was a bad place to put the parrot: as I unlocked the door, the lights came on and I stepped into what was one of the cleanest rooms in the building. Almost everything in here was behind glass; some controlled substances under the additional protection of locked cabinets. But the temperature was kept constant and the air purified. There was no view, but, really, it might have been the safest place for Randolph.

That didn't mean he had to like it.

"Hey, how are you doing?" I approached the cage, which had been placed on the work table where Doc Sharpe prepared various compounds. Randolph had his head tucked beneath his wing, as if he were asleep. That could have been because the room had been dark until I came in. For some reason, I doubted it.

"Bugger off." Randolph stirred enough to be heard. "Ignorant slut."

"I'm glad you're feeling better." I leaned against a ceiling-high shelf. "You were pretty sick there for a while."

"Squawk!" Randolph straightened up long enough to shoot me a sideways look, then he started preening. I couldn't help but think of Wallis.

"So, are you ready to go home again?" It wasn't the best idea, but I was hard pressed to think of an alternative. The thought of Wallis had extinguished the one other option I'd been halfway considering.

"Ha!" Randolph sat up and fluffed his feathers, and I was reminded once again just how big he was. "Ignorant."

"I don't know, Randolph." It seemed like he was just repeating words, but I couldn't shake the sense that we were having a conversation. Just in case, it seemed sensible to act as if we were.

"Good girl!" With a whistle, Randolph jumped to the side of the cage and wrapped his powerful beak around the wire.

"You want out, don't you?" Another whistle, as I started to formulate a plan. "And I'm willing to spring you. But first, you'll have to give me something."

The low whistle that followed could have been an interrogative. It could have been nothing. If Doc Sharpe came in right now, he'd be locking me away in another kind of room soon.

"I need you to tell me what happened that night."

A whistle and that horrible noise—"ka-da-KLUMP!"—convinced me that I wasn't crazy. As the parrot shifted from foot to foot, I tried to catch one of his eyes. At moments like this, I felt so sure that Randolph was aware—that he did have some higher sense of himself, of me, and the world. That ran counter to everything Wallis would say, but I had to try, and as I caught one eye—that separated vision was unnerving—I focused my thoughts. Birds have excellent vision: they're better at seeing movement and amodal perception, "filling in the blanks," than we are, and I felt that Randolph's eyes were key. Or eye, as I stared into the little black pupil.

I don't always have luck reaching out with my thoughts, but I did my best now. *"What was that? Can you tell me?"* It would be so easy for me to project onto this poor animal, to ascribe a human sense of tragedy and loss. I'd seen that too often with my clients. Still, parrots have excellent memories and they are known to bond with people. He might be repeating noises, nonsense sounds. Or his vocalizations could mean more. I had to know. *"Randolph—if that's your name—are you trying to tell me something?"*

"Be quiet!" Randolph's voice was loud and strangely deep, and it startled me, coming as it did just when I'd been focusing so much on the silence. I don't like to be taken off guard, but I must have jerked back and in the small room that had consequences. I hit the shelves behind me, sending a wall's worth of vials and bottles rattling. Instinctively, I reached back, only shaking them up more, and, it seemed, disturbing the parrot. "Shut up, won't you?" Randolph shifted on his perch, staring at me. "Shut up!"

"Randolph." I worked to keep my voice level as I stepped forward, away from the shelf. "Are you telling me off? Or are you repeating something you heard someone else say?"

"Shut up." His voice was quieter now, almost distant. I paused. I was reaching, and I knew it. He could have learned this particular phrase anywhere. Dozens of people had probably told this foul-mouthed bird to shut up. Perhaps Doc Sharpe had, here, when he'd tried to house the bird in his consulting room. "Quiet." A soft whistle, and I waited. I had to figure out some way to ask. To find out. With all these drugs around us, you'd think there would be something that would help, but I was on my own.

"Randolph—" Before I could say anymore, I heard the crash. Something—a vial, a bottle—had rolled to the floor and the splintering of glass was unmistakable. I turned, and with that, the bird erupted: flapping those large wings, almost throwing himself against the cage. "Randolph!" I kept my voice steady, but I was looking around for something, anything, to cover the cage. If he kept up this way, he was going to hurt himself. "No!" He yelled in his frenzy. "Stop! *Stop!*" The last word was almost a shriek, as I peeled off my jacket and wrapped it around the cage. "Ka-da-KLUMP."

The bird was still, at last. It was my turn to be agitated. I'd been pressing Randolph, verbally and mentally, to tell me something—anything. But I was a relative stranger, in a decidedly strange place. Plus, the way I had jumped back must have been scary. Only one vial—an individual dose of an antibiotic—had broken, but it had startled me. I'd worried briefly that the wall of shelves was going to come down. To a parrot, it might have seemed like his small world was collapsing.

The coolest part of my mind dismissed what I had heard, analyzing it as I cleaned up the broken glass. I had agitated an animal that was already under deep stress. It had acted like an upset parrot, spewing phrases from its distinctive vocabulary, perhaps incorporating words and phrases it had heard recently.

But I couldn't entirely dismiss another thought, one that nibbled at my mind like that powerful beak at the cage's wire. I had asked the bird some questions, and he may have answered them. Had my actions helped liberate a thought or a memory? It was possible. After all, I didn't see Randolph as a creature who would scare easily. And his world, as he knew it, had already collapsed.

Chapter Twenty-two

I wasn't sure how I was going to explain it to Wallis, but one thing I was sure of: Randolph was coming home with me. Going back to LiveWell wasn't an option. I still had no idea what had sickened him, and with Jane continuing to pack, the possibility of dust or other pollutants being stirred up made the apartment unsafe. Nor had I completely dismissed the possibility that the parrot had been poisoned. Even if not—or not intentionally—there was too much hostility in the air, between Genie and Marc Larkin, for one poor parrot to be left safely in an empty apartment.

Doc Sharpe, at least, had been relieved. "Thanks," he had sighed, showing more emotion than I could recall seeing from the old New Englander.

"No problem." I made a mental note to follow up. Either he was overwhelmed—and I needed to insist on helping him out— or something else was going on. He was too good an ally to lose.

This was not the time, though. Between the parrot, the raccoon, and the aspersions on my honesty, I had my hands full. Literally, for a few moments, as I carried the big bird out to my car. Randolph had been strangely quiet as I transferred him to a borrowed carrier, and I had time to think about what he'd said back in the dispensary. It was probably nothing. For all I knew, the reason Doc Sharpe had looked so tired was because he'd been listening to that bird all day. I couldn't recall him ever telling anyone, particularly an animal, to "shut up." Stranger things happened, though, especially when everyone was busy and creatures were squeezed into tight quarters.

Speaking of quarters, I realized I needed to get going. My car was warm with the engine running, the soft patter of rain on the roof slightly soporific. But it was also of a vintage where I didn't want to think about what fumes might be leaking in. I'd already battered my own brain cells with enough substances. I really didn't need to sicken Randolph, too.

Still, there were legalities as well as logistics to consider. Jane wanted the parrot retrained; she'd originally suggested I take Randolph. But I'd been accused of pet-stealing before, I wanted to make sure I had explicit permission—and that I was covered for any liabilities.

Those potential liabilities included one very self-motivated tabby, of course. That's where the logistics came in. Being able to communicate with Wallis gave me a leg up. She knew what I did for a living, how I earned the food and firewood that kept us warm and comfortable. However, that understanding went both ways: Just because she could hear me did not mean she was any less a cat. If anything, I was less willing—or able—to try any kind of "training" on her. And as often as I'd been party to her thoughts, I knew how she considered birds, or any prey animals. It was kind of funny, really, how being able to communicate with animals made me less prone to anthropomorphize them. Wallis was a cat, all cat, and Randolph, for all his size and language skill, was a bird.

Wallis, well, I'd deal with her when I got home. For now, I fished out the notebook with Jane's contact info and dialed her cell. At the very least, I needed to keep her informed.

"Hello?" The voice on the other end sounded even more tired than usual. Too late, I remembered she'd been at the hospital today. Might still be there, for all I knew.

"Jane? This is Pru, Pru Marlowe. Am I catching you at a bad time?" I asked for form's sake. I had no idea what I'd do if she said yes.

"No." A woman like her never did. "But—" she paused in a rare moment of self protection, "I'm on my way home now. Did you need me to come by LiveWell?"

"No, not at all." This made things easier, and I decided on a tack. "I'm actually calling with good news. Randolph is doing fine. The vet has released him."

"Oh, that's great." Her voice sounded anything but happy, and I couldn't tell if she was disappointed or simply fatigued. "Do I have to pick him up?" Fatigued.

"No, I have him. In fact," I drew out the word, to make it sound like I had only now come up with the idea. "I was wondering how you would feel about me taking him home for a few days. I hadn't wanted to disrupt his habits, but since he was already removed to the hospital, I figured it might be easier."

"That would be great," she said, with the most enthusiasm I had heard yet. She hadn't even let me get through my other reasons. "That would be perfect," she said again. "I'll be back at LiveWell tomorrow, if you need me."

"That's fine. There is one thing, though." I tried to sound more casual than I felt. "I don't think it will really be a problem. I have a large house, and Randolph is a large bird. But you should know, I have a cat."

"Oh." Poor little Jane had sounded so relieved before that I was somewhat taken aback. Then I thought again of where she'd been.

"I'm sure it will be fine." I crossed my fingers. "How did the meeting go?"

A sigh so big I could almost feel it provided the answer. That was my cue to express sympathy and hang up, but I waited. Not out of fellow feeling; I save that for the animals, the ones that can't defend themselves. But because any discussion of old Polly Larkin's last days might provide some insight into how she had died. Not that I got any details, only another sigh and what might have been a sob.

"That bad?" I said, trying to prime the pump. "I'm sorry," I added, belatedly.

"Thanks." The word came between sniffs. "It was pretty awful. I'd *said* I didn't want an autopsy, every time they'd asked." More sobs, but I was intrigued now. It was interesting to hear that someone besides me had had questions.

When the sobs seemed to have subsided, I tried again. "I am sorry, but they must have had their reasons…" Nothing. "When my mother passed, I said 'no autopsy,' too."

"I guess I should count myself lucky." Jane continued on as if I hadn't spoken. "All they talked about were the blood tests. I mean, I knew they were saying she had too many prescriptions. They were talking about her like she was some kind of a junkie. Calling her a 'drug seeker.' But they didn't know Mother. She was the opposite of a drug seeker. She never wanted to be 'all fuddled up,' she always said."

I smiled. Knowing Randolph, I bet old Polly hadn't used the word "fuddled."

That thought almost made me miss what Jane came up with next, though. "But the tests proved it. They showed there was nothing in her system, even though that wasn't what her care sheet called for."

That supported what Genie had said. Polly had pain meds, but she wasn't taking them—at least not the night she died. Then again, old and infirm, she might not have had a choice.

"Could she—do they think that was why she got up at night? Maybe someone had forgotten, and she wanted to get her pills?" Chronic pain could drive even the most feeble old woman from her bed.

"I don't know." Jane sounded worn out. "They didn't say. Just that her doctor—Dr. Wachtell—was to be cautioned on overprescribing narcotics, even when requested. But the tests cleared it all up. She wasn't—wait, 'death is not viewed as caused by an overuse or misuse of medication.'" That last bit sounded like she was quoting. In other words, I translated, the doctor was getting off.

"At least it's over," she said, with another ear-busting sigh. She was self comforting, like a cat who purrs when injured.

"They didn't say anything else?" I was pushing her, and I knew it could backfire. Jane Larkin had no more fight in her, though.

"Nothing." Another pause. "I can pick up the ashes anytime, I gather."

That was my cue. And as much as I didn't want it, I found myself mouthing the words. "Do you want me to go with you? I've done this before," I said. What the hell. Maybe I'd be able to learn something.

"No, no." I should have known Jane Larkin would never impose. "But if you could take Mother's bird for a few days, it would be a relief."

"Not a problem." I hoped it wouldn't be, and as we rang off, I had to admire the woman. Somehow, she'd managed to make my request, the one I was a little hesitant to ask for, into a favor I was granting her. It was like passive aggression in reverse. It was also, I realized, a sign of just how manipulative the long-suffering daughter probably could be, when she wanted to be.

Maybe, I wondered, some of that fatigue I heard in her voice sprang from relief. After all, the doctors had talked about both how many drugs the old woman had been prescribed—and how few were in her system. But, at least from what Jane was telling me, they hadn't asked where those drugs had gone.

Chapter Twenty-three

Randolph was so quiet on the drive home that twice I pulled over and checked under the cover. Both times he turned his head to look at me, and I had the uncanny sensation that he was thinking about his situation, too. Not to mention what he might have overheard.

I decided to leave him in the car, briefly, while I scoped out the situation. I'd toyed with the idea of sneaking Randolph in. My old house is big enough, I could have put him in one of the warmer rooms upstairs without much notice. But Wallis had already demonstrated an uncanny ability to open doors.

Better, I decided, to brazen it out. If nothing else, it was well past lunchtime. I'd left Wallis' breakfast eggs for her, and she had a bowl of kibble, too. But cats are social eaters, just like humans, and if I was going to eat, she'd want to as well. Better to scarf something quickly, and then deal with introducing the parrot.

"*Parrot?*" Wallis greeted me at the door, eyes narrowed in concentration, the tip of her tail lashing back and forth. "*Lunch?*"

"Wallis, I hate it when you do that." Hunger was making me cranky, although having one's mind read—as Wallis can—is never comfortable. That was the other reason I'd decided not to try to keep the parrot a secret. "Randolph is…a client. You know that."

I led the way into the kitchen, where I immediately began shredding roast turkey slices into a dish.

"*That's cold.*" Wallis sniffed at the dish and sat back down. I stared at her. Cats' senses can dull as they age, same as with any of us, and warmth intensifies aroma. Still, I had the feeling I was being toyed with.

Wallis cocked her head.

"What?" I asked. It wasn't my most genteel tone, but I had already had a full day, and I had a recently hospitalized parrot waiting in my car.

"*Oh, bring him in.*" Wallis walked to the window and jumped neatly up, as if mocking my speculation about her age. Her eyes were on the trees outside, scanning them for movement I couldn't see, but her thoughts, I knew, were on the carrier in the car. "*This will be interesting.*"

"Okay, Wallis. But remember: Randolph, the parrot, is in my care. He's important to me. To us."

She simply flicked her tail, and I watched her for a moment until our silence was broken by the rumbling of my stomach. Damn, it was after two. I rolled up a turkey slice and ate it in two bites.

"*That's a bird, too.*" The voice was so soft I could have mistaken it for my own thought. "*Doesn't it taste good? Now, warm...*" That last bit decided it.

"Wallis." I approached the window. "Let's not make this difficult."

"*Forget it.*" She jumped down and sauntered down the hallway, before I could pick her up and bodily remove her. "*I'll interrogate the witness later.*"

◇◇◇

She was taunting me, I knew that. But she was a feline, with all the instincts of a small house tiger. I waited until I saw her walk through my living room, out to the old covered porch that serves as a sunroom behind the house. Only then did I go out to the car, to retrieve Randolph.

"You okay in there?" The car had cooled more quickly than I'd expected, and the parrot who glared at me when I lifted the cover had fluffed up his feathers to stay warm. "I'm sorry about that."

"Asshole." I deserved that, and hurried the bird into the reasonably warm house. Without pausing to look for Wallis, I ascended the stairs, choosing the room that had been my childhood bedroom, in the sunny front of the house, and placing the cage on my old desk. Closing the door carefully behind me, I removed the cover. Randolph started hopping around, checking out the room. I moved the carrier so he could see out the window. It was a lovely view, but mentally I cursed myself.

"I know that's not the most spacious cage, Randolph. I'm sorry." I hadn't thought this far ahead. A cat could just roam free. But even if I wanted to deal with the mess, I didn't like the idea of letting the parrot have total freedom here. The cage might not be much of a barrier, but anything that would stand, however briefly, between him and Wallis was a good thing.

"Look," I tried to catch those beady black eyes. "I'll see if I can get your cage tomorrow. Jane will be back at her mother's place then, packing everything up."

"Hand's off." Randolph punctuated his words with a sharp whistle. "Stop that. That's mine."

"Yes, it is yours." For argument's sake, I decided to assume the bird was making some sense, if only acknowledging Jane's name—or the mental image I had unwittingly conjured of the LiveWell suite.

"Stop that!" The bird was getting louder, agitated. Well, it was to be expected in an unfamiliar environment, especially one that probably smelled of cat. "Bugger off."

The assorted whistles and squeaks died down as I covered the cage once more. Better the parrot be sensory deprived than hurt himself against the bars of the cage. Besides, he'd made me wonder: Jane had been cleaning up her mother's apartment for days before Dr. Wachtell had stopped by to find those drugs missing. She had also, clearly, been a frequent visitor in her mother's final days. Despite her protestations, I had to wonder where she really stood on her mother's prescriptions. And if downtrodden little Jane Larkin had been, even before her mother's death, a secret beneficiary.

Chapter Twenty-four

I made sure the bedroom door clicked shut when I left the parrot. Not that this would necessarily stop Wallis from getting in, but it would, I hoped, signal my very strong desire that she not disturb the parrot during what I trusted would be a brief stay. If I could have, I'd have stayed around, maybe had another talk with my tabby housemate. But the afternoon was getting on, and I was beginning to feel a bit guilty about my other charge.

As I drove back to the shelter, however, I had a realization. That raccoon was healthy. We were keeping him locked up illegally. I needed to let him go. In the interest of not getting him poisoned—or whatever other horrible fate Jerry Gaffney and his inbred brood could conjure up—I'd drive him farther away than Albert had. There was preservation land a few miles out of town that would be perfect. The young male would be at a disadvantage, landing in unknown territory. But that was the lot of young male animals everywhere. Better he should wrangle one of his peers than a Gaffney. Another raccoon would at least fight by the rules.

The only question, really, was whether to involve Albert in my decision. True, he was the animal control officer for Beauville. And he'd managed to trap and remove the poor animal. But as I pulled up to the new brick building that housed the shelter, I rather thought I wouldn't. It's not that Albert is that much into following rules. He is, however, both a coward and a guy. Whether he was afraid of crossing Jerry Gaffney or would simply spill it all the first time they ran into each other at Happy's, I didn't want to deal.

"Hey, Albert." I swung into the shelter office with a sense of purpose. I wanted to get the raccoon and get out. Not only was Albert a possible hindrance, but the fact that Jim Creighton might be around—the police station was right next door—was another complication I'd rather avoid.

"Pru! Glad you're here." Albert started to get up from behind his desk, and I sped up. But even though the whiskered man wasn't built for speed, he had the edge on me: the door to the cage area was pretty much right behind his desk. I stopped and waited, arms crossed.

"Yes?" I'd already started tapping one toe. With a specimen like Albert, there's no point to subtlety.

"Were you, uh, going back to see Rocky?"

I cocked my head, wondering if there were any new developments. "You have any other animal back there?"

"No, Pru." He turned back toward his desk and started to shuffle through some papers. "But something came in. Wait, here it is!"

He turned toward me, holding out a piece of stationery. I reached for it, expecting some state update, maybe on rabies or nuisance animal removal. As soon as I saw the letterhead in that too-bright green—"Evergreen Hills: Your Home in the Pines"—I knew this was worse. Sure enough, it was from Jerry Gaffney. In his position as property manager of Evergreen Hills, he was following up with the request for a rabies test on the animal removed from the premises. For the safety of the homeowners, the legal counsel of Evergreen Hills was insisting…blah, blah, blah. It took two paragraphs to get to the point: they wanted that raccoon dead, and they wanted proof.

"When did this come in?" I admit, I crumpled the letter a little bit as I gestured with it. Albert's filing system left something to be desired, and his trash can would be an easy shot. He looked down and muttered something as he shuffled. "Did you read it, Albert?"

"I had to." His fumbling produced an envelope with something green stuck to it. "It was one of those special deliveries. They made me sign."

"Great." I took the envelope, and looked at it. Registered mail, addressed to Albert in his role as Animal Control Officer, Town of Beauville. I tossed it back on the desk and pulled up the guest chair. We'd had the raccoon in here for four days. If he were a dog, we could simply observe him for another six and let him go. Rabies shows up within ten days in domestic animals. Probably in raccoons, too, but there was no proof of that. The research hadn't been done, probably because nobody had bothered to spend the money on it. Raccoons were just pests. Nuisance animals, easier to kill than to get to know. Unless I could come up with something, the raccoon was screwed.

"It's what we're supposed to do anyway." Albert didn't dare look me in the eye, and for a moment, I was glad. It would have been easy to acquiesce. To just do it. Outside, the rain had started again, and I could hear it pound down on the roof, the perfect accompaniment to my mood.

"Up, up! Dry branch, dry."

"Excuse me?" I turned toward Albert, who blinked back.

"Up on the branch. Climb!" There was an urgency to the voice. *"Up!"*

"Sorry." I shook my head. This wasn't a human reaction to rain. "Did you bring Frank in today?"

"Nuh uh. He didn't want to leave his cage." Albert shook his head. Of course not. Why would a sensible animal want to leave a safe place on a stormy day? A sensible animal who had a steady supply of food, and probably a good cache of purloined treats as well. Which made me wonder if there was another reason for the pressing need in that voice.

"Albert, did you feed the raccoon today?" That voice was coming from somewhere.

"Yeah." He nodded. "Sure did."

The double, no triple, assurance was what did it. "No, you didn't." As much as I didn't want to see the doomed animal, I would be damned if he'd go hungry. Albert didn't dare contradict me as I went for the door to the cage room.

I opened it in time to hear a soft thud, and a grunt of what might have been frustration.

"Hello?" Turning on the light, I tried to mentally apologize. Raccoons have excellent night vision, but I needed to find the kibble. I needn't have worried. As I approached the cage, I saw the lithe animal scrambling at the far wall. It wasn't hunger bothering the young animal, though. As the young male turned—I got a distinct sense of anxiety—I saw he wasn't looking at me. Instead, he was peering at the far end of the cage, really a pen on the cement floor, which had a small puddle in it.

"Great." I looked around, hoping to see an incompletely closed window. No such luck. The leak seemed to be welling up slowly from the base of the wall. I did some quick calculations: this was an external wall, so it wasn't likely that the water came from a pipe. No, it seemed that our new shelter, which shared a space with Creighton's office, was as permeable as a sieve.

"*Up! Up!*" I turned from the small puddle, which was already growing visibly against the painted cement floor, to the panicked animal pacing by it. "*Up!*" Animals understand floods. They know about rain and rising water. This raccoon wanted to climb, as high as he could, to find a safe place to sleep. Except that the bars of his cage didn't allow for much of a foothold, and even his dexterous little pads couldn't grip anything that would hold him above the cold, increasingly damp floor.

"Hang on." I looked around me for something, anything, the raccoon would climb on. Whatever it was, it wouldn't be what he wanted: a tree with some good, yawning branches that would allow him to get safely above ground. Anything, though, would be better than nothing.

Then I saw it: a pile of packing cases, doubtless left to rot once whatever was inside had been removed. Heavy cardboard, they would melt into mush if the water reached it. But maybe, if the rain stopped, the leak would recede. I found myself cursing the town under my breath. Beauville, its shoddy workmanship, and its deference to yuppies. All of them played into my creative invective as I carried two of the boxes over to the raccoon's pen. Randolph would have been proud of me, I thought, as I unlatched the pen door and pushed in first one, and then the other, reaching to toss the smaller one on top to roughly approximate a rocky hillside.

It wasn't an immediate success. The raccoon drew back, frightened by the movement, and as he neared the puddle, I saw him recoil further. He wasn't that big to begin with and the stress was clearly taking its toll. Already, I thought, his fur had lost some of its luster.

"You need some dinner." I remembered my initial reason for being there and, gate latched, went to find the kibble. I overfilled the bowl, unsure when I'd get back next and slid it into the enclosure, waiting. A healthy animal, a hungry one, he should have caught the smell right away. I held my breath, wondering how he'd acknowledge the food: would it be "grubs"? "Eggs"? Instead, I got nothing. The scared beast simply shrank back further, his tail nearly in the puddle.

"Come on, guy, you've got to eat." I found my own stomach tensing up. "Hungry?"

This is what I hate about wildlife rehab. Too often, it doesn't work. Whatever we think of them, wild animals are actually more fragile than we know. Fear, anxiety—any of these things can keep an animal from ignoring its own survival instincts. My presence—that water—could be viewed as enough of a threat that the raccoon would starve, rather than eat. In my first practicum, doing emergency work with raptors that had misjudged skyscrapers and electric wires, I'd seen birds drop dead of heart failure, die of pure fear. All of us had.

"Kibble…." I did what I could. I tried to conjure up images of fat and juicy beetles, of acorns, half-rotted and fragrant. Of a clutch of robin's eggs—and then of the young birds themselves. Nothing. The raccoon was staring at me, and I could sense his heart beating faster.

Images were getting me nowhere. Scent, that was key. If I could get the young male close to the dish, then maybe the smell of the kibble would trigger his hunger. But how? He was wedged so far against the far side that I could almost feel the bars pressing through his fur. I knew Albert would have an answer. Over in the corner, propped up against the wall, was the long-handled net that he'd probably used to capture the animal.

I couldn't see poking him. He was already so freaked out. Instead, I slowly opened the door. Crouching down low, so as to be as unintimidating as possible, I began to push the bowl closer. "Come on," I kept my voice low, just a gentle, reassuring sound. "Aren't you hungry? Don't you want to eat?"

I knew he wouldn't speak English. He was a raccoon, not Wallis. But if I could just conjure up the emotions, the intent of my words, maybe something would come through. Something would spur him on. I crawled into the pen, pushed the bowl toward him. Tried to visualize a nest of eggs, the sweet, juicy taste of something fresh and warm. Biting down. Tasting. I pushed the bowl a bit closer.

"No! No! NO!"

"Ow!" I jerked back so fast, I hit the opened door behind me. Suddenly, we were one: the feeling of cage, of trapped. Of sheer panic like lightning between us. Only as it faded, I realized who I was—and what had happened.

Scurrying out of the cage, I locked it behind me, and stepped under the light to examine my hand. It was bleeding, blood welling out of a small puncture wound at the base of my thumb. I had gone too far. In my effort to reach the raccoon with my own particular gift, I had forgotten the basic training of my profession. A wild animal is just that: wild. And a wild animal, when cornered, will strike out, no matter how kind your intentions may be.

"I'm sorry." I was talking to the raccoon now, even as I washed my hand in the utility sink. "I really am." I pressed a clean paper towel to the wound, which was starting to throb—along with my conscience. I'd not only gotten too close, I'd thought about eating, about biting—any message that had gotten through might have been that I was the predator. That I was looking for some smaller animal to eat.

This was my fault, entirely, and yet what I had just done had sealed the poor creature's fate. Before, the raccoon had simply been a nuisance animal, the request for a rabies test just a mean-spirited attempt to assert human control over what had once been a wild environment. But now the raccoon had bitten someone—bitten me—and the prescribed regimen was clear. He would have to be tested for rabies now. Killed, and his head sent to the state lab. Or else I would have to get the painful series of shots that were the only way to prevent the disease from dragging me down.

"I'm just—I'm so sorry." I forced myself to look at the beast who was both my attacker and the innocent victim of my own foolishness. At the far end of the cage, he looked up at me. For a moment, we held each other's gaze as he brought his paws together. Those amazingly agile little hands clasped each other, and I could almost believe that he was feeling my pain, recognizing my hand as something like his. In his eyes, beyond the fear, was something else—something sad and lost.

"*Hurt?*" It was just a flash, a memory of a littermate taken, or a parent killed. I just nodded. And then, to my surprise, the raccoon began to eat.

My own sigh surprised me. I hadn't realized I'd been holding my breath. But as I watched the bear-like creature hunch over the bowl of kibble, I relaxed. Picking at the pieces, one by one, he examined them, and then as his hunger kicked in, he began to gorge, sticking his snout deep into the bowl.

"Don't rush." I sat on the floor, exhausted. "You'll make yourself sick."

My own words caught me up. What was I doing? This animal was doomed. I had condemned him, only moments before.

"Pru? Everything okay?" As Albert opened the door, I shoved my wounded hand in my pocket. The decision was made before I even spoke.

"Everything's fine, Albert." I called back. "I'm just spending some quality time with Rocky back here. I think he's going to be just fine."

Chapter Twenty-five

I took the letter with me. Albert, in all fairness, was loath to let it go. He's enough of a coward to want to toe the line sometimes. But he can't stand up to me, or any woman, really, and so I got it. What amazed me, as I drove off, was that he didn't seem to notice how I reached for it—with my left hand—and how I kept my right hidden in my pocket until I was safely out the door.

Good thing Frank wasn't there, I thought, as I pulled out of the lot. Once I was a few blocks away, out of range of Albert or any other prying eyes I stopped to look at the bite. Blood was still welling up; the raccoon's teeth had gone deep. But I'd washed it, and I would keep it clean. I pressed the paper towel to the wound. I wasn't going to kill that animal, or let Albert kill him. That decision had been made. If I was wrong, I was condemning that raccoon to a horrible end. I didn't think I was, however. And he deserved a chance.

Still, on the slight possibility that I was wrong…In the back of my mind, I began doing the math: How long did I have?

It was all, I quickly realized, ridiculously complicated. I'd gotten the vaccine, years before, when I'd signed up for that practicum. The prophylactic treatment—a series of three shots—had become standard practice with the newer vaccine. It didn't necessarily block the virus, but it did make treatment easier. The trouble was, once I'd dropped out of the program, I'd also stopped getting the booster shots every six months. I might still have antibodies, but I might not.

As I drove, I pressed my right hand against my leg and tried to remember anything else I could about the disease. I knew that time was important, that it could take anywhere from days to months for the virus to make its way to my brain. I seemed to recall something about infection site. It was my hand that had been bitten, not my neck or my body. Did that mean I had more time before the virus got to me? Less?

The disease itself wasn't something I wanted to deal with. Yes, there was a case—we had studied it—of a girl who had been bitten by a bat somewhere in Wisconsin. They had put her in an artificial coma, and hoped for the best. She had survived. But she was the exception. What usually happened was simple, inexorable, and horrible: You came down with what seemed like the flu. That led to insomnia, confusion, and the classic hypersalivation that led to foaming at the mouth. By the time you were hallucinating, maybe it didn't matter anymore. You were dead.

Rabies. A suspect bite. We had learned that treatment for a bite was considered medically urgent—not necessarily an emergency. I had a day or two. Maybe three, on the outside, if I wanted to be completely safe. It was pointless to speculate. I would start the shots as soon as I'd freed that raccoon.

First, I had to deal with Jerry Gaffney, and whoever had masterminded that letter. It felt good to think about something other than my hand, and this was a real puzzle. Jerry Gaffney hadn't drafted that letter. Jerry Gaffney wasn't the kind of guy who invoked legal counsel. If he knew the word "counsel" at all, it was from his own scrapes with the law. As our prior confrontation had shown, he had a much more direct take on animal control. No, there was someone else involved here, someone using the oafish property manager as the heavy.

Driving relaxed me, even as my hand started to throb, and as my car ate up the road, I realized that I was probably making the situation more complicated than it had to be. Why was I going to the Evergreen condos at all? What I should have done was simply taken the animal. Released him. Then I could have left Albert to deal with the consequences. Or, no, I had too much pity for dumb beasts—then I could have explained that we'd crossed wires. Between our full roster of responsibilities, Albert and I had simply mixed our messages. He'd gotten the letter and signed for it, sure. But by then, I'd already removed the animal somewhere far, far away.

Would there be legal ramifications? I didn't want to reread the letter as I drove. Didn't want to move my right hand, truth be told. But I didn't see what they could do, really. It wasn't like anyone else wanted Albert's job. And mine, well, I was freelance anyway. Who else would be affected?

Doc Sharpe, that was who. If Jerry or his colleagues wanted to, they could make trouble not only for me, but for the old Yankee. And Doc Sharpe had been not only a good source of employment, but a friend as well. As different as we were, he had respected me. He'd also overlooked the lapses in my training and certification while referring me for jobs with his own credentials as backing. He had vouched for me, more than once. I didn't want to bring more down on his head, not now.

I needed to confront whoever was behind this. Have it out, once and for all. With a renewed sense of purpose, I accelerated. Evergreen Hills—or, at least, Jerry Gaffney—was in my sites. It was getting dark, and the rain had turned patchy, but I'd be damned if I let that overgrown bully get away with causing trouble for anyone—two- or four-legged—I cared about.

Not that he was easy to find. The rain had let up again by the time I turned in at the gaudy sign, once again wondering how the color green could be made to look so unnatural. But the light was dimming, the autumn afternoon fading fast. This time, I parked right in front of the office. The door was locked, and nobody answered when I knocked, so I set off on foot, convinced that the slovenly manager had to be somewhere in the complex.

It was beautiful, even soggy. As much as I didn't want to admit it, as I followed the slate path between two of the buildings, I had to admire the setting. True to its name, the development— four buildings, total—was surrounded by towering pines. Deep in their greenery, I heard a cardinal singing, the usual macho boasts, and I stopped to look around. In the dimming light, I couldn't see any sign of his red plumage, but that's what the song was about, after all. And as I kept walking, it occurred to me to wonder just how thick these woods had been—and how many similarly majestic trees had been cut down to make room for these upscale homes.

"*Mine! Mine! Mine!*" The cardinal kept singing, the last call of the day. Yes, I guess the desire for a home was universal. But it wasn't like folks were clamoring for condos up here. In fact, I had yet to meet a resident, although I knew that the development had been open—and supposedly selling—for more than a year.

"*Mine!*" Well, birds had their seasonal homes, too. Though I'd have thought the foliage would have drawn some of the owners. Maybe they were weekend nesters; maybe they'd be snowbirds, coming in a few months to ski.

Something bright caught my eye as I turned toward the last building. A pickup was parked by the farthest building, the one that the raccoon had invaded. Its side advertised the condo complex, with the logo in green and yellow highlighting. And its bumper, which I recognized from having cut me off, was that same acid yellow as the sign. Another color not found in nature. Well, that was interesting. I doubted Jerry Gaffney or any of his minions had intentionally tried to drive me off the road the other day. Our near accident had been too random, and, besides, whoever had been driving had sped off. However, it had been careless—if not worse. I made a mental note to check the vehicle out. Maybe there'd be something I could use for leverage. Maybe I—and the raccoon—would get lucky.

"Pru." As if on cue, Jerry Gaffney appeared in a doorway. "What brings you back here?"

"Nice truck." I walked up to the vehicle and made a show of examining it. I wiped some beaded raindrops off the painted side. "Yours?"

He puffed out his chest, as I knew he would. That cardinal had nothing on the human male for attitude. "It's one of my rides."

I checked the back. Sure enough, the rear gate had a ding in it where the yellow paint had been chipped away. "You should be more careful with your driving, you know." I ran my hand along the ridge. It looked new, and there was no rust. "You could get hurt."

"That?" He had come up next to me, and I pulled my hand back. The movement had irritated the bite mark, and I didn't want to have to explain the blood on my palm. "That's from one of the yuppies. They're city drivers."

He said that like it was a bad thing, but I just smiled. I didn't want to threaten him, not yet. What I needed was information. "Some of the owners are here?" The birds had gotten quiet as we talked, or maybe I'd managed to tune them out. No other voices had replaced that cardinal.

"A few. Nobody full time. Not yet."

I nodded as if this meant something to me and looked around. Granted, it was a dull, damp afternoon, but I hadn't heard or seen a sign of any other person on either of my visits. "Someone must live here," I said finally. "Someone complained about the raccoon."

"I figured that was why you were here." Jerry Gaffney had piggy little eyes, and they weren't improved as he squinted at me. "Albert showed you the letter."

"Yeah, I was surprised." I squinted back. It helped. "You didn't write that."

"My name's on it." He leaned back on the truck as if to present his pelvis. What really extended was his belly. "I'm the one in charge here."

"Uh huh." I neither backed away nor crossed my arms. I needed him compliant. "But the idea of legal counsel, of demanding test results. That's not your way."

He shrugged, so I continued. "No, you were talking about having Joey set some traps. Taking a more direct approach." I almost said "manly." It wouldn't have been too obvious, but he'd already taken the bait.

"City folk, like I said." He looked around. "This place is big money, and that means they let the lawyers run it."

"They?" I leaned in, trying not to hold my breath.

"The board." He shrugged again. "But I don't have to deal with them, mostly. They've got some guy in town, runs it all part-time like. He handles the paperwork."

"Maybe I should speak to him then?" I reached for the letter in my pocket. My hand had pretty much stopped bleeding.

"I'm the guy you deal with," said Jerry. "That's why I signed the letter."

I nodded. You hire someone like Jerry because you want a heavy. Or a fall guy. "Well, there may be some problems with this," I said as casually as I could. "And we over at animal control wanted to discuss the options."

"There are no options." He jutted his chin out. He was beginning to look annoyed. The rain had started up again, which didn't help. "You've got it all in the letter."

"Look." I leaned in. "Can't we go somewhere? Talk about this?" I didn't have a plan. I didn't think Jerry Gaffney would be that hard to manipulate.

"You come in? Nope." He shook his head. "I've locked up the office for the day, and I'm going home."

"Can't we just step in?" I gestured to the building, quiet and dark, before us. "Just to get out of the rain?"

"No, no way." He started walking up to the cab of the truck. "These are the exclusive property of Evergreen Hills, and you'd be trespassing." He climbed into the cab. "I'm sorry, really, but it's not allowed. Just do what the letter says, Pru, and we'll be fine."

With that he got in his truck, leaving me to hike back along the wet stone path to my car. The cardinal had long since left, retreating to some warm, dry nest for the evening, and I was ready to do the same. I was soaked, and my hand hurt. What really bothered me though were the questions that Jerry had raised. I understood why he would want to claim to be the boss, but he'd just about admitted that he took orders from someone—the director of the development. And he'd held me off when I'd pressed for a name. I knew Jerry Gaffney from the old days. He didn't respect authority, and the way he treated that truck showed that property, like money, was something you got and used. No, there was a different note in his voice when he talked about the director. A note that had given him some steel when he'd ordered me off, and then retreated. I thought, maybe, Jerry Gaffney was afraid.

Chapter Twenty-six

Attraction is a funny thing. You'd think that having studied animals, I'd have some insight. Truth is, I barely get it: I know what I want, but I don't always know why. Jim Creighton, for example. Sure, he's good looking, in that healthy boy-next-door way. And there's something about that short, light brown hair that begs to be touched. But he is a cop, through to the bone. And while I'd dated cops before, I'd never really spent time with a clean one. Not voluntarily. Tom, my ex from the city, barely counted. He'd been on the job when we hooked up, but giving me my switchblade, which he'd taken from some young thug, had been the least of his transgressions. Last time I'd seen him, he'd gone into the private sector. He'd also gone to seed. I'd let him go, thinking I'd seen the last of him. When I thought of Tom, it was of somebody far out to sea. He was going to sink, and I couldn't help him.

Creighton, though, he was different. And as I sat in my car by the side of the road, I found the good-looking detective preying on my mind. Part of that was because of the time. Going on eight, there was a good chance he'd be dropping by the house soon. He'd probably have another pizza, or maybe a six-pack. He didn't need an offering, though. We'd gotten into a good routine.

He wouldn't find me at home tonight, though, not any time soon. I was waiting by the side of the road for Jerry Gaffney to leave work, and wondering why he hadn't. There was something going on with the Evergreen Hills condos, that much was clear, and while I seemed to have developed a taste for a law and order man, my own methods were more direct. Then again, maybe that was why I liked Creighton. Contemplating what I was about to do wasn't that far from ruffling his neat, short hair.

The thought was tempting, almost enough to make me give up and drive back home. Besides, my hand needed a proper bandaging, and I needed some aspirin and bourbon. As I reached for the key, however, I finally saw the headlights. Jerry Gaffney in that fancy truck pulled onto the main road and drove back toward town. I was ready to go.

While I'd waited, the storm had passed, and a bit of faint moonlight lit my way back up the condo road. Driving slowly— my engine can be loud—I bypassed the main office building and pulled in by that last building, a little back from where Jerry had parked. If anyone looked, I hoped the dark and the trees would keep my car from being obvious. At least in this light, the baby blue paint job wouldn't be particularly noticeable. Before I got out, I reached into the glove compartment for my flashlight, and I was set.

My time with Tom had taught me a few things. One was that burglars could be stupid. A set of break-in tools—jimmies, and the like—will secure a conviction as quickly as fingerprints. I traveled light. Sure, my switchblade was illegal, but even Creighton knew I carried it. Self-defense would be my claim, if I had to make one. That and the flashlight were all I needed. The blade was thin and strong, and I had the simple catch unlocked in under a minute. Maybe the developer told buyers crime wasn't a problem out here, away from the city. Maybe they just didn't care.

The flashlight was a big one, metal and heavy. It was as much a weapon as my blade, and I didn't turn it on until I had stood inside the door for a full minute. If anyone approached me, I wanted to be able to back out unseen. The quiet, though, told me I was alone, and so keeping the beam aimed low, I turned it on and began to explore.

Evergreen Hills was nicely set up, I'd give it that, made up primarily of side-by-side townhouses, each slightly angled for the illusion of privacy. The door I'd unlatched had let me into some kind of a foyer, with what proved to be a coat closet right at hand. The floor seemed to be stone, practical and cool-looking. To the left was a great room, made larger by its emptiness. Keeping the light low, I could see the big bay window facing the back, and I could imagine the view. I wondered if anyone had seen it. Nobody lived here; it hadn't even been staged to sell. Which meant that no resident could have complained about the raccoon rattling around upstairs.

The stairs were off the great room. Once I found them, I turned the flashlight off. No sense in risking a light when I could use the curved banister to find my way up. I stepped carefully, still, aware of every creak in the wood. Just because the downstairs was empty didn't mean there wasn't a surprise waiting for me on the top floor. Maybe Jerry was letting one of his relatives crash here. Maybe more than one. I stopped where the stairs did, and waited, listening. No sounds, animal or human, greeted me.

When the silence had lasted a good fifteen beats, I risked the light again. Nothing. Shiny hardwood floor and white-painted walls, broken only by more hardwood—what looked like closets or bedrooms. I stepped into one, large enough to be a master bedroom, and saw where the ceiling had already begun to leak. A gap not much larger than my fist separated the closet frame from the wall. That must have been the corner where the raccoon got in. For all these fancy finishes, the construction on the condo had been shoddy. At least, I saw with a sigh of relief, there were no traps set. Unless—I crossed the room—there was an attic space, where poison could have been set down.

I walked over to the corner with the gap and raised my flashlight to examine the space behind it. I couldn't see much. Nothing to indicate a crawl space or storage area. Running my light around the rest of the ceiling, I saw a few more damp spots. One in particular caught my eye, over by the window, and I looked around for something to climb on—a box or a step ladder—when I saw it. A flash, coming from outside. A car was pulling up slowly, its engine nearly silent.

Cursing my foolishness, I dropped to the floor, switching off my own light as I did so. I smacked my hand on the way down, starting it throbbing again, and I bit my lip to avoid crying out. I was too tired for this. I wasn't a kid anymore, and I was hurt.

I was also, it seemed, safe. No other lights came through the window above my head. No sounds of entry or footsteps from the floor below. After another minute, I dared to move. Cradling my injured hand against my body, I made my way slowly out of the bedroom and back down the stairs. Heart in my throat, I stood at the front door for several more minutes, before daring to open it. Nothing waited but the night, and if the usual animal sounds were quieter than usual—no murmurings of prey or predator—well, that could have been because of the rain, which had moved in again. Crouching low, I ran to my car and started her up. Nobody stopped me as I rolled back to the main road, my heart racing loud enough to give me away.

Chapter Twenty-seven

My first thought on getting home was to pour myself a drink. My palm was sticky with blood as I reached for the bottle, though, and I realized I'd lost the paper towel somewhere in the night. That didn't help me relax, but as I slugged back the golden warmth, I waxed philosophical. Odds were, the soggy rag was in my car. At any rate, I wasn't going back to Evergreen Hills to look for it.

At least, I thought as I balanced my glass on the edge of the sink, my little adventure had distracted me from the problem of my hand. The wound, under the harsh bathroom light, looked nasty, swollen and red. But it had obviously bled freely, which reduced the risk of an anaerobic infection, so I daubed some antibiotic cream on it and taped a patch of gauze over it. Puncture wounds were bad, but I could have Doc Sharpe look at it—once the raccoon was safe. Hell, in a day or two, I could even start the rabies shots, as long as things worked out.

Back on the sofa, I looked around for my cat and tried to make sense of what I'd seen. No resident had complained, but really, what did that mean? If one of the development over-seers—someone from the mysterious board of directors—had noticed raccoon activity, that could have sparked the whole thing. Though if that were the case, then why wouldn't Jerry be working on fixing the eaves? Those damp spots were going to hurt sales more than the occasional wild guest.

The only good thing, I thought as I contemplated my whiskey, was that everything seemed sort of once removed. Jerry hadn't written that letter, and he hadn't told me who had dictated it. Maybe it would all be bluster and no follow up. Maybe I could just let the raccoon go, with no repercussions.

I took another sip and thought about it. Tomorrow, I'd go see Doc Sharpe, see if I could suss out what was going on. See if he had any more work I could take off his hands, to our mutual benefit.

Work. Hell. I sat up with a start. I hadn't checked on Randolph, and suddenly Wallis' absence seemed suspicious. "Wallis?" I called as I climbed the stairs. "Are you there?"

"*What?*" She was sitting on the second-floor landing, washing her face. A little too nonchalant. "*You seemed otherwise engaged when you came home, so…*" A slight feline shrug expressed her disdain and something else, too.

"Wallis, what were you doing today?" I didn't want to mention that parrot. I didn't want to give her any ideas. As soon as I had the thought, though, I realized she had heard it, too.

"*Please.*" She stopped washing and turned away, pausing to bat at something on the floor. "*As if there was anything to be gotten from that bird.*" Tail high, she stalked off. "*Anything worth the effort.*"

"Wallis." I was tired, my hand hurt, and I was also, by now, a little buzzed. "Please, Wallis." I called after her, pleading. This was what I was reduced to. "Randolph is a guest."

"*And you've never…*" The voice was faint, almost subsumed in the rumble of a purr. "*Interrogated…a guest?*" She was gone, but a movement caught my eye. She'd been amusing herself as I came up the stairs. Batting at something. I leaned over, the whiskey rushing to my head. It was a feather. A long, gray feather.

◇◇◇

"Wallis!" I tore down the hall. Sure enough, the door to my old bedroom was slightly ajar. "Randolph?"

The look of surprise that greeted me could have been because of the way I slammed the door open, making my hurt hand scream with pain. Randolph, his cage uncovered, did indeed look startled, his smooth gray head jerking up and down as he watched me storm into the room. Wallis, sitting on the windowsill, seemed much calmer, those wide green eyes projecting an innocence I didn't trust for one moment.

"You're okay." I addressed the bird, who merely clucked to himself.

"*Of course he is.*" Wallis jumped down and came over to rub against my shins. "*Though I do think it was unfriendly of you to leave him here, all alone.*"

I glared down at her. I was not going to apologize. On his perch, Randolph whistled softly.

"*Don't you want to know what we talked about?*" The soft pressure against my legs was as relaxing as the whiskey I had drunk, as Wallis well knew. And as the adrenaline of this most recent shock wore off, I slumped into a tattered armchair. Wallis jumped up to my lap and began kneading.

"If you want to tell me, Wallis." I stroked her back, completely beaten.

"*Too late.*" She jumped down. "*You've got a call that I think you'll want to take.*"

I heard my phone begin to ring then, and gathered my strength to stand up. I'd dropped my bag downstairs. "We're going to talk, Wallis." Fatigue gave my voice an edge. "As soon as I handle this."

"Bugger," said Randolph. "Bugger all."

Chapter Twenty-eight

"You at home, Pru?" It was Creighton.

"Good evening to you, too. Jim." I kept my voice cool, matching his.

"I'm sorry." He sputtered briefly. "It's that—well, are you alone?"

"Wallis is staring daggers at me." That wasn't quite true. She was really smirking. "But, yes, you've reached me at home. Alone."

"I'm sorry I didn't come by tonight." He sounded like he meant it, and I felt my shoulders unclench a bit.

"Yeah," I could tease him now. "I'm getting used to my pizza delivery. And my pizza delivery boy."

"Have you been home all evening?" There was a note in his voice I couldn't identify. He knew better than to try being possessive of me.

"What's it to you, Jim?" I could nip that in the bud. "We have a date that I forgot about? And that you stood me up for, apparently?"

"No, I'm sorry." He sounded tired now, plain and simple. "I had a…thing. Something came up and I wanted to touch base with you."

This was intriguing. "A thing?"

"I had to swing by that new condo development, Evergreen Hills."

"Oh." It was the best I could do. "Really?" I looked at Wallis. She looked at me, and I tried to convey what was racing through my mind. First off, Creighton is a cop. A good one. He doesn't just chat about what he's working on. Suddenly, the fact that he was checking in on me was worrisome. "No trouble, I hope?"

"Nothing major." I waited, cursing my clumsiness. Someone must have seen my light, back in the empty unit. That must have been Creighton cruising by. And Creighton knew my car. I'd parked away from the condo, back in the trees. Far enough?

"So you've been home?"

"Since I left work." Nothing to do but brazen it out. Besides, that was more or less true. "You thinking of coming by?"

"No, I'm bushed." So the call was simply to check up on me. I smiled at Wallis. I'd passed the test. "But Pru? I do think we should sit down and talk, sometime soon. There is something going on up there. And it's getting dangerous. We found blood."

I was cursing like Randolph for a few minutes after that, and Wallis chose to make herself scarce.

"Wallis? Where are you?" I checked Randolph's room, but either he was sleeping or doing a good approximation, head tucked neatly under his wing. It was just as well: the cat had gotten something from the parrot, and I had no idea if the bird had wanted to share.

"*You don't have to yell.*" Wallis appeared in the hallway in that maddening fashion cats have. I swallowed back my retort and simply looked at her. "*Come along, then.*"

I followed her back down to the kitchen, where she waited while I shredded more turkey. Then I watched her eat, and bathe, until finally I could stand it no more.

"Spill, Wallis." I stared at her. Cats hate to be stared at. "What did you learn from the parrot?"

She jumped up to the windowsill. I had the window closed—the rain had brought a chill—but she liked to be eye-level with me. It was a status thing.

"*You act like you're expecting answers.*" She had her back to me, while she surveyed the yard. "*I mean, this is a* bird *we're talking about.*"

"Yes, I know." I was working very hard at not losing my patience. "But we also both know that this parrot, Randolph, has said some very interesting things. And besides, parrots are not just any birds. They're larger, they live longer—"

"*Next you'll be saying they can think.*" Wallis lashed her tail.

"They can, after a fashion." I let my mind wander over everything I had read. The research on parrots was tantalizing. "There's evidence that they do connect some sounds with meanings, like a child would—a human child," I specified. "They can remember things they've seen, and that they can form attachments to people." She looked up at me, so I hurried on from that. "But, yeah, sometimes they just repeat sounds for no apparent reason. Still, if that bird witnessed something and is repeating it back to me—"

"*I know, I know. You want to know if what the bird is telling you is something that really happened, whether or not understands what it's telling you.*"

That was pretty much the whole question in a nutshell. So I waited, while Wallis completed her survey. From her, I got an image of a vole, three squirrels, and something larger: a fisher?

"*Something weaselly, that's for sure.*" Wallis turned toward me finally. "*Now, where were we? Oh yes, that parrot...*" Her ears went up, and she turned back to the window

"Yes?" I was beginning to think that my tabby hadn't gotten anything, the way she was stalling.

"*I wasn't stalling. That squirrel was being distracting.*" She turned back toward me and settled into her Sphinx pose. "*What you have to keep in mind is how that creature thinks. It's all pictures for it—okay, him—shapes and movement. Half the time, I didn't know if he knew I was there, or if he was just checking out the room.*"

That made some sense, from what I knew of parrot vision, and it could explain why the bird's vocalizations had changed when he moved from LiveWell to County. A bird, even a big bird, is a prey animal. They have to be sensitive to their environment.

"Huh, some environment. More like an overheated henhouse, with those old biddies."

Polly and Rose, I assumed. Wallis closed her eyes slightly, the feline equivalent of a nod. *"There were others, too, but they were the main ones. The ones that bird responded to."*

"Responded to?" I was beginning to sound like a parrot. "You mean, in terms of what he said?" I thought of the parrot's various outcries: "hands off, that's mine," and, more recently, "shut up."

"I wouldn't credit too much what that bird says. Most of it is gibberish, sounds he's picked up. Words that he likes."

"That he *likes?*" I was going to squawk soon if this kept up.

"That got a reaction." Luckily for me, Wallis was in a tolerant mood. She does enjoy explaining things to me. *"He's grown fond of attention from your type, and he's learned what makes you jump."*

"Huh," I nodded. "That is interesting." Wallis closed her eyes in satisfaction, and I wondered silently. Was Randolph repeating that awful noise—the sound of the walker keeling over—because it had made an impression on him? Or because I reacted to it?

"Oh, I don't think he's thinking much of you personally, Pru." Wallis could be a bit condescending, but what she said made sense. *"He's had a lot to deal with recently."*

Of course, I was a newcomer in his long life. That could be why I wasn't connecting with Randolph—and why I was having trouble retraining him.

"I'm sure that's part of it." Wallis' eyes were closing for real now, and I felt her growing fatigue. *"You have some sense, after all."* Sleep was coming on her quickly, a trait I often envied. *"But there's more to it, Pru. That's what I found so interesting."*

"Wallis?" I didn't want to wake her. No good could come of that, but I was intrigued.

"He keeps replaying scenes in his mind, Pru, in that cranky old mind. He feels—how would you put it? He feels responsible, Pru. He feels—what would be the word?"

I filled in the blank. "The parrot feels guilty."

Chapter Twenty-nine

It was what I had thought, that first time I met Randolph, only I hadn't been sure. And with that puzzling statement, Wallis was out. Drained by bourbon and pain, I wanted nothing more than to follow her lead. There were a few too many questions, however, so as I dragged myself back up the stairs, I made myself head to my old bedroom—Randolph's room—to check in once more on the gray parrot.

"Hey, Randolph. Randy." I was buzzed, I knew it. I didn't care. "Do you really feel guilty about something—or are you just having a laugh at my expense?"

The large bird shifted on his perch and eyed me. I knew I should let him be, should cover his cage to re-create some semblance of routine for him. We'd both be better for a good night's sleep.

"You let something slip to Wallis—to the cat." I pictured the tiger-striped tabby and got a low whistle for my efforts. "She thinks you don't care about me, about what you tell me. That you're just responding to the environment. To the room you're in."

Nothing. "Is that true?" I leaned back against the doorjamb. If I wasn't careful, I was going to slide to the floor and fall asleep there. "What aren't you telling me?"

"Shut up." It was so soft, I could have missed it.

"Thank you, Randolph." My own eyes were closing. "I'm sure that means a lot." There was too much to piece together. "Is it true you feel responsible? Do you feel guilty about Polly's death? You were in a cage. You couldn't help her. Don't you know that?"

"Shut up," he said softly. "Shut up."

The next morning dawned cool and crisp, the front that went through had brought with it that New England clarity for which our autumns are famous. I was glad of the cold. It was just a nip in the air, really, but it helped clear my head of whiskey and bad dreams. Besides, it gave me an excuse to wear gloves. No way did I want to explain my bandaged hand to anyone, particularly Tracy Horlick.

"Late night?" She greeted me on her doorstep, in the same faded housecoat she always wore. Maybe the haze of stale smoke protected her from the cold.

"Not particularly." I felt rather smug. For once, her gossip was off kilter. I might feel like crap, but with one thing and another, I'd been in bed—alone—before ten.

"Cause I hear that cute policeman, James Creighton, was burning the midnight oil."

I'm not the sort to get jealous, but even if I were, I wouldn't show it. Instead I smiled even more broadly at the old hag. "He's got a tough job," was all I said.

"Maybe it's all the new people in town." She took a hit off her cigarette, and I watched the ash extend. "As well as the ones who've come back."

"Maybe." I wasn't rising to her bait. "Where's Bitsy?"

With a snort that was probably supposed to put me in my place, she turned. A minute later, I was in the company of Growler. That company wasn't much more congenial.

What are you thinking of, walker lady? He looked back over his shoulder, those black button eyes conveying scorn. *Tackling that one?*

"Tracy Horlick?" I didn't want to refer to the old lady as the dog's owner. "Old smoke teeth?"

Huh! The dog chuffed, the closest thing to a laugh he'd give me, but he kept charging ahead. *No, that bear-thing. The little bear.*

"The raccoon?" I paused without thinking, and Growler tugged at the leash. "Sorry," we resumed walking. I was holding his leash—a formality, really—with my left hand. I hadn't thought he'd noticed.

"*I didn't. But the smell.*"

I'd washed the wound again in the morning, before rebandaging it.

"*Huh.*" That laugh again. "*It's in your blood. I can smell it.*"

"Great." I had successfully avoided all thoughts of rabies for a good twelve hours. Some of the first signs were similar to those of a cold or flu. But it was soon—too soon—to worry. "I'm trying to save an animal's life here, Growler."

"*Stupid animal. Young and stupid.*"

I chose to believe he was talking about the raccoon, and not my own decision to delay treatment. "Growler, it only fell afoul of people because it was looking for a safe place to stay." Considering the bichon's domestic situation, I was careful to tread lightly here.

"*Old smoke teeth isn't a killer.*" So much for not mentioning things.

"If I have my way, Jerry Gaffney won't be either." The dog gave me a quizzical look, and I realized he had no reason to know the name. Instead, I figured I'd pick the small dog's brain. "So let me tell you the latest about the parrot," I began, before stopping myself. What was I going to say: that I'd let my cat interrogate Randolph? How would that play with the small, but macho canine?

"*Huh!*" This time it was clearly a laugh. "*As if you could understand what either of them was trying to tell you.*"

I'm human, I'll admit it. And that shut me up for the rest of our walk, which seemed to suit Growler just fine. He kept his commentary to himself as we made our rounds, leaving me to pick up bits about the neighborhood dogs, their diets, and general health.

As soon as I'd returned him and touched base—I couldn't call what Tracy Horlick and I exchanged pleasantries—I made my way to LiveWell. Randolph had been in good shape when

I'd left, and Wallis had made herself scarce. I'd raised the shade to let the big parrot view the world, and he'd started twittering softly to himself, sounding more like a bird than I'd yet heard. Maybe, I'd thought, the poor creature had simply spent too long with humans. Not that I could do much about that. And while Wallis and I did seem to have an agreement, I wanted the bird out of my house. His presence was not only too much of a temptation for my tiger-striped tabby, it was a bad precedent to set for clients. I do not run a boarding service. Nor am I, as the Tracy Horlicks of Beauville would probably have it, a hoarder.

Guilt. I thought about that as I drove. What did that mean? Wallis had picked up a lot of human concepts from me, but I couldn't always count on her understanding them perfectly. Responsibility, for example, seemed a particularly unfeline concept—there were things one did and things one didn't. "Should" or "shouldn't" didn't really have a place in the animal world.

The question was rattling around my head as I pulled in to the assisted living center and parked by an SUV with MD plates, distracting me as I walked in the front door.

"Ms Marlowe?" It was the receptionist, Nancy. "I have a message for you."

Damn, I knew I should have called first. I hadn't in part out of the fear that Jane Larkin would find a way not to meet with me.

"It's from Mr. Larkin," Nancy was saying.

"*Mr.* Larkin?" I'd assumed Polly was a widow.

"Marc? Polly's son?"

"Oh, right." I was fuzzy-headed. I nodded, once again regretting last night's bourbon.

"He says he'll meet you at eleven. He needs to speak with you."

"Thanks." It wasn't Nancy's fault that Marc phrased his request as a demand. I checked my watch: it was a little after ten. Pity. I'd have loved to have left a message of my own, and not been here when the conceited schmuck arrived.

As it was, I confirmed with Nancy that Jane had in fact returned to her packing, and I headed up to the second floor to meet with her. I hadn't made any progress with Randolph, not of the kind she had hired me for. But I wanted to keep in touch. I knew how easy it was for a client to not deal with a troublesome animal, and I did not want to become the parrot's default guardian.

Jane was alone when I arrived. She looked worse for wear than I did.

"Oh, hi." She looked up from a box that seemed to contain nothing but crumpled newspaper. "You didn't bring Randolph, did you?"

"No, he's still at my place." I moved a lamp off a chair and sat down. "But I think we need to talk about him."

I hadn't thought she could deflate any more. "You can't retrain him. I knew it." She reached for a china figurine, one of a dozen I only now noticed in shades of pink and gray.

"It's not that." I reached for one, too. I needed to bond with this woman somehow. "I can, with time. There's been a lot else going on, though." I was thinking of what Randolph kept repeating—and Wallis' take on it. Jane, however, had her own interpretation.

"It's just too much, isn't it?" She paused and looked around. "Sometimes I wonder why I'm packing everything. Marc doesn't want it, and I don't have room for it."

The priority she gave her brother bothered me, but it didn't surprise me. "I don't think he'll want Randolph either." I made my voice as gentle as I could. "Even if I can retrain him. Are you sure you can't take him?"

I was already thinking of options. I'd heard of an African gray rescue group back in the city. If there wasn't one closer, I could probably arrange transport. Jane, however, was on another track.

"Maybe Marc was right. I should have bought." I didn't understand, but she explained. "He kept telling me I should buy a condo. After our father died, I could have. He could have gotten me a deal, too."

"He's a realtor?" I couldn't see the bullish little man selling anyone anything.

"What? No, he's in business. One of his clients got him in, though. It's a new development, and he was very excited about it. Originally, I thought I'd do it. The units are bigger than my apartment, and I'd have had room for Mother's treasures."

The thought of this washed-out woman buying a place just so she could display her mother's china left me speechless. Luckily, she kept talking.

"And Randolph, of course. But it was just so much money— and it was going to be so long before I could move in. Then Mother got sick, and I was afraid to spend any more than I had to. Marc kept saying I could rent it out, make more than enough to take care of Mother, but I don't know." She smiled up at me, her face pale. "I'm not much of a risk taker, and I guess I missed my chance."

"There are always other opportunities." I smiled back. I didn't want to say that I'd trust her brother's idea of a good investment about as much as I'd trust his sense of fashion. Everyone said the economy was recovering, but Beauville was hardly a boom market. I thought of that empty unit at Evergreen—and found myself wondering. "He wasn't talking about Evergreen Hills, was he?"

"You know it?" She brightened briefly. "It would be so nice to own a place right near town. So convenient."

"You're better off." I was thinking fast. I'd be meeting with Marc soon, and I bet he could tell me who was on the board of directors. No need to involve Jane in that, though. "I hear the construction is shoddy."

"Oh, no." She shook her head. "They spent a fortune. Everything top of the line."

I didn't respond to that. I knew what I had seen. Besides, Beauville might be a small town, but this was still too big of a coincidence. "You wouldn't happen to know a Jerry Gaffney, would you? He works there."

"Oh, no." She had resumed wrapping and packing, so I reached for another figurine. A shepherdess. Of course. "We didn't get that far. It was all just plans, then. But Marc took me out to the site. So pretty."

It had been. I did some quick math. Evergreen Hills had opened a little over a year ago, which meant it had been under construction for a year or maybe two before. I'd bet the development had been planned in the go-go years before the housing bust, and by the time Marc was trying to get Jane to buy, its investors were probably getting a little frantic.

"If you want to buy, I bet there are other places around that can offer you a good deal." I was beginning to sound like a realtor. If she could take the parrot, though, that would be a load off.

She was shaking her head. "No, it's not for me. I only looked because Marc was so adamant. And he knows my budget."

To the penny, I bet. Jane had had a lucky escape. Randolph, however, wasn't so fortunate. "So, Jane, about Randolph."

"Oh, yes." She was suddenly very involved in the figurine she was wrapping. A little boy fishing, it looked like. "You don't think you could, maybe, permanently…?"

She couldn't even say it. Loyalty to her mother, she would say, if pressed. A lifetime of bullying is what I would have called it, resulting in this kind of passive push.

"No." As in any training, I needed to be both firm and clear. "Yesterday, you were overwhelmed, and County needed to discharge Randolph, so I took him home with me. I did not want to bring him back to LiveWell until we could figure out what had made him sick, but my house is not a permanent solution."

"What did the doctor say?" It took me a moment to realize that she'd only heard part of what I said.

"Didn't he call you? We aren't sure. It could have been something he ate, or something in the air." I looked around the packed suite. "Dust, or other allergens. If someone had been painting, or using some kind of spray cleaner…"

She was shaking her head. "Genie wouldn't. She knew. She was with Mother for months."

I knew what the aide thought of the parrot and didn't respond. I did, however, find myself eyeing Jane anew. Randolph was a burden, and despite her protestations to the contrary,

I'd just seen how eager she would be to get rid of him. Before I could phrase a question, however, we were interrupted by a knock on the door.

"Who is it!" Jane jumped up with a little too much alacrity. The conversation had discomfited her, as well. "Oh, how nice." I checked my watch. Marc didn't seem like the type to be early. Then again, maybe he'd read me as the type to run off without seeing him. But it was a woman's voice that rang out from the doorway.

"Good morning, dear. Just checking in." Rose, with Buster and Genie in tow. "Ah, hello!" She turned to me, even before I could say anything. Not too soon to stop Jane from loudly announcing: "Miss Marlowe is here too, Rose. She's sitting on the green armchair. Oh, I mean, the armchair in the corner."

Maybe it was her blindness that kept Rose from masking her disdain. Maybe not; Genie, behind her, ducked her head to hide a smile.

"Hi Rose, Genie." I stood to greet them. Rose took my hand in her cool, wrinkled one. Genie nodded. Buster just panted. I didn't need to be a psychic to know that they'd come back from a walk, and that she found the small suite to be overheated.

"Hi, dear." Rose looked up at me. "How are you—and how is Randolph?" I noticed she didn't address Jane.

"He's doing much better, thanks." I moved over to lean against the sill, and let Buster guide the old lady to my chair. *"One step, turn—box. Stop!"* The service dog was good at her job, and I wondered how much Rose picked up, at least subliminally. "The vet couldn't find out what was wrong with him. It could have been an irritant. Or simply age and stress."

"Poor old bastard," said Rose, settling into the armchair. "None of us likes the changes here."

"Changes?" I was watching Genie, but she'd kept her face blank. That could have simply meant she'd heard all this before.

"Oh, the usual. There's always something they want to treat you for."

"Are you having health problems?" I remembered what Genie had told me. It didn't seem to me that Rose needed to be medicated, but I didn't know her that well.

"I'm old, that's all." She waved her hand to dismiss it. I also remembered what Genie had said about her finances. "Just like Buster: two old bitches making do!"

The dog didn't seem elderly to me, but I smiled in acknowledgment of her joke—and her stoicism. So did Genie, I noticed. Jane only opened her mouth and quickly closed it.

"Well, I'm happy to tell you that Randolph seems to be doing fine. In fact, I was just talking to Jane about his future." I looked over to see Jane standing up, and realized that we'd been joined by Marc. "Hello, Marc." I didn't want Rose to be taken unaware.

"Miss Marlowe." He didn't, I noticed, acknowledge Rose or Genie. "Jane, I need to talk to Miss Marlowe." He paused, as if suddenly taking in his surroundings. "When you're done. I've got a half hour."

"I'm glad we're all here." I had my own questions for Marc, but I wasn't going to let this opportunity pass. "Jane and I were talking about Randolph's future." I'd used the bird's name deliberately, to stress his individual identity. Marc looked blank, however. "The parrot?"

"Yeah, mom's bird." Marc nodded. "Go on."

Well, that was interesting. If the bully brother hadn't come over to talk to me about his mother's pet, what was on his mind? I'd find out, I was sure. For now, however, I plowed on.

"I have temporarily taken the parrot over to my house. He was released with a clean bill of health by County, the animal hospital, and I obtained Jane's permission." I didn't trust Marc, and I really didn't need to be accused of anything. "And I would like to keep working with him. He's an intelligent animal, and I know he can be retrained to everyone's satisfaction. However, that isn't going to happen overnight. And I don't think that coming back to this suite, what with the dust and fumes of packing and cleaning, is the best thing for him."

"Why not? He lived here as long as Mom did." Marc said. I knew he was intentionally ignoring what I'd said, but I tried again.

"Either the dust or a cleaning product—"

Jane interrupted me. "It's not healthy for him, Marc. He could have *died*."

"Well, if you think I'm going to take him, with that mouth on him, you've got another—"

"I'll take him." A soft voice broke up what was building up to be a battle royal. "He's spent enough time in my place, and I'm not packing. He'll be safe there, while you work with him."

It was Rose. I turned, and realized we were all looking at her. Even, I noted, Genie.

"Oh, we couldn't." Jane was flustered, I could tell. Genie, her mouth set tight, was simply shaking her head. "He's such a bother."

"I like hearing him talk." Rose was warming to her theme. "He'll keep me company when Genie's off duty. We can curse like old sailors together."

I looked at Genie. She'd be the one stuck cleaning up after the bird. She shrugged, ever so slightly, and I nodded back. I'd try to do some of the work.

"It would have to be temporary." I looked at Jane and Marc. No way did I want them unloading the bird on Rose, not without at least making some financial accommodation for his care. "I can provide what he needs, and add it to my bill. I'll bring everything over with him later today, if that's acceptable."

Nods all around. "And I'll need both of you to be available to continue his training."

"Is that really necessary?" Marc was close to whining.

"Yes, it is. Unless you want me to start making other plans for surrendering the bird."

"Marc." Jane's voice had a little steel in it, something I'd never heard before.

"All right." The kid brother actually kicked the carpet.

"How about five this evening. Does that work for you two?" They nodded. "Rose, Genie?"

"We'll be at dinner then," Genie answered.

"That's fine; they'll have the place to themselves," Rose said, then turned to me. "The door's always open. Who's going to break in here, anyway?" She laughed a short bark of a laugh. Buster looked up at her, ears alert. *"Ready to go?"* Sure enough, she was beginning to push herself up on the arm of the chair. Genie rushed to help her before I could. "You just bring him by anytime, dear," she said to me, as she made her way toward the door. "I'll be watching my stories all afternoon. Jane," she nodded to her neighbor's daughter as she made her way. "Pru. We'll be talking."

"Blind old bat." Marc said, even as the door closed behind her. "Always fishing around."

"Seems to me, she's helping you out of a jam." I stood, too, wiping my hands of the sill's dust. "Now, do you want to talk here, or shall we go over to the coffeehouse?"

Chapter Thirty

I wanted privacy. I had my own questions. The way he looked at his sister, though, that answered some of them right away. "Starbucks," he said. "I gotta get out of here."

We walked to the corner in silence, and I let that continue. He was the one who'd called this meeting. I could let the pressure build.

"Can't believe we finally got one of these out here." He forced a chuckle as we waited for our drinks. I'd let him pay. "About time, huh?"

"You're not from here, are you?" I didn't know if it mattered. But he was uneasy, for a change, and I thought I'd take advantage of that. The way he was concentrating on his coffee—half and half, then some skim milk, then enough sugar to make my teeth hurt—made me wonder what was really on his mind.

"Not for years." He said, with a touch of wistfulness in his voice. "Moved back for the kids."

"Uh huh." If he'd grown up here, he knew it wasn't paradise. I rescued my coffee before he could dump sugar in it, too, and followed him over to a table. Then I watched him stir his oversweet mess. Finally, I broke.

"You wanted to talk?" This was a Marc I wasn't used to. My questions would wait. I needed to get a handle on what was going on first.

"Yeah." The coffee must be thrilling, the way he was staring into it. I sipped my own—black and bitter—and waited for him to go on. "It's about the bird."

I nodded. Drank some more. I hadn't thought it was about my taste for fast cars.

"You see, I'm trying to cut back on unnecessary expenses." He looked up. I doubt he liked what he saw on my face.

"Unnecessary? Marc, unless you're willing to adopt Randolph the way he is now—"

"No, no, I didn't mean that." He was quick to cut me off. "I just mean, well, it's just a bird, you know? Couldn't we just, maybe, have it put down?"

"A healthy animal? For no reason? Randolph is not just any bird, Marc. He's an African gray parrot. They're extremely intelligent and long-lived animals." I could imagine Wallis' response to that, but I wasn't talking to her. "In addition, Randolph was your late mother's beloved pet. Besides," I was warming to my topic, "you're not footing the bill. Jane is."

He looked at the door as if dreaming of escape. "Yeah, that's the problem."

I waited, actually curious. Besides, unlike Marc, I was drinking my coffee.

"You see, Jane isn't paying you out of her pocket. She's paying you out of my mother's bank account. We had our names put on her accounts early on when she went into LiveWell. It just seemed to be the safe move."

I bet, I thought. Out loud, I said nothing.

"LiveWell," he continued, "is a top of the line facility, as I'm sure you're aware. And my mother had one of the nicer suites."

I put down the paper mug. I knew what he was getting at, but I didn't like it. "I gather the place is pricey, Marc. But really—this was your mother's pet, and my rates are not that high." Hell, the few weeks' work I'd sketched out probably cost less than one of the old lady's prescriptions. "Surely, there's enough for Randolph's care. Jane certainly isn't worried."

He was squirming now. "Jane isn't the best with money. She just, well, she just doesn't have the head for it." I bit back my thoughts on that. Marc was still talking. "You see, I'm in business. I was with one of the big firms before we moved back, but for the sake of my family, I decided to go independent. Investments, financial planning. You know." I nodded. I did. More than he knew. "But it's hard getting a new venture off the ground." He paused and seemed to realize that it was time to make eye contact. "I won't lie to you," he said. "I've had some reversals. And my mother, bless her heart, was helping out me out."

He stopped there. Drank some of his milky mess as if he were giving me time to digest what he'd said. I didn't need it. What he'd said was clear: baby brother had drained mom's accounts, and big sister didn't know. I thought of the check I had already deposited and wondered if it would clear. He had given me an opening, however, and peeved as I was about his financial finagling, I had no mercy about pressing it.

"Does this have anything to do with Evergreen Hills?" I was watching his face. Sure enough, he blanched, his ruddy complexion turning pasty.

"Did Jane say something?" He ducked down into his drink, which had to be cold by now.

I wasn't going to rat her out. "This is a small town, Marc."

"Don't I know it." He put down the cup with a little moue of disgust—I'd been right—and started staring at the door again as if it would call to him. He wasn't getting off that easily.

"So, is that one of your 'reversals'?" He shrugged. I thought it was as much of an acknowledgment as I was going to get, and was going to move on when he started talking.

"Five years ago, it seemed like a win-win, you know?" His voice sounded soft. Dreamy. "People needed housing. The area needed the jobs, needed development."

"So this is purely altruistic, huh?" Another thought hit me. "Is that why you moved up here?"

"I had multiple business leads in the area. Plus," he back-tracked, remembering his story, "I love the area. Fresh air. The mountains. I'm a family man now."

A family man who steals from his mother and sister. I nodded. "So who are your associates?"

"Excuse me?" He'd blanched again, his face going pale before a wave of color rose up his cheeks. "My who?"

"The people you're doing business with—the ones in charge. You know, the general manager, board of overseers over at Evergreen Hills?" I watched as his color began to normalize. I'd missed something, so I pressed on. "Who knows? I might be ready to downsize. Buy a condo myself."

"Evergreen Hills is a professionally managed consortium—"

"Yeah, but who runs it?" I cut him off. "Who's on the board of overseers, the condo board? Whatever you call it."

He sputtered a bit. Took a sip to cover up.

"I can go down to the county clerk and look it up, you know." I was reasonably sure of that. At any rate, the bluff worked.

"Several prominent local citizens are on the board." Marc looked hurt, as if he'd forgotten how this conversation had started. "I am, of course. Dan Weatherby of Weatherby Real Estate. Mal Jones from Jones Construction." He listed a few other locals—all in the building trades or real estate—and then hit on a name that surprised me. "And George—George Wachtell from LiveWell." He said it like it was an afterthought, but I wasn't buying.

"So that's how your mother ended up here? Or did her move come first?" I wasn't sure what was going on, but I could see a web of connections forming. An investor, a builder, a realtor—and now the doctor who had treated Marc's mother. Some of these players had an obvious vested interest. The others may have been roped in, I didn't know.

"George Wachtell—Dr. George Wachtell—is a prominent medical practitioner. And Beauville is, as you've said, a small town." Marc was getting back into bully mode, a mix of smarm and force I didn't care for. "I don't know what you're implying." He started to stand up.

"I'll spell it out for you." I stood too—sick of this verbal dancing. I also had the nasty feeling that I'd asked the wrong question. Let him get loose somehow. "You've had money problems. So bad that you want to euthanize your mother's pet rather than care for it. I get it: the bird's a big responsibility. But your sister hired me to do a job, and I'm going to do that job. If you want to tell her you've bilked the estate, that's up to you."

I stood up, looking down as Marc flushed with rage. When he didn't respond, I figured he couldn't. Well, he was in a public place. If he had a coronary, someone would call over to LiveWell. With a nod at the glaring little man, I tossed my empty cup into the trash and walked out.

I'd enjoyed my little outburst. Marc needed to be put in his place. Of course, the truth was more complex. It always is. But I'd talked to Jane about rescue groups, about giving Randolph up for adoption. She was the client, not this minor league bully, and she'd rejected the idea—at least for now. Besides, I hadn't wanted to give Marc any ammunition to go after his sister. From what I'd seen that morning, she was at the end of her rope, and I didn't want to be responsible for it snapping. Which reminded me: I'd promised to bring Randolph over to Rose's. If this was ever going to be resolved, I needed to spend some time with the big bird. Besides, now that I had more experience with Marc, I was looking forward to talking to the old lady again. Rose Danziger might be blind, but she had seen enough to know what was going on.

As I walked back to my car, I looked into the wide glass doors of LiveWell. I had no real idea how long the assisted living residence had been around, or who had been behind it. Was it the same shoddy construction, I wondered? Or had changing times justified cutting some corners in a new development, to be marketed more at out-of-town yuppies than the local elders? As I stood there, I saw a white coat walk up to Nancy and say something that started her laughing. When he turned, I saw it was Dr. Wachtell, smiling at his own wit.

Or maybe I was simply feeling bitter. Either way, his exit was a reminder that some of us did have work to do. With more questions than I had answers for, I went to pick up the parrot.

Chapter Thirty-one

"Don't worry." Wallis greeted me at the front door when I walked in. I'd gotten home as quickly as I could, rushing through my remaining regulars. Still, a few hours had passed. *"I haven't eaten our guest."*

Something about the way she said it made me wonder what was going on, but I did my best to clear my suspicions from my mind before the sleek tabby could catch them. As it was, she stalked off after our greeting, her tail cocked in a defiant exclamation mark.

Sure enough, Randolph looked a little ruffled when I got upstairs. "About time," he barked at me, making me pause in the doorway.

"Are you talking to me, Randolph?" I asked the parrot.

"Some people!" He whistled in reply.

It could have been the new environment. The parrot's phrases certainly sounded like something he could have picked up from a crotchety old woman. Then again, if Wallis had been sparring with him—and if the bird had, as I suspected, gotten the better of the match, we could be in a new phase of communication.

"That's mine! Hand's off," he yelled as I reached for the cage. Wallis was waiting at the head of the stairs as we came out of the room.

"Told you I could get him to talk," she said, with the beginning of a purr.

◇◇◇

I was a little earlier than I'd planned, returning to LiveWell, and I was hoping to run into the good doctor. If he was on the board of the condo, that might explain that awful letter. The chances I could talk a doctor out of a rabies test were slight, but it would be worth a try. However, he was nowhere in sight as I crossed through the bright lobby of the oldster's home, carrying Randolph's covered cage. It was early enough that I did catch Rose, though, and she explained he rarely was.

"We go see him, dear. He doesn't come to us," she said. Her tone conveyed everything I needed to know about the power structure implied by that arrangement.

"And your medications?" I'd seen one of those divided plastic boxes by Rose's sink, the same kind as Wachtell had checked at Jane's.

"Oh, the aides handle those." With Buster silently guiding her, Rose had come over to where I'd set Randolph's cage. "Now, how's my old friend?"

"Hands off! Stop that!" As I unwrapped the cage, Randolph started right in. "That's mine, you! Bugger off!"

Rose chuckled, but Buster's ears perked up. I knew she was too well trained to go for the bird. Still, I was curious. Under the guise of friendly petting, I crouched down to make contact with the dog.

"That's mine!" Randolph was loud, I'd give him that. Buster seemed fascinated, and I moved my hand from her black back to her oversize ears. *"What do you hear?"* I asked the dog silently. *"What is it?"*

"Protect!" The response came back as loud as a bark, and I drew back. I'd almost forgotten: I'd reached out with my right hand, my bandaged hand. Could Buster have picked up the trauma of the bite? The scent of raccoon? Growler had. Neither Rose nor Genie had said anything, but just to be sure, I switched hands, using my left to fondle the velvet base of those ears. Buster remained silent, the most uncommunicative creature I'd ever met. Then again, she was a service dog, and every fiber of her was

focused on her person. And, I thought, on the parrot. *"Protect!"* I heard it again, softer, though whether directed to the woman or the bird—or both—I couldn't tell. I sighed and gave up. At least I didn't have to worry about Wallis-style harassment here.

"Bugger off!"

Maybe Rose did, though. As the parrot continued his tirade, I saw her reach for Buster's harness. She had been standing since she came to greet me at the unlocked door, and her jolly face was hanging slack.

"Oh, my, she is on a tear today." Rose was turning, trying to return to her chair. Buster, however, was now clearly fixated on the bird, to the point of ignoring her mistress.

"Buster?" I reached for the dog again, wondering what could distract her from her duty.

"Oh, she's just got a crush on that old blabbermouth bird." With a yank, Rose got the dog's attention. Buster was too well trained to complain, and even from a foot away I could catch a hint of her self-reproach as she turned to guide the old lady back to her seat. It was curious, though, that something could distract this disciplined guide—an animal whose first response was "protect." It was also odd, I realized as I took my own seat, that Rose would behave so roughly to the dog. Maybe she had forgotten just how loud the parrot could be.

"Is he going to be too much for you?" I asked as gently as I could. I knew it would hurt Rose's pride to renege on a deal. "I mean, I could find another place for Randolph."

"Nonsense." Seated, Rose seemed to recover a little of her composure. It was after four, close to her dinner hour. I could put down what I'd witnessed as low blood sugar—or the fatigue of an elderly blind woman. "Randolph is family," she said. "He was with Polly till the end."

"We should be getting downstairs to dinner, dear." Genie must have had the same thought I did, as she came over with a thick gray cardigan. "Want to put your sweater on?"

"Give it to me." Rose snatched it from the aide's hands and began fussing with it. Ignoring her words, Genie eased the soft weave around the old woman's shoulders and then began to button it. "Everybody fussing. You'd think I was an invalid."

Genie didn't make eye contact with me. That could have been loyalty. I know I wouldn't take kindly to being upbraided for a simple kindness. Then again, I doubted I'd last a day in her job.

"She's just trying to help, Rose." As soon as I'd said it, I regretted it. I liked the old lady. More than that, I needed to keep her sweet on the bird.

The look Rose gave me was as sharp as a hawk's. Then she relented. "I know," she grumbled. Putting her hands down, letting Genie push the last few oversized buttons through the soft cloth. "This place. It gets to you. God's waiting room." Genie stepped back as Rose leaned forward and then pushed herself upright. Buster, meanwhile, stood, her flag of a tail wagging once. There was a routine at work here that kept the old lady going, and I stepped back. "Have fun with my boyfriend, won't you?" Rose called over her shoulder. "But not too much fun. I want him back!"

Genie looked up at that, and we smiled at each other over Rose's head as she made her way to the door. There was life in the old dame yet.

"Sqwah!" Randolph seemed to know he was being talked about. "Ignorant slut!"

"Well, it's just us now, Randolph." The moment the door closed behind them, I approached the cage. "I think you'd like to fly free, but I'd like to do some work first."

I had no idea what the bird was picking up, and after my misadventure with the raccoon I wasn't going to make any assumptions. This was going to be animal behavior 101. However, if I talked through my plans, I figured it couldn't hurt. At the very least, maybe Randolph would start picking up on my language. Not that this would necessarily be an improvement.

"Bugger off." Now that we were alone, Randolph seemed to have calmed down, his volume reduced to nearly conversational levels.

"Hello, Randolph." I stood close to the cage, so he could see me and feel my breath. "Would you say, 'hello?'"

"Would you?" That was something. I gave him a treat. He whistled.

"Hello?" I repeated, pitching my voice up. It was possible that he'd picked up so much foul language because of how we talk. When we're agitated—angry, upset—our voices get louder and, if we're female, higher pitched. "Hello? Pretty bird? Pretty bird? Hello?"

"Shut up." He shuffled on his perch to face away from me. I couldn't say I blamed him. I sounded like an idiot. "Ignorant slut."

"Hello to you, too." This bird was pissing me off. "Come on, Randolph, say 'Hello.'" I held a treat up, moving so he could see it.

"Who's that? What!" I had agitated him, so I stepped back. "Hand's off! Stop that! That's mine!" He craned forward. For the treat or to see, I couldn't tell. I held up the treat. "Hello," I said again, as he ate it. "Say 'hello,' pretty bird."

"Stop that! Awk!"

This went on for a while, and I was about to give up. Randolph must have sensed that—or maybe the treats were finally paying off. Because suddenly the parrot gave a loud squawk, flapped his wings, and said, quite clearly, and in a voice eerily like my own, "Hello! Pretty bird. Hello!"

"Hello yourself." I jumped and turned. That voice had come from the opened door behind me. George Wachtell, still in his white coat, stepped in, smiling.

"You don't knock?" Being caught off guard makes me grumpy. Randolph was still flapping though, his large wings hitting the bars, so I began to wrap the cover over his cage.

"I thought the unit was empty." As I closed the bird up, the doctor walked up to the tiny kitchenette area and browsed the shelves. "I saw Rose on her way into dinner."

"She's letting me keep Randolph here, for a little while." He'd barely given the parrot a glance.

"That bird is a nuisance." He was shaking his head. "We should never have allowed Polly Larkin to keep it here." As he spoke, he pulled out the plastic pill dispenser, and opened the first of its little containers.

"It's only for a short while," I was buying time. I knew it, and worked to change the subject. "I thought the aides dealt with the drug trays?"

"Basically, they do," he said, closing the first section and popping open the one marked "Tuesday." "Our medications are delivered already sorted by the pharmacy, and the aides do an admirable job of dispensing them to the residents. The aides are, after all, an integral part of many residents' lives, and I couldn't function without their help. And for the most part, they are honest and valued partners in our healthcare system." He paused to close the compartment, and maybe to give his insinuation a moment to sink in. I didn't do him the honor of responding.

"However," he picked up, "I do believe in spot checking. I am ultimately responsible for the medical well-being of the LiveWell residents, after all."

"And that's what you're doing now? Spot checking?" He seemed to be counting, poking at the pills with his fingertip. I wondered how many pills there were supposed to be, and if any were missing. I leaned in to look.

"Exactly." He snapped the compartment shut. "Some of these pills do appear similar, and I wouldn't want to have a mishap."

"So what's Rose on, anyway?" I had seen enough to note that there were several different pills or capsules in each compartment. And I remembered the old lady's complaint.

He looked over at me, dark eyebrows arching above his glasses. It was a flirtatious move, as well as questioning, but I was in no mood.

"I am working with her." It didn't mean I had access to privileged information. Then again, LiveWell didn't seem big on privacy.

He nodded and turned back to the task at hand, opening another compartment. "Rose had a little cerebral vascular incident, a stroke, a year ago. So that means blood thinners, medications to keep her pressure in check. The usual."

"The usual?" Looking over his shoulder, I counted at least three pills for that day.

"Our Rose doesn't like to admit it." He had moved on to the last compartment. "But age is catching up with her. Surely, you've noticed how she moves? The trouble she has getting out of a chair?"

"Arthritis?" My mother had had it in her hands.

"Exactly." He replaced the container. "Complicated by cartilage and bone density issues. The combination can be a cause of considerable pain."

I thought of the old woman's newly sour mood, of how slowly she had moved. "She doesn't want pain meds," I recalled out loud. "She said something to me about that."

"Rose talks tough." That look again, the one over the glasses. "Late at night and when she comes to see me, I hear a different story." He closed the cabinet and reached for the door. "Are you done in here?"

"What? No." I turned back to Randolph's cage. "I closed it to calm him down, but I'm hoping to work with the bird until Rose gets back from dinner."

He nodded. "Do me a favor, will you? Don't tell her I was here." He opened the door. "If any of the residents hears I'm willing to make housecalls, I won't have any peace."

I nodded. Let him think I'd agreed. "Hey, Doc?" I had my own questions, and figured using his title might help me get some answers. He turned in the doorway, waiting. "Are you on the board of Evergreen Hills? I was over there the other day, and I had some questions."

"I'm afraid I'm not the best person to answer any questions." He was smiling and shaking his head. "That's purely a sideline, an investment I'd made. Maybe not the wisest one. As you can see, I'm keeping my day job." With that, he stepped out.

"So much for caring professionals," I said as much to myself as to Randolph, as I uncovered his cage. The whole visit bothered me. He clearly didn't trust the aides. Nor did it seem he liked the residents much. Then again, I thought of Doc Sharpe, he might simply be overwhelmed—and I had had my own questions about Genie. "What do you think, Randolph?"

"Stop that!" The bird whistled softly, almost as punctuation. "Ka-da-KLUMP!"

◇◇◇

"Randolph—" I paused. Now that I was attuned to it, I heard the door to the little suite open. Genie was holding it open as Buster led Rose in. "Hello," I tried to sound cheerful, wondering what they had heard. "I didn't think you'd be back so soon."

"Rose got tired, didn't you?" This time, the old lady didn't complain as Genie took her hand and placed it on her own firm forearm. "We left before dessert."

"Is she okay?" I didn't like the way Rose was shuffling. She hadn't said anything—hadn't even looked up at me—since she had entered the apartment. "Should I go for the doctor?"

The look on Genie's face said it all, but before I could respond—could say that the doctor was indeed still around and making the equivalent of housecalls at the ripe hour of five-thirty—Rose interrupted.

"I'm fine," she snapped. "We don't need that doctor."

I looked from Rose to Genie, waiting for her to argue. Instead, she got Rose settled on her chair. "Rest here while I get your nightgown, Rose," Genie said, and went to the far side of the room, where a wardrobe stood against the wall.

"I don't like the way the doctor talks to her," said Rose, as if Genie weren't less than ten feet away. "I know she doesn't have the education he does. None of us do. But that doesn't mean she's a thief."

I nodded, thinking of Wachtell's snide little comment, and then remembered who I was talking to. "No, it's not very nice," I said.

Genie returned with a flannel nightgown over one arm, and knelt to begin unbuttoning the old woman's cardigan. I kicked myself. I could have started on getting Rose ready for bed. It wasn't like I hadn't done the same thing during my mother's final days.

"You know, the doctor was on the floor not that long ago." I knew what he'd said. In this case, though, my loyalty was entirely to the old lady. "If you want me to hunt him down, I bet I could find him, bring him back."

I was talking to Genie, but it was Rose who responded. "I said, I don't want to see that bastard. He's got creepy eyes."

Even Genie smiled at that. "Rose, do you want to use the bathroom?"

"Of course." Rose's temper hadn't improved, but she got up by herself and stalked off with Buster, shaking off Genie's arm.

"Is she always like this in the evening?" I'd leaned in, unsure of how sharp Rose's hearing was.

Genie shook her head. "She's getting worse. She thinks it's the drugs that doctor has her on."

"The doctor said she's just putting on a show. That she wants the medications." The truth was in here somewhere.

We heard a flush, and Genie stood, shaking out the nightie. "That doctor," she shook her head. "He thinks everyone needs to be on pills. Because it makes things easier for him. Easier to blame us, too, when things go wrong."

I looked at her. Of course she was aware of the insinuations, the accusations. All the aides probably were.

"I think he'd just as soon have them all die, as long as he could pin it on us," she said. "He's the bastard. He's, how do you say it? He's a son of the bitch." There was such animosity in her tone that I found myself staring at her, even as she went to meet the old lady halfway, helping her out of her shirt and bra and lowering the flannel gown over her head. "Okay, let's sit down and do the shoes," she said, her voice soft and warm. The contrast was startling.

The doctor's comments I had taken as class-based insults, and Rose's defense had been made out of loyalty, if not love. That love might be returned. I wanted to believe it was. But underneath it all, Genie was simmering with rage. As much as I didn't want to think about it, that much anger didn't come out of nowhere.

Chapter Thirty-two

Whatever I thought about Genie, it was Randolph who was my responsibility. That said, I had no choice but to leave when Rose went to bed. As I drove home, I found myself wondering, though, about the odd tangle of relationships at LiveWell. Marc was a sleaze, there was no doubt about that. And even if Dr. Wachtell wasn't in bed with him, financially speaking, the gerontologist's smug disregard for his patients and his staff wouldn't endear him to me. That didn't mean Genie was innocent. I'd heard her, just now, and I'd seen the looks she'd given Randolph, too. Plus, it seemed Wachtell was right about one thing: Rose Danziger was in worse shape than she wanted me to know. Had she been stealing her neighbor's painkillers? I didn't want to think about it. I could use some painkillers of my own.

"Took you long enough." Wallis sidled up to me as I stood in the kitchen, pouring myself a water glass of bourbon.

"What? To get home?" I looked down at her. "I'll feed you in a minute."

"Oh, don't worry about me." The way she rubbed against my shin put the lie to her words, and I left my glass to retrieve a chicken leg from the fridge. *"I meant the people."*

Damn, this mind-reading thing really messed with me. "What part of what I was just thinking do you mean exactly?" I spoke out loud as I pulled the cold chicken from the bone. I didn't need to, obviously, but I was hoping to make this conversation a little more conscious, at least to me.

"*Hmmm, bird.*" Wallis sauntered over to examine this evening's offerings. I hardly ever gave her canned food anymore. It's hard to keep my refrigerator stocked, even for me. We were more like roommates than pet and person now, anyway, and so what I got she got. Within reason.

"*That so-called drink is disgusting.*" She filled in my thoughts as she began to eat. Soon she was purring and kneading the floor. I felt strangely gratified.

Finishing my whiskey, I contemplated a second, then decided I should wait. Wallis clearly had something to tell me, and I'd understand it better if I had my wits about me.

"*Such as they are.*" She sat back and began washing her face. To me, it looked spotless, but she rubbed her white front paw over her fur as if she were scrubbing a stained sheet.

"*Interesting thought.*" I got that. I hadn't realized Wallis understood metaphors. "*A sheet, where you sleep. Those two old ladies. You were wondering about the one who takes care of them, yes?*"

Genie. "Yes, I was." A wave of sadness hit me. Bourbon can do that. "I like her, though."

A flex of the ears dismissed this all too human weakness. "*And she survives, how?*"

"By helping the old people. That's her job." Wallis understood jobs, after a fashion. She knew that I had to do certain things in order to bring back food.

"*And that other one?*"

I looked down into emerald eyes. Wachtell? Or did she mean Jane? "Wallis, can you explain?" I lifted my glass as an excuse.

She didn't need one. She only sniffed a little as she led me to the living room. Cats like to have the upper edge. "*The one the bird was talking about.*"

"You said he felt guilty, right? You mean about Polly?" I stood while she jumped up to the sofa and began to knead the pillow.

"*He feels guilt?*" The tabby glanced up at me, and I could have I kicked myself. "*What is this guilt?*" No matter how well we communicate, Wallis is still a cat. She translates my thoughts, and in some way, I do the same with hers, automatically putting the gloss of human emotions on them. That leaves a lot of room for misinterpretation.

"Shame. Feeling bad." I was grasping at straws, trying to remember the sense of the original. Not only did I have a buzz on, Wallis was beginning to nod off. "He feels like he's responsible."

A spark of interest. Those green eyes focused on me once more. *Yes, that's it. He did it. He knows that. The rest…animals in a cage.*

The parrot did it? Wallis fell asleep after that, not that she'd deign to explain herself anyway. I was stuck trying to figure out how Randolph could believe he was responsible. Maybe he'd cried out, and that had woken Polly in the middle of the night? Maybe she'd been the one yelling for him to shut up?

I thought of those bare spots on his breast. Maybe they had pre-dated her death; maybe he'd been distressed about something else and had begun the self-mutilating behavior. There were certainly a few possibilities that could unsettle a bird: his person's declining health, her increasingly medicated state. The fact that the aide didn't seem to like him and that somebody might be stealing from her only added to the list. And if he had been in distress and she, his longtime owner, had heard him cry…

There was only one thing I could be sure of. Randolph didn't intentionally kill Polly. I was beginning to doubt that anybody had. He might have been responsible for her death, though. Stranger things have happened.

The concept gave me something to think about as I made my own way to bed. If some form of avian guilt was the cause of both his feather-plucking and, possibly, his self-destructive verbal behavior, then maybe confronting it with him might give me an edge. I wasn't sure, exactly, how parrot psychotherapy would work. Then again, they use therapy on children, and Randolph was at least as intelligent as some kids I knew. It was something to think about. Better that than the throbbing in my hand, or the angry color of the wound as I changed the bandage, a fresh glass of bourbon balanced on the edge of the sink. Better than wondering why I was going to bed alone before midnight, yet again.

It was just as well, I thought, pouring on the hydrogen peroxide. I'd told Jim about the raccoon. He was smart enough to put two and two together. Besides, he and I didn't have that kind of relationship. We were too different, for starters. I could never be completely comfortable with a straight-shooter cop.

I did wonder, as I rewrapped my tender hand, how it would end. Would he get sick of my solitary ways? Trade me in for a local girl with her eye on a ring? It made me smile, and almost made me reconsider the Tylenol with codeine that I slugged back with the rest of my drink. I rarely bothered to look that far ahead. Old Jim Creighton must have gotten to me.

Or maybe it was Beauville. Being back here, I'd fallen into the slower pace of my old hometown. Maybe I'd be the one looking to settle down soon. As my relationship with Wallis proved, almost anything was possible.

Either way, I promised myself, I could deal with it tomorrow. Creighton. Randolph, and that damned raccoon. My hand was still smarting as I drifted off to sleep. Another thing on my list. Tomorrow was going to be a busy day.

Chapter Thirty-three

The phone call that woke me, rather to my surprise, was about none of the above. Instead, the voice that penetrated my sleepy whiskey fog had a lilting Haitian accent—an accent that softened the words she said.

"It is Rose," Genie was talking quietly, but with an urgency that quickly brought me around. "She is being taken to the hospital. I only just arrived myself."

"Hang on." I grabbed the clock. A little past six. I could get over to LiveWell and be back in time to walk Growler no problem. "I'm on my way."

I didn't have time to look for Wallis and only downed a large mug of water before hitting the road. The previous night's excess should have had me driving more slowly than usual, but I was taking the turns hard. I knew I should have insisted, last night, that Rose see a doctor. Wachtell wouldn't have been that hard to find. My tires squealed as I pulled up at LiveWell, and I jumped out while the engine was still rumbling. Talk about feeling responsible.

Rose was gone by the time I got to her room. Nancy had simply waved me past, but I didn't even see the EMTs as I ran down the hall. Only Genie, making the bed, was there to greet me.

"Genie!" The face that rose to greet me looked bereft. "Is Rose...?" I was afraid to go further, but she shook her head.

"They took her to the hospital. She was not conscious, but she was breathing when they came."

Relief, in the form of exhaustion, hit me, and I found myself sinking into the chair that Rose had been sitting in, only hours before. "What happened?"

Genie shook her head. She'd moved on by then, and was folding what appeared to be Rose's morning outfit, all laid out on the dresser. "I came in to get her ready for breakfast. Rose says she does not want help, but these days…" She didn't need to finish that sentence. I had seen how weak the old lady was. "She was still in bed. I should have known. Her dog—she was barking fit to wake the dead."

As if startled by her own turn of phrase, she shut up suddenly and blinked. And I woke up a little, too. "Buster." I stood. "Where's the dog, Genie? They didn't take her."

"No, no." Genie pointed toward the restroom. "She was making so much noise. I couldn't think."

I ran over to the bathroom and put my hand on the door. The dog inside was silent, as she had doubtless been trained to be. Someone had shown up, a person was taking charge. She must have heard me, though, or felt the thoughts that were reaching out to her. A faint whimper—*"what? what?"*—came through.

"Hey, Buster." I opened the door and got down on my knees. To Genie, it would look like I was hugging the dog. Comforting a confused animal. I was, but I was also making as close contact as I dared. *"What happened? What did you see?"*

"Help!" The dog barked once, so close to my ear I pulled back.

"Help?" I repeated the word, as I'd heard it, in my head, looking into those large and soulful eyes. *"Did you call for help?"*

"Help!" The bark was softer, and I made myself hold still. Poor Buster really wasn't capable of a whisper. Nor, I decided after another moment of holding her, was she capable of complex thought.

"You called for help." The dog only whimpered, and I found myself looking at her as Wallis would. Loyal, certainly. Articulate? Not so much.

"She has calmed down, certainly." Genie was standing right beside me. "I'm glad you asked. I almost forgot. Her and that bird."

"Randolph!" Standing so quickly I startled the dog, I ran over to the cage. Still covered, the parrot inside was quiet, and it was with a shiver of trepidation that I whisked off the cloth. A yellow eye blinked at me.

"Hello!" Randolph cocked his round gray head. "Sqwah?"

I could have laughed. Maybe it took another tragedy to make my training sink in. Or maybe the parrot was more intelligent than I'd thought. "Hello, Randolph." I said out loud. "Hello." Silently, I asked, as best I could. "*Did you hear anything? Rose? In the room?*"

"Hello!" The bird repeated. "Pretty bird!"

"At least he's getting better." Genie was right behind me, watching the parrot, who began to groom. "That's good, yes?"

"Yes, it is." I was thinking fast. "Maybe being with Rose was good for him."

We were both silent for a moment. So much depending on one frail old woman. "Did they say anything? When they took her?"

Genie only shook her head. Of course. Why would they talk to an aide? I wondered if I would have better luck. I could say I was a relative. Being white wouldn't hurt.

Genie had finished folding everything in sight by then and was simply wringing her hands. "I should be moving on. Alice will have covered for me, once I called for the EMTs, but still…"

I nodded. Life went on. She was waiting for something more though. "Randolph." Her face relaxed as soon as I'd said it. "Genie, I'll come back for him later today, I promise. I just need to sort things out." Sort out Wallis—or Jane. I doubted the bird's sudden quiet heralded a permanent change. If anything, it meant I needed to keep working with him. I couldn't leave him with the aide, though. She had other, paying charges to care for.

"And, maybe, the dog?"

I looked over at Buster. Buster looked up at me, whining again softly. "*What?*" For an inarticulate dog, she sure picked up on people's moods. "Yeah," I said to them both. "I'll think of something." Another whine. Rose didn't have family, Genie had said, but there had to be protocols. A service dog association.

Someone I could call, even on a Saturday. "In the meantime, she probably hasn't been out this morning, has she?"

"No. With all that went on, I didn't think." Genie looked exhausted, and I had the feeling she had a good twelve hours left to go.

"I'll take her." I reached for the harness. "I may bring her back here for a while, but I promise, I'll think of something by the end of the day." I saw my day eaten up by phone calls to answering machines. LiveWell had to have some arrangement for service dogs, didn't they? Buster whined again, softly, and I realized she had more pressing concerns. "I should take her now."

"Thank you," Genie said as she walked us to the door. "And, I'm sorry."

Behind her, I heard Randolph skitter along his perch. "Hello?," he called. "Pretty bird says, 'Hello!'"

◇◇◇

I took advantage of Buster's guide harness to take her into the Starbucks. We all have our morning needs. Other than that, I let her guide me around the block. "Go wild," I said, sipping from the hole in the plastic lid. "Wherever you want."

With a dog whose routine is that tightly regimented, I didn't expect much deviation. But if there was anything to be gotten, beyond that basic call for aid, I thought this might be the way in: Dogs love the outside world. The scents, the life. Buster was a good guide dog, maybe even a great one. Life with an elderly woman, however, could not have indulged all her doggy fantasies.

Already I could feel her, fighting her own impulses. A squirrel scurried up a nearby maple. The smell of wood smoke—and another dog. Still, she kept to the path, too well trained to do more than tilt her head.

"What are you thinking, Buster?" The connection—my hand on the lead—wasn't the best. Still, I'd communicated with Growler with much less. "Are you thinking of Rose?" I pictured the old woman, not as I'd seen her last but as I'd first met her. Feisty and foul-mouthed and full of fun.

"*Bite!*" That wasn't what I'd expected.

"Bite? You mean, you wanted to bite Rose?" A wave of revulsion hit me. "Rose wanted to bite." I laughed, thinking of her fearlessness. "Yes, she did, didn't she?"

"*Bite!*" Buster stopped and looked up at me. "*Bite!*" She barked again.

"Wait, you don't mean her attitude. She wanted to attack. To fight?"

That big tail whipped the air. We were getting somewhere.

"She didn't like Wachtell. Didn't like Marc, either." The names got me nowhere. "Do you mean last night? This morning?"

Another series of wags and a little whine. "*What?*"

"She might have been fighting, Buster, but she was a sick old lady. The sickness got the better of her." I put it as gently as I could. The dog was having none of it.

"*Help! Help! Help!*" She started barking, making so much noise that I looked around. I really didn't need anybody complaining that Pru Marlowe couldn't control an animal.

"What are you saying, Buster?" I knelt on the sidewalk, reached one hand up to cup those sensitive ears. "What did you hear?"

"*Help!*" The internal voice rang out in my head. Out loud, Buster's bark had changed to a whimper, her training kicking ing. "*Get help! Raccoon?*"

That startled me, until I realized I'd been stroking her with my right hand. "Sorry." I sat back on the sidewalk and took a moment to think.

What if Rose had been fighting with someone? Had called out for help—a cry that her dog had echoed into futility? A possible sequence of events played out. Genie had said she'd found Rose and been unable to wake her. Then she had locked the dog in the bathroom and called for help.

What if that wasn't what happened? I'd heard of other cases—nurses whose patients begin to die. I liked Genie, but then I would relate to her. Everyone else in that place was abhorrent.

"Did Genie do something, Buster?" I tried to picture the aide, her calm face and gentle manner. "Did Genie think she was helping?"

"Help! Help! Get help!" The ears were sagging, the tail now hanging flat. Still, Buster whined, *"Help! Get help!"*

Chapter Thirty-four

I don't know why I was surprised to see Wachtell when Buster and I got back to LiveWell. He had duties here, and it sounded like the EMTs had taken Rose to a competent medical facility. Still, I paused when I saw his white-coated back, joking again with Nancy. Maybe it was the laughter, after all that had happened.

She must have said something, because he turned to greet me with a smile. I nodded back, unwilling to fake happiness this morning. I was being unfair; I knew that. As the staff gerontologist at an assisted living residence, he undoubtedly had a lot of mornings like this one. Maybe a day that started with a sick resident carted off to the hospital was one of the good ones. Still, I was unsettled. Partly, I realized as Buster led me forward, that was because I wasn't sure how to greet him.

"*Help!*" Buster barked once, her voice loud in the nearly empty reception area.

"Enough!" I used my command voice, low and stern, and reinforced it with a gesture, holding my hand out flat to signal "stop." I understood her impulse: she must have recognized the white coat, if not the man. This was not the place, though, and I didn't want her to get into bad habits under my care.

"So that's where it went." Wachtell turned from me to the shepherd mix. "We were wondering."

"Genie was busy, so I took Buster for *her* walk," I explained. I could feel Buster's tension—the desire to bark again, to alert the doctor—but the only sound she admitted was a low whine. "Good dog," I said to her, to reinforce what seemed a great effort of will. To Wachtell, I did a version of the same. "I'm glad I ran into you."

I wasn't, not really. For starters, I wasn't sure how to ask what I wanted to know. Wachtell would be only too glad to suspect Genie, or any aide. I almost did myself. What I needed was an honest account of who might have been in her room either overnight or early this morning. Someone had been, I was pretty sure. In truth, though, all I had to go on was what I'd picked up from Buster.

"I was hoping you could tell me about Rose." I started with the basics. "And what her prognosis is."

The doctor raised that famous eyebrow of his. "I don't believe you're family, Miss—ah—Pru."

"No, but I am a friend." I was using the same tone as I'd used with Buster, low and firm. "And I am helping care for her service animal."

He nodded. "She's over at Berkshire General. It's too soon to tell, but I did get a call from the admitting M.D. It seems that perhaps she took a few too many of her sleeping drugs."

"Rose?" This wasn't making sense. Even forgetting her objection to medication, the woman I'd seen last night was half asleep before she'd even undressed. The reality of what he'd said sank in. "An overdose? How is that possible? You were checking her medications only hours before."

"That's what we'll have to look into." He looked down at Buster. *"Help!"* the whine picked up. "She had an aide with her last night—and this morning, too."

I didn't like what he was implying. "Was anyone else with her?" Wachtell only shrugged.

"Nancy?"

The blonde shook her head. "I worked till eight, and there were no visitors. There's nothing on the overnight log, either. Except for you, Miss." She looked at me, and Wachtell turned back toward me as well, that eyebrow raised again.

"Well, that's interesting." He paused, letting the implications sink in, before throwing me a lifeline. "Of course, seeing as how the medications are administered by the aides, I'm afraid we're going to have to do a little in-house investigation."

I was right about one thing. Wachtell was going to blame Genie. Maybe I should have been grateful.

I wasn't. "I'm going to visit Rose," I said. "See what I can find out." At the mention of her person's name, Buster's tail thumped on the carpet.

"You think maybe she meant self harm?" That smile again. "I don't know if she was competent enough for that."

"I'll talk to her." I didn't like him talking about her in the past tense. "I'd like to take Buster to see her." A visit would do them both good, I was sure. Besides, with the two of them together, I'd have a better chance of piecing together the events of the night. "Once she's receiving visitors."

"I'm sure Nancy can find out for you." He turned to walk away. "Oh, and since you've already formed such a bond with the dog, maybe you'll continue to take care of it while Mrs. Danziger is indisposed?"

I nodded. I wanted to say something about billing, about fees for services rendered. That was the kind of language he'd understand. But I knew he'd simply have the costs passed along to Rose, and from all I'd heard, she had enough to deal with right now anyway. Raising Buster's harness, I prepared to lead her back to Rose's apartment. I had to think through what to do with her—and with Randolph—and the quiet, empty room seemed like the best alternative.

"Miss—Pru." I turned. Wachtell was looking at me quizzically. "What did you do to your hand?"

Of course, I had my right hand on the harness, and not only was it bandaged, but I was holding it gingerly, the result of the continuing soreness.

"Oh, an accident." I wasn't sure what to say. "Occupational hazard."

"An animal bite?" He was a little too perceptive for my taste. I didn't respond. "You should have that looked at, you know." He nodded at my wrapping. Done the night before, in a bourbon haze, it hadn't weathered the night well. "Such things can turn septic. Or worse."

"Thanks," I said, not meaning it. I was relieved when he didn't offer to do the honors.

Chapter Thirty-five

"Hello, Randolph." I opened the door to Rose's apartment to find the parrot looking at me, head slightly tilted. "Hello."

"Bugger off." With one scaly foot, he brushed something off his beak in what looked for all the world like a rude gesture. So much for new behavior.

In the vague hope that some mild aversion training might help and partly, to be honest, because I was bushed, I ignored the bird, instead heading straight for Rose's armchair. Buster, whose halter I'd released as soon as we were inside, padded around, whining softly. I knew how she felt.

"I'll bring her back, Buster." Even as I said it, I wondered if I was lying. "Or I'll bring you to her, I promise." That I would— even if it was to say goodbye to a corpse. Animals understand death, better than most humans. To not give Buster a chance to say farewell would be cruel. It was the meantime, though, that was the problem.

"Buster, would you be okay if I left you here?" I looked around the unit. It was small, too small for a big dog. Buster was used to working, and even if Rose wasn't much of an athlete her minor needs—getting up, going to the bathroom, going to meals—kept her dog focused. Without Rose, Buster would quickly go stir crazy. "Just for a day or two?"

She whined, coming back from the neatly made bed to lie at my feet. *"Protect?"* No, this dog needed a job.

"Let me find out what's going on with Rose. Okay?" I reached to pet that strong back and mentally added another item to my list. Maybe this would work out: I could visit with Rose, or at least talk to her doctors, and start the rabies shots. Berkshire General was big enough that I could probably lie. Say I'd been bitten in the wild, that the animal had escaped. There'd be a report to fill out, but I didn't care about that, as long as Doc Sharpe didn't get dragged in.

Randolph, however, was another problem. I wondered about his brief transformation. Earlier, he'd been all sweetness and light, his usual round of abuse replaced by inane, but inoffensive chatter. Had he been cowed by Rose's illness? I knew too well what the scene must have been like. Genie, increasingly agitated, trying to wake an unresponsive Rose. Then the EMTs charging in with their gear, their radios squawking. The parrot's cage had undoubtedly been covered through all of this, but that would have been worse—hearing, unable to see.

"*Guilt.*" Wallis' words came back to me, but I shook them off. Somehow, according to my tabby, the parrot had felt implicated in Polly's death. Maybe he actually had been, luring her out of bed late at night. Here, though, I couldn't see how that would apply. There was no way Randolph had sickened Rose. He certainly couldn't have given her an overdose of her pain meds—or prompted anyone else to.

"Randolph?" The idea was just too tempting, and I've learned these days that when a thought pops into my head sometimes its because somebody—some animal—suggested it. "You didn't tell anyone—" No, it made no sense. "Did you hear something? Something you can tell me about Rose? About Rose here, last night?"

I didn't know how to make myself understood. The concepts were too complex—transferring thoughts of Polly to her neighbor. Of noises to actions, of time past to time now. The big bird shifted on his perch and looked at me, though, and I had the damnedest feeling he was trying to figure out what I was asking. "*Guilt.*" Was that Wallis' voice reverberating in my head or was it something coming from Randolph?

"Hello?" His voice was soft, quizzical. "Hello?"

"What did you hear, Randolph? What can you tell me?"

"Bugger off! Stop that! That's mine! Hands off." Out of nowhere, Randolph's mood changed. Suddenly, he was flapping those large wings, hitting the sides of his cage in his frenzy. "Shut up! Shut up! Shut up!"

"Randolph, calm down!" I jumped up to cover the cage. An agitated bird could hurt himself, and I didn't need another complication to this day. "Randolph, it's okay. It's okay."

Once covered, the parrot settled down, whistling and muttering curses under his breath. I was doing the same. Despite living with this so-called gift for more than a year already, I was no closer to understanding its implications. Clearly, what I had done had agitated Randolph, but I had no idea how. Perhaps the intensity of my thoughts had been painful somehow, like a probing spike in that round gray head. Maybe I had awakened memories of Polly, and the loss of his longtime companion. Maybe there were simply underlying issues that I didn't understand. I hadn't examined that bare patch on the parrot's breast for a day or two. It had seemed to be getting better, but I had a sinking feeling that the next time I looked, it would be plucked raw again.

"Bugger all." He was settling down, his voice softer. "Ignorant slut."

"Oh, hell!" I grabbed my coat, glancing at the clock as I did so. "Sorry, Randolph, Buster, I've got to run." I'd totally lost track of time. Growler, I knew, would forgive me. Tracy Horlick, however, would be wanting an explanation.

Chapter Thirty-six

"I was wondering what happened to you." Twenty minutes later, I was at the Horlick house, facing a heavier than usual barrage of smoke. "Expected to hear you'd been found dead. Eaten by your cats."

"One cat." I did my best to smile. I was, after all, forty-five minutes late. "I'm sorry. My Saturday schedule is a little different." Old lady Horlick had only recently decided to hire me through the weekend, and I was wondering if the extra five bucks per visit were worth it.

"Whatever." She flicked her ash into the bushes at the side of the door and picked a stray thread of tobacco from her lip. "It's not like I have all day, you know."

I nodded, afraid to say anything. The fact that Tracy Horlick was still in the faded yellow housecoat that she usually greeted me in made me doubt that she had any pressing engagements that morning. "Is Bitsy ready to go?" I managed an upbeat note at the thought of the bichon.

"Huh." Another drag. "Like you care." Without waiting for a reply to that one, she turned. Hearing the familiar scrambling sound, I reached in the door for Growler's lead, but his mistress' claw-like hand came down on it first.

"I hear they've had some excitement over at the old-age home." Her eyes, small and mean, focused in on me. She was exacting her toll for my lateness. "You involved with any of that?"

I shook my head reflexively, impressed as usual by the speed of gossip in this small community. "I'm just helping retrain a parrot," I offered, sounding as neutral as I could.

"Retrain a parrot. Ha!" Her squawk of a laugh would have startled Randolph. "Funny what the kids do with their money, isn't it? And I hear they came into quite a bit of it, too, after parking their own mother in that place to die."

I couldn't smile. Just couldn't. But I kept my mouth closed as she handed me the lead and I snapped it on the little white dog's collar. Tracy Horlick was a mean gossip, like some people were mean drunks. I didn't know how much she knew, and how much was her just chumming the water—knowing the bloody bits drew best.

Growler seemed strangely uninterested when I told him what was going on. I had thought the little dog, as social as he was, would at least be interested in Buster. In truth, I had thought he might have some tips for me, some ideas as to how I could get the guide dog to tell me more.

"What do you care, walker lady?" The little dog huffed and puffed as we trotted up the sidewalk. Growler depended on our daily walks for more than exercise or bathroom breaks. Locked in the Horlick basement or backyard most of the day, this was his one chance to catch up on the neighborhood goings-on. *"Huh,"* I overheard a brief analysis of another dog's urine. *"Butch was eating the cat's food again."*

"But Growler," I had waited until the little dog had made his own mark on the corner birch and was growing a little tired. "I do care. Buster might be the only witness to what happened. The only one who saw anything."

"Huh!" The bichon kicked at the ground, his way of dismissing anything as so much trash. *"Like you'd understand, anyway. Completely misses the point...."* Muttering to himself, he turned and started home. *"Doesn't see what's right in front of her. Stupid bitch."*

As I fell in line behind the fluffy little creature, I mentally kicked myself. I should have known. Growler had picked up, from me, that Buster was female. Still, the little dog hadn't expressed such a virulently misogynistic thought in quite a while. As we walked silently back to his home, I also considered the effects of my tardiness. Who knew what Tracy Horlick had put him through?

I didn't think it was mercy that kept Tracy Horlick silent as I delivered the dog back into her care. I heard voices in the back of the house, and I figured she was getting her gossip fix for the day. That was fine by me. I drove a few blocks off and stopped by the side of the road. It had been a full day, and it wasn't yet noon. What I wanted was to go home and sleep off the rest of the hangover. What I needed was more coffee.

What I did, however, was make a phone call. Poor Rose had been in worse shape than me when they'd taken her away, and I'd left two animals in her empty apartment. There were service-animal groups in the area that would undoubtedly take Buster if Rose was permanently incapacitated—or worse—but that was a last resort. Before I made plans for either animal, I needed to find out what was up with the old lady.

"Berkshire General." Calling the hospital made me think of my own mother. She'd had hospice care at home, at the end. We'd made our share of trips, though, and I remembered the drill.

"Patient information. I'm calling about Rose Danziger. She would have been brought in from LiveWell Assisted Living this morning."

"Just one moment please." Saccharine strings filled the space as I waited. Through my windshield, I could see a bit of sun. Despite everything, this was shaping up to be a nice day. "Are you a relative?" The voice was back.

"I'm her niece," I lied. "I'm the only family in the area." In for a penny, in for a pound. The music came back and two songs later, I heard a different voice—male—on the line.

"I gather you're asking for Rose Danziger?"

I was, I assured him, to which I got more hemming and hawing.

"She's still being evaluated," he said eventually. "Is there a number we can reach you at?"

There'd be hell to pay if any real family turned up, but it was too late to worry about that. I gave him my cell and thanked him, for not questioning me further, if nothing else.

When my phone rang, less than a minute later, I was still parked. The car was warm, and I'd been drifting off. The sound shocked me upright, however, and I answered with a gasp.

"Yes?"

"Hey, Pru, are you all right?" It was Albert, not the hospital. "I didn't wake you or anything, did I?"

"It's almost noon, Al." Being caught out made me grumpy. "What's up?" I was expecting some tale of woe. A skunked dog that he didn't want to deal with. Another newcomer who couldn't figure out how to squirrel-proof his attic.

"It's that raccoon." Of course. He sounded almost guilty, as if at some level he did recognize that this was his job.

"That condo association send another letter?" I stretched. "'Cause I'm on my way to talking to the man in charge."

"No, it's the raccoon—the actual raccoon, Pru." Damn, he sounded glum. I waited. "I think something's wrong with him. He's not eating, and, well, he just looks bad."

I kicked myself. I hadn't been back to check on the poor creature. Sure, I'd given him some boxes to climb on, to get him out of the puddle and provide a bit of stimulation. Still, a cage was no place for a wild animal.

"I think maybe he's sick, Pru." Albert was still talking, although his voice had sunk so low I had to strain to hear it. "You know, like those condo guys said."

Rabies. Hell. I didn't want to hear it.

"That's one idea, Albert, but there are a lot of other possibilities, too." I scrambled for excuses, for a reason to delay. Luckily, Albert provided one.

"I don't know, Pru. I think we should, you know, do the test." Euthanize the animal, he meant. "I was hoping you'd, uh, you know, help me?"

He wanted me to do the dirty work. I didn't know if he was squeamish about administering the injection or simply afraid of the animal. After a second, I realized it didn't matter; he'd given me my edge.

"I understand, Albert. This isn't a one-person job." I was improvising. "Look, I'm really busy right now, but I'll be by as soon as I can." He started to protest. "By the end of the day, okay?"

He grumbled at that, but it wasn't like he had a choice. There was an awkward moment when I almost asked if he could put his ferret on the line. That I couldn't find an excuse for, though, so I let him go. Sitting in my car, the day suddenly looked less bright. With even Albert pushing for euthanasia, that raccoon was running out of options. I needed a consult with someone I could trust, so I did the sensible thing: I drove home.

Chapter Thirty-seven

"Wallis?" I'd rushed out so quickly that morning, I hadn't seen her before I left. Nor did she appear as I made my way to the kitchen. Only after I had the coffee brewing did she make her entrance, brushing ever so slightly against my legs.

"Want some late breakfast?" She eyed me, and I took that as a yes. I couldn't really tell how much she picked up from me, and an offering of food is always a good opener. "You know I had an emergency this morning," I said, as I cracked two eggs into the pan.

"I know you've been running around like some headless bird," she purred. I cut off an extra pat of butter and dropped it in her dish. It was a bribe, and she knew it. *"Speaking of brainless creatures,"* I could hear her voice despite the soft lapping. *"Are you going to be bringing that parrot back here?"*

"I don't know, Wallis. I have to figure out what's up with Rose." I looked down at her, at the way her stripes converged to a black badge between her ears. She might be small, but she was as beautiful—and as pitiless—as a tiger. "Do you think that would be okay?"

"You're asking me?" She sat up and began washing her face. I stirred the eggs and took them off the heat. *"I'm not going to burn myself, you know."* She blinked up at me. *"I am not a kitten."*

"Sorry." I slid the eggs into her dish. "I have a lot on my mind."

"Like that raccoon." Her tone, even as she began to eat, was clear. *"You're such a human."*

From anyone else, it might be a compliment. From Wallis, it was anything but. Watching her eat, I thought about what she meant. For starters, I knew, she was worried about me. As she might put it, we'd formed a neat little pride, an ecosystem in which each of us played a part. Plus, although she'd be loath to admit it, I suspected she was fond of me. As fond as she could be.

That was it, of course. By pointing out my humanity, she was letting me know that I was thinking emotionally—something no animal ever did. I pitied the raccoon, sympathized with his plight. In her eyes, this was clearly wrong.

"Of course it is." She looked up, licking her chops. *"Things die, Pru, that's the way of nature. And, yes, I'd prefer you not be one of them."* She had a point. I got a flash of what could happen if I released the raccoon. If he were sick, he'd be the one to die alone and in pain. He might infect other animals before the end. Other humans, possibly. I swallowed, aware suddenly of a swelling and soreness at the base of my throat. Rabies is a horrible disease that kills with fever and hallucinations and an endless deadly thirst. It had been nearly forty-eight hours since I'd been bitten; the window of safety was closing. I needed to take care of myself. To think of myself first.

Still, it went against the grain to destroy a healthy animal. I poured my coffee and turned to find Wallis on the counter, eying me. "What?" I asked.

"You're not going to do it, are you?" I got a note of something. Amusement, maybe.

"I don't know. I'm going to go see him. Maybe Frank will have a take on all of this."

"Oh, she's talking to the weasel again." I smiled. We were back on familiar footing. *"Maybe you should introduce that dog to the weasel."*

I thought, for a moment, she was making fun of me. Cats do have a very cool sense of humor.

"It couldn't hurt." She turned away, a little offended.

"What now?" I reached to pet her. "I'm sorry."

"You're clueless, Pru. You really don't listen." Her back arched slightly as I rubbed down her smooth fur. An involuntary reaction, I knew. *"Sometimes, you know, I am serious. If you can't understand what an animal tells you, you can ask another animal."*

I felt, rather than heard, a soft purr starting. She was beginning to forgive me my many sins. *"You may bring that parrot back, you know. I did find him interesting to talk to, even if you didn't get half of it."* I kept petting her, musing on our interaction. *"But you're not bringing that dog here, and that's that."* With that she jumped off the counter and left the room.

Since the pan was dirty anyway, I made myself some eggs and ate them at the window, staring out at the tapestry of trees. Saturday. If the rain were over with, the tourists would be hitting us hard. That could add to my workload as they brought their inevitable troubles to Doc Sharpe at County. I should call him, let him know I was available. Whatever I was going through, he'd looked bad.

At least I had some resources. Wallis might have been serious about enlisting Frank. The slender mustelid had a keen insight, born out of his sense of smell and the acute instincts any small animal must develop to survive. I didn't know what she'd meant about translating for Buster, though. I'd heard what the dog had said. It just hadn't been that much.

Unless I was missing something. That would fit with Growler's rude comments, too. Maybe there had been some other sign—some signal I wasn't getting from scent or posture. All I'd heard were a few words, the key phrases of a well-trained service animal.

Or maybe Wallis was simply talking. For all her smugness, she hadn't actually gotten that much out of Randolph for me. Just that he felt responsible for Polly's death. Guilty, even if she didn't understand the word. I found it curious that Wallis would have communicated an emotion to me—she'd made it clear just how worthless she thought those were. Then again, she didn't have much respect for Randolph either. Maybe his having an emotional response to Polly's demise was part of it.

Unless I was the one who was misinterpreting everything. I drank more coffee, willing my tired brain cells to spark, when the phone rang again.

"Pru, where are you?" It was Creighton, his voice sounding strangely clipped.

"Jim, long time no see." I didn't like being interrupted in the middle of a thought.

"Pru, I'm sorry I haven't been around." He was talking fast, and I could hear the tension in his voice. "I've been busy, but, please, talk to me. Where are you right now?"

"I'm at home, Jim. I was just looking out the window." It's in my nature to tease him. "The trees are beautiful from here. There's one maple—"

"Good." He cut me off. "Do me a favor. Stay there for a few hours?"

"Are you placing me under house arrest?" I realized my error in suggesting that and kept talking before he could respond. "I've got things to do, Jim. I've got to get over to County and Albert's office, and back to LiveWell, and—"

"Those are fine, Pru. Just, look—please listen to me for once."

"Will I see you later?" The words slipped out before I knew what I was saying.

"If not tonight, tomorrow, I promise." He was so focused, I doubted he'd even noticed that I was asking for him. Well, that was fine, because he'd also ended up telling me the one thing he didn't want me to know: he didn't want me to go someplace I'd been recently. It had to be Evergreen Hills.

Chapter Thirty-eight

Going to the condo development wouldn't solve any of my problems. Not directly. Then again, if I could find out what was going on over at Evergreen Hills, maybe it would help me with the raccoon. Then I could continue on to Berkshire General, get my first shot, and I'd be in a better place to deal with Rose and Buster and Randolph.

That was what I told myself as I grabbed my jacket and keys. Wallis, however, was staring at me with a look I knew well. *"You don't really believe that, do you?"*

I smiled back. "Not necessarily, Wallis. But wouldn't you be curious?"

She flicked her tail, which I took for agreement, and I left.

The day had turned clear and bright, one of those New England days that make the postcards look faded. That meant traffic as the weekend tourists filled our roads to gawk at nature's finest. If they hadn't been in my way, I'd have felt a bit of pride, actually, though my role in the loss of chlorophyll was about on a par with theirs.

As it was, the fact that I couldn't let my GTO flex her muscles pissed me off. What was the point of driving if you couldn't feel it? And so I leaned back, revved my engine, and took off, weaving between the out-of-towners like a hawk through a flock of pigeons. They didn't scatter, not exactly, but my baby's got enough of a growl so that they started pulling over as they saw me coming. It was cruel, about as fair as anything else in nature, but it was fun. And when I saw the shadow on the road—a redtail taking stock overhead—I began to remember what I'd liked about this old town, small as it could feel.

I was so caught up in the flow of the road, passing with a roar and easing back in, that I almost missed it. Jerry's truck, its noxious green and yellow standing out among the sedate sedans. It didn't cut me off this time—we were heading in opposite directions. And instead of pulling onto the highway, it was turning onto that cutoff. But the driver—Jerry or one of his brain-dead cousins—had no respect for traffic patterns, and had braked abruptly enough so that someone honked. I saw a raised middle finger poke out of the driver's side window as the truck cut the sharp right, disappearing down what looked like a dirt track.

Interesting. I let myself glide along, thinking. That was the second time I'd seen the company truck this far from the condo development. It was Saturday. Jerry could be taking some time off: that track could lead to his favorite fishing hole or, more likely, the beer cooler at a buddy's cabin. I didn't see Jerry Gaffney as having an incurably strong work ethic. But unless he had free use of that logo'd truck, there was an off chance that his errands were business related. If the brains behind Evergreen Hills were planning another development, they would be looking for more investors. I didn't envy Jane Larkin's chances at the next family get-together.

Or, I realized as I pulled off for Evergreen Hills, Jerry could simply have been hiding out. The road to the development was as empty as always, but once I turned the last scenic curve, I was greeted by more activity than a bear-raided beehive. Cop cars from all over the county lined the road. Dun-colored uniforms, some holding flashlights, patrolled the grounds. I braked as quickly as possible, but one thing about a baby blue vintage Pontiac: it isn't inconspicuous. With all the stern looks I was getting, I figured smiling and staying put was the thing to do. Luckily, someone who looked vaguely familiar talked into some kind of handheld device, and a minute later, I saw Jim Creighton walking up the drive.

I rolled down the window as he got near. He leaned in, but I knew better than to expect a kiss.

"Didn't I tell you not to come here?" He sounded tired rather than angry, which piqued my curiosity.

"You asked if I was going anywhere. At the time, I didn't think so." I smiled. Batting my eyelashes would have been too much. "But once you mentioned it, I remembered an errand that I needed to do."

"Pru?" He'd pulled back to get a better look at me. His voice was level, but there was strain behind it. "Why are you here?"

"I told you, I had an errand." A smile wasn't going to work. "I needed to see someone."

"Who?" He wasn't going to give me anything.

"Whoever's in charge." That sounded weak, even to me. "I need to speak to the head of the board of overseers, or whatever he's called." I figured it was a he. "He's never around during the week, so I thought I'd try this afternoon."

Creighton wasn't buying it. "It seems to me like Jerry Gaffney runs things here."

"Jerry Gaffney is a tool." I realized I had something to trade. "Besides, I passed his truck on the way here." Creighton nodded, waiting. "He pulled off onto a dirt road about a quarter mile south. The truck's pretty unmissable. Bright green and yellow."

"You come here on an errand for him?"

"Jim, cut it out. Please." I didn't know where that last word came from. "I told you. I've got no involvement with Gaffney, and no desire for any. I really am looking for whoever is in charge. Legally, I mean."

He had a stare, I'll give him that. Those blue eyes were more metallic than my car. "It's about an animal, Jim. A raccoon we removed from one of the buildings."

He considered that for a moment. "What happened to your hand?" He nodded toward my bandage, and I remembered he hadn't seen it.

I had to fight the urge to tuck it underneath me. Instead, I just opened it in a careless wave. "I got bit, Jim. Sometimes that happens, even to me."

"Not by the raccoon I hope." He was making conversation. I could hear a certain warmth creeping back into his voice. This was too close for comfort, however.

I forced a laugh. "No way. This was a regular. Crazy, huh?"

I'd gone too far. Those blue eyes narrowed again, trying to see the lie. "Pru, what's going on here? Really?"

"Just what I told you, Jim." I raised my bandaged hand. "Swear to god. We picked up a raccoon and I need to clear some things up before we release him. So, can you tell me who's in charge around here? I mean, for real?"

"Sorry, Pru." He stepped back and stood up. "No can do. But I'll tell you one thing: whoever's in charge has got bigger things to worry about than a raccoon."

With that, he slapped the top of my car, and walked off. I took my cue and started up the engine. As quietly as I could—no way I could be inconspicuous—I drove back down the entrance road to the highway, wondering all the while just what the hell was going on.

The good news, I realized once I was back on a real road, was that Jim had given me as much information as I'd given him. Maybe more. For starters, he didn't know who really ran the condo development either. I suspected that officially it was all set up that way, incorporated on paper with a million loopholes so none of the principle investors would ever have to take responsibility. He'd probably tracked down some of the board—Wachtell, for example, or Marc Larkin—but he seemed as in the dark about the real boss as I was. He'd also as good as told me that whoever it was had enough heat on him so that he'd never bother to follow up on that letter.

I'd given him Gaffney, maybe. I had no qualms about that. Whatever that thug was hiding, it would do him good to be hauled in by Creighton. In the meantime, I needed to act. I wasn't sure yet what I'd say to Albert, but that didn't worry me overmuch. I'd check out that raccoon. If he looked okay, I'd take him today—somewhere far beyond this rattrap development. If he didn't, well, I'd deal with that then. I flexed my hand as I drove. The wound was still sore, the base of my thumb swollen and hot. I needed to take care of it—to take care of myself—while there was still time.

Chapter Thirty-nine

Heading toward the shelter, I really didn't want to be bothered by anyone else. So when my phone rang the first time, I ignored it. I'd check my voicemail when I got to Albert's, in case one of my regulars was having an emergency. When it rang again, almost immediately, I was a little curious. It was possible that Creighton wanted to apologize, after all. Or that he had something more fun in mind. But with any animal, consistency is the key to training, and the lesson I wanted to teach was that my time was my own, and so I let it go. The third time, I reached to turn it off. But the combination of bite and bandage had made my fingers clumsy, and before I knew it, I heard a familiar voice, calling frantically from inside my bag.

"Miss Marlowe? Pru? Are you there?" It was Genie, her accent making her voice more clipped. With a sigh, I raised the phone to my ear.

"I'm here, Genie. What's up?" I didn't slow down, but I heard the touch of guilt in my own voice. I should have left a note, when I left the dog and parrot in the room. She had no way of knowing I'd be back. "If this is about Buster—"

"You have to come. You have to come now." She interrupted me. "They are going to take the dog away. They are going to call the police."

"Good luck with that." I murmured to myself. All the police in Beauville were down at Evergreen Hills, and any call about an animal would be routed to Albert anyway. Still, I had left her—and the animals—in the lurch. "Don't worry, Genie. I'm on my way."

This time, I made sure I turned off my phone. I couldn't imagine what had prompted the panic in the aide's voice, but it was an excuse to drive fast, traffic be damned.

I'll admit, I swept into the lot with a bit more flourish than necessary. That might have been why the aides gathered outside for a smoke looked up as I walked up to LiveWell's main entrance. There was no way Nancy could have heard my squealing tires, however, so it had to be something else that had her eyebrows raised to her bangs.

"Miss Marlowe!" She nearly jumped out of her seat.

"Reporting for duty." I gave a mock salute. "I hear Buster's been causing some trouble?"

"That dog's gone crazy." She leaned forward, her voice a hush. "Nobody knows what caused it, but it's scaring all the residents. You've got to get rid of him."

"I'm sure she's fine." As I've said, half my job is training humans. More than half. "With Rose in the hospital, Buster has had a shock, and I'm sure she's just acting out." Even as I said it, I wondered. A well-trained service dog does not simply go off without provocation. "I'm going up there now."

She breathed, what might have been the first time since I walked in, and I realized that maybe my stop here would be useful. "Once I've seen Buster," I turned. The elevator tended to take its time. "I'd love to talk to Dr. Wachtell again." I really wanted to grill him on Evergreen Hills, but I'd let Nancy think it was about Rose, if that would help.

It didn't. "He's not on duty today." She must have seen the surprise on my face. I'd seen him only that morning. "He handled the overnight," she explained. "So he won't be in again until tomorrow."

"Ah well." The chime announced the arrival of the elevator, so I got in line behind two walkers and wheel chair. "Maybe you can tell me how to reach him when I'm done upstairs?"

She nodded, but I wasn't optimistic. The look on her face said that disturbing the doctor on his day off was not something in the LiveWell handbook.

As soon as I got off the elevator, I understood the urgency. LiveWell's walls were probably more solid than those at Evergreen Hills. They only muted the loud, deep barks, however, the sound of a dog in distress. I panicked for a moment, remembering that I didn't have keys, and then caught myself. Rose never locked her door. As far as I could tell, nobody here did. Which might, I thought, be part of the problem.

The scene that greeted me, though, was not what I had feared. In the few seconds it took me to reach Rose's unit, I had visions of an intruder, lying dead. Or of Rose herself, returned from Berkshire General, and once more lying unconscious. *"Help! Help!"* was what I had heard in each round of barks. *"Help! Help! Help!"* A cycle repeated long enough for Buster to grow hoarse.

"Buster." As I stepped into the room, she shut up even before I could make the hands-down "silence" gesture. She'd been facing the door, standing, and now she sat. She even wagged that big flag of a tail, as I knelt in front of her, thumping it on the floor two or three times in greeting. "What is it?" I reached out to put my good hand on her head. "Tell me?"

"Help?" she woofed softly, almost a sigh. And it hit me. "Randolph!" I jumped to my feet so fast that Buster scurried backward. Racing to the shelf, I ripped off the cage covering. And found myself face to face with the quizzical eyes of a perfectly healthy parrot.

"Randolph?" He whistled softly. "Are you okay?"

"Mind your own business!" He tilted his head, as if to get a better look at me. "Ignorant slut."

I laughed with relief, a sound that started the parrot cursing again. "Bugger all! Shut up!" Buster even came up to lean against me, that big tail thwacking against my leg.

"You two gave me quite a scare. You know that?" Randolph whistled again, and I made for the armchair. Buster lay by my feet, undoubtedly exhausted by barking. "Either of you want to tell me what happened here?"

I was talking as much to myself as to them. I don't have any kind of easy rapport with anyone but Wallis. I certainly didn't expect a response. But even as I settled into the chair, I realized the dog before me had raised her head. She was looking at the parrot, and Randolph was looking back at her. The room was suddenly very silent.

"Anyone want to start?" I didn't want to disturb what seemed to be a communication here. I did want in. Leaning forward, I put my good hand on Buster's back. I couldn't reach Randolph from here, but I looked up at him, trying not to blink as I met his small black eyes with mine. "Randolph?"

"Hello," he said, softly. "Hello. Pretty bird."

"Buster?"

I felt the dog's response, rather than hearing it. A low rumble, the precursor to a growl, and for a moment I wondered if I had miscalculated. A bored dog might just see a large bird as legitimate prey.

"Hands off!" Randolph squawked, his voice louder. "Hands off! Bugger off! That's mine! Stop it!" He was getting louder, shuffling on his perch. Beneath my hand, I could feel Buster's growl getting louder. Could almost hear it.

"Hands off! Stop it!" Randolph shrieked. Clearly, Buster's growl had set the parrot off. "Stop it!"

"Okay, that's enough." I stood up and reached for the cage cover.

"*Help! Help! Help!*" Buster stood too, and began barking.

"Quiet." I turned toward her, my voice low and firm. "Quiet, Buster." Using both hands, I motioned for her to sit and be still. Good dog that she was, she sat.

"Sorry about that." I apologized to Randolph as I began to spread the cover once again over his cage.

"Hello," he responded, much more quietly. "Hello." I paused. The dog was no longer barking, nor could I sense that incipient growl. But the cage wasn't covered yet, and Randolph and Buster could clearly see each other. Still, the parrot had clearly calmed. "Hello," he said. "Pretty bird?"

Did my command to the dog work with the parrot, too? Was Randolph intelligent enough to have picked up some of Buster's training? For a moment, I paused, the implications racing through my head. Maybe I did have a future in animal behavior. Maybe there was even a thesis in this.

Or, at least, a content client. Backing carefully out of the room, I went across the hall and knocked on the door.

"Come in." Jane, sounding more tired than the day before.

"Jane, great news." The woman I saw sitting cross-legged on the floor looked like she could use it. "Would you come with me?"

Her sigh could have been a jetpack, launching her upright, only it took too long. "I believe we've made some progress," I said, hoping to jolly her along. The look she gave me was both doubtful and confused, and I realized I'd lost her. "Randolph? The parrot?"

She nodded without saying anything, and I realized that she'd disengaged. Granted, she had her hands full, but I needed her to realize that even if the African gray was currently in my care, he was her responsibility.

"He's really coming along," I said, glad to have the excuse to reintroduce them.

"Oh, good." She paused to brush some dust from her sweatpants, and paused again at the door, looking at her sweater.

"He's right across the hall." I was doing my best not to lose my temper. "At Rose Danziger's, remember?"

"Of course." There was a bit of snippiness in her tone. "I didn't know if you left him there, after—well, after all that fuss."

"You were here this morning?" I didn't remember seeing her. Then again, with everything going on, it would have been easy for someone so pale and nondescript to go unnoticed.

Jane nodded. "I can't sleep," she said by way of explanation. Looking back at the boxes behind her, she added, "Sometimes, I think I'll never be done."

"Well, one problem may soon be solved." I was using my happy voice. I really didn't have time to waste. "Come see."

With a flourish, I opened Rose's door and ushered Jane inside. The worn-looking woman took two steps and then started, holding her hands up as if stifling a yell.

"That's just Buster," I reassured her. "You've met Buster. She's very well trained." Just the same, I made the calming gesture with my hands—palms down. None of us needed another barking fit. The dog obliged, tilting her triangular head to consider the newcomer.

"This is who I wanted you to see." Hands low, pitching my voice in as calm and unthreatening a tone as I could, I drew Jane over to Randolph's cage, and turned to him. "Hello, pretty bird. Would you say, 'Hello'?"

There was a moment, I'd swear to it. The bird looked at me, turning that round gray head side to side to examine me with each of those yellow eyes. Then he looked over at Buster, and then at Jane. "Hello?" I tried again. Something was going on. Something I didn't like. "Pretty bird?" I could hear the hope drain out of my own voice.

"Well, this is better than all that foul language," said Jane, coming up behind me.

And that was it. "Sqwah!" Randolph flapped his wings. "Hand's off, damn you! That's mine!"

"Quiet." I tried using the same voice, low and commanding, to Randolph. "Be good now."

"That's mine!" The parrot was on a roll now. "Screw you! Hand's off!"

To make matters worse, Buster started barking. "*Help! Help! Help!*"

"Buster, no." I spun around and caught her in mid-bark. She shut up, but Randolph was still at it. "Screw you! Your own damned business."

"I'm—" Jane flapped her hands, in a sad mockery of the parrot. "I'll be across the hall."

"I'm sorry." I watched her go. "Randolph really was doing better." The door closed behind her, and immediately the parrot settled down.

"And what," I turned back to the bird. "Was that about?"

"Ah, bugger all!" He was quieter, now, as if he'd made his point. "Bugger all and be done, you ignorant slut!"

Chapter Forty

"Well, that was useless." I wasn't talking to Randolph, not really. Nor to Buster, although the guide dog was staring at my face as if trying to make sense of my words. "Worse than useless. And I still don't know what to do with either of you."

Both animals were quiet, now that Jane was gone, but my thoughts were anything but. I could understand some of it. Jane was not an easy person to be with. I'm not into psychobabble, but I knew enough about depression to recognize it. And I'd had enough experience to know that the quiet ones were the ones who turned. Jane clearly didn't want responsibility for her mother's pet, even though I doubted she'd ever admit that, and I wouldn't be surprised if the bird had picked up on some of that. Even a big bird, like Randolph, was essentially a prey animal. You see any of your family become dinner, and you learn pretty quick to recognize hostility—and to do what you can to chase it away.

And Buster? Well, the parrot's voice had sounded enough like an old lady's—Rose's, though also, I imagined, Polly's—that the dog might have been responding as she would if her person had been yelling. She had been calling for help, trying to alert me to a problem. And she had shut up when I'd told her to.

Animals make sense. They don't know any other way. It's people who act erratic, and Jane's mixed messages were the cause of the commotion, of that I was sure. Though as I sat there, being stared at by three inscrutable eyes, I realized Jane's behavior had raised some alarms in the back of my mind, too. For starters, where had she been that morning? You hear cries for help, you hear emergency techs racing down a hallway, isn't it natural to stick your head out? Especially when you know that your beloved mother's beloved pet parrot is in the room where the emergency is happening?

I already suspected that Jane wanted Randolph gone. Unlike her brother, she would never dare voice the words out loud. It was clear, though, that she'd love for me to spirit the parrot away and never bother her again. We still had no explanation for Randolph's seizure. Come to think of it, we didn't yet know what had happened to Rose, either. Could Jane be some kind of closet killer? And could Randolph have been yelling his gray head off to save himself—or to warn me? No, I realized. I couldn't bring that bird back to his old home. Not yet, maybe not ever.

I couldn't leave them here, though. Buster was clearly too bored, and it wasn't fair to Genie to expect her to keep cleaning up after a foot-long bird. I toyed with the idea of bringing them over to my house. It was big, and, on paper, it was mine. Well, except that the paper didn't reflect the reality. Wallis might agree to the parrot being there. Even that was pushing it, I feared, as I thought of the tabby's "interrogation." The dog? No way. Wallis had been clear about that, and our old house was her territory. Besides, I had too much to do to try to convince her. Albert had as good as told me the time was running out for that raccoon, and although I had every intention of stalling him, I had to do something for the poor beast. Odds were, if he was getting sick, it was from being stuck in that back kennel for days now.

That's when it hit me. A little over the top, maybe, but with a little luck, it just might work.

I ran into Genie on my way to the elevator. Buster was leading me, in her fashion, and I saw the wave of relief wash over the aide's face as she looked down at the now-silent dog.

"Ah good." She looked up at me with a smile. "Thank you, Pru. This is for the best."

Something in her wording made me worry. "I hope this is just temporary. Genie, have you heard anything?"

She stared at me, blank faced, for a moment. "About Rose?"

I lowered my voice.

"Ah." She nodded and glanced around. Of course. Aides may wash the residents and dress them, deal with all kinds of intimate care. They're not officially family, though, and I doubted they were supposed to be privy to much information. However, healthcare workers talk to each other, and clearly someone had said something. "I have heard," she leaned in, and I did the same. "Our Rose is doing well," she said quietly. "She took too much of something, and so they want to keep an eye on her. But she will be back."

Something about Genie's phrasing, her slightly stilted English, gave her words more weight. Rose would be back—it was almost like a declaration of war.

"I'm so glad." I meant it. "But, they're still worried?"

A shake of the head. "You said, they're keeping an eye on her?"

"Oh, that." The aide's contempt was clear. "They think our Rose maybe tried to kill herself. How silly is that?"

I shrugged. Aging, blind, with health and money problems. I'd have thought her aide would see the possibility, but Genie seemed oblivious. "You don't think she might have?"

Another shake. "Not our Rose."

"But something happened." I was weighing the factors. Genie was Haitian. Probably Catholic. Maybe the idea of suicide was inconceivable. Still, working here, with so many old and frail people, she must have known other residents who wanted to end it all. She might have been enlisted. The memory of other cases, of so-called angels of mercy, crossed my mind. "Are they saying it was an accident?"

"They are not saying anything." Her mouth was set, firm. "Not to me. Not yet." So she did expect to be blamed. Immediately, I was sorry for my own suspicions. She seemed to sense a change, because she looked down at Buster. "But she will not need her dog for now. She's a good animal. She works hard. If you can take her…"

"I can. But Genie?" A questioning look. "I'm leaving Randolph in Rose's apartment for a little while longer. I'll come by and clean the cage, tomorrow at the latest. Is that okay."

A nod, as Genie stared down the hall. She was probably used to people dumping duties on her, and I made a silent promise that I'd make it up to her. "I'm not going to stick you with bird care," I said. That got me a smile—and another glance down at Buster. "I guess we better get going."

"Goodbye, Buster." She called softly as we walked to the elevator. "See you soon."

It was interesting, I thought as we waited. Genie never petted Buster, never got down on her knees, as I would, to greet the dog. Then again, Buster was a service dog, and service dogs should not be pet: it distracts them from their job. Genie had spent enough time with Rose so that maybe this had become second nature. At least she'd praised Buster. Randolph, however, was clearly never going to be a favorite. Poor old guy. I could never let Wallis know, but I was beginning to sympathize with him.

Chapter Forty-one

As we took off from LiveWell, I opened the window a bit for Buster. I don't care what their job is, dogs love car rides. Still, the shepherd mix was so quiet during the ride that I felt her thoughts were elsewhere. Maybe it was just as well. I had a crazy half-thought-out plan in mind, and before we reached our destination, I was hoping to work it into a more manageable shape.

"Hey, Albert!" I let Buster lead me into the shelter as if she were working. I could see her nose quivering, the smell of all the other animals that had passed through here playing like a Technicolor movie through her head. She was too well trained to react, though, and with a steady, gliding pace led me right up to Albert's desk. "What's up?"

"Huh?" The bearded animal control officer slammed his desk drawer. Porn, I hoped, and not Frank was quickly closed inside. "Pru! You here for the raccoon?"

"Not right now, Al. As you can see," I nodded down at Buster, "I've got some other business to take care of first."

"What? Oh, yeah." He looked over his desk as if seeing the dog for the first time, and started back in fear. "What is that, a German shepherd?"

"She's a mix." I was scanning Albert's desk as I spoke, looking for Frank. I could use an ally with what I was planning. "She's a trained service dog," I said, trying to reassure him. A nervous Albert was even less attractive than usual.

"Oh, you brought her because of the raccoon?" Albert began nodding, as he settled back into his seat. For a moment, I was concerned. There was no way he could have guessed my plan, could he? Then I realized the nodding was another nervous tick, like the way he kept petting the down vest he wore over this month's flannel.

"Excuse me?" I'd seen a movement inside Albert's vest, something too big for fleas. *"Frank?"* I silently mouthed the words. *"Can you help me here?"* I could use a hand, even a tiny, clawed one.

"Like those cancer dogs?" Albert was still talking.

"Albert, what are you talking about?" It didn't pay to be too polite to the man.

"I was just wondering if, you know, the dog was trained to sniff out rabies. You know."

"Oh, we're working on it." I smiled. Out of the mouths of idiots come the best alibis. "Hey, did you bring Frank in today?"

"Why, yeah." He peeked inside his vest and then glanced nervously at Buster. "You think it'll be okay?"

"Buster is very well trained." I had my hand firmly on her halter to be sure. "Hey, Frank," I called to the small mustelid.

A damp nose inched out of the vest, followed by the rest of the masked face. I could sense Buster's interest, but true to her training, she held still. Frank, however, seemed doubtful. *"Wolf?"*

"Buster is a good dog." I was using my command voice, low and calm. I figured it would work on everyone there. Even Albert nodded, and slowly Frank emerged, climbing down to the cluttered desktop.

"Interesting." Frank's nose was as busy as Buster's, and I'd have given anything just to be able to observe the two animals interacting. I had other plans, however, and Frank could help me. As simply as I could, I visualized what I was going to do. It was straightforward; it should work.

"Okay, Frank?" I smiled at Albert as I said it, hoping he'd think I was talking about the dog. "We're good here?"

"We're good here." Frank and the dog were still staring at each other, but the ferret had inched forward so that their noses almost touched. *"We're good."*

"Good." I nodded to Albert and headed toward the back of the shelter. "I'm going to have to leave Buster here, temporarily, Albert." Let him think it was to sniff out disease. The shelter was nearly empty, and this would solve one big problem. It also gave me the perfect excuse.

"Be careful with her," Frank's thoughts caught me by surprise, as Albert buzzed me in. *"She is tryin'; she always tries. But she doesn't understand."*

I appreciated it, I really did. Frank's a good friend. I didn't need Buster to understand, however. I just needed her to obey commands, and that's what she did as she led me into the back. "In," I opened an empty cage, down at the far end of the room. "Go inside, girl." I shut the door.

"I will be back," I said, trying to make eye contact. With what I had in mind, I couldn't be sure I'd be able to keep my promise. I knew I would try.

Buster seemed content, even in the strange setting, and so I walked over to the one other occupied cage in the back room, and gave its resident a good hard look. The raccoon had seen better days, that was certain. A certain dullness in the coat showed that either he wasn't eating or grooming properly. It could also indicate disease. Without thinking, I flexed my right hand. The swelling had gone down, but when I moved my thumb, I could still feel the deep bite Rocky here had inflicted. What I couldn't feel was if there were any further damage. Any of the virus multiplying inside me, infiltrating my bloodstream. Making its stealthy way to my brain.

"Hiding, hiding. Burrow—good!" The interruption startled me, it was so strong and sudden. *"Dig away!"*

The raccoon was staring at me, his eyes bright. Bright with fever? I blinked, and the bear-like creature brought his hands together. For a moment, I was touched. Those little hands, so human-like, seemed to be praying. Begging me for a chance. But if I were to try this, I would not only be endangering my career—relocating raccoons and other wildlife is against the law in Massachusetts—I would also be putting an unknown amount of wildlife at risk. Yes, rabies was endemic in the raccoon population. However, I was planning on releasing my captive here in a different section of the woods than where he'd been caught. If he were infected, I could be spreading the disease further, or at least exposing an uncountable number of new animals to it. In addition, if this raccoon were sick, I would be condemning him to die alone, a horrible and painful death. Better he should be euthanized, cleanly and without pain.

Those hands came together again. No, I was thinking like a human—a stupid, sympathetic human. *"Away!"*

Then it hit me: this wasn't a supplicating gesture, the begging of a poor trapped creature. It was a digging motion. This raccoon was acting out what he wanted to do. What he'd tried to do, I suspected, in the still-damp concrete corner of his enclosure. As young as he was, this creature had already learned about fences and since he couldn't climb over it, he'd been trying to burrow beneath it. Concrete, even damp, wasn't as yielding as soil, but he'd tried—and now he was letting me know what he wanted to do.

I took a breath. I'd gotten myself in trouble once with this beast already, seeing him in too human terms. It might well be a mistake to assume he was trying to communicate with me now. A deadly mistake: lack of fear can be a symptom of rabies.

"Away?"

Or the dullness I had noticed in his coat could be the result of three days of bad food and no activity. Three days of desperation and despair. No, it was no use. What I was about to do might be crazy, but I didn't really have a choice.

"Try to trust me, okay?" I let my plan run through my head, as simply and as visually as I could, while I assembled what I needed. An old animal carrier, thrown in a corner. A blanket, probably from some rescue attempt. And, because I'm not a complete fool, that long-handled net. In the back, I could hear Buster whining softly. She had enough good dog sense to know that I was taking a risk. If she'd known all of it, she'd doubtless be barking to raise the alarm.

"Quiet." I said it as calmly as I could. Both Buster and the raccoon seemed to respond.

Within minutes, I was ready. I had the carrier set up by the opening to the raccoon's cage, and I'd piled the blanket on top. I'd already checked that the back door could be unlocked and that the tiny dog run was empty. The fence would be a problem. At six feet high, it wouldn't have been much of a challenge for the raccoon, but I had no wish to release the animal right here, in downtown Beauville. Back inside, I poked around, finally finding another, larger carrier that I hoped would support my weight. When I took it outside, I also took a harder look around. The shelter lot was empty, and the adjoining lot—belonging to the police department—seemed quiet as well, our small town force still tied up at Evergreen Hills. I could only hope it stayed that way. As much as I enjoyed Jim Creighton's company, his sudden appearance would put a crimp in my plans.

Back inside, I took a breath, rehearsed everything in my head one more time. And made my move.

"*Now, Frank!*" From the front, I heard Albert yell. "Ow!" Good, Frank had nipped him. It was risky, but Albert was fond enough of his pet that there likely wouldn't be any repercussions, and I needed the distraction. "Ow, stop it! Stop it!"

"*Good luck…*" The faint thought reached me, and I smiled as I unlatched the raccoon's enclosure. The sound of running water reached me. Albert had finally learned to wash his hands after a bite, and I only hoped he'd stay in the small bathroom, with the tap on, for a few minutes.

"Come on." I didn't want to use the net. Didn't want to panic the already distressed raccoon. And as I began to raise the cage door, he responded. With one glance at me, he scurried through the door and into the carrier. I dropped the net and shut the cage, letting the blanket conceal its masked occupant.

"Here's hoping." I prayed to nobody in particular, and hefting the carrier, threw my shoulder against the back door. Buster in her enclosure looked up, and I shook my head. She held still, and I was out, the door closing behind me. It was a matter of

seconds before I was on the larger carrier and lowering the raccoon's box over the fence. Back inside, I straightened my shirt
and brushed off some stray hairs from the old blanket. Well, that
would give the raccoon something to think about. Then, taking
a deep breath, I walked back into the main room of the shelter.

"Be quick!" Frank, standing upright on Albert's desk, caught
me with his sharp gaze. I nodded.

"Heading out, Albert!" I called over to the bathroom. "I'll
pick the dog up soon."

The sound of a toilet flushing obscured his response, and I
was out. Through the glass double doors, away from the shelter—and away from the front of the police headquarters next
door. There was still nobody in the parking lot, as I grabbed the
raccoon's carrier, still covered by the blanket, and slid it onto
my front seat.

"Sorry about that," I apologized softly as I shoved the cage
in securely.

"The woods! Into the woods!" I had a brief flash of an oak tree,
half rotten, a sweet, moist opening high up between its boughs.

"I'll do what I can, little fellow," I said, as I gunned the engine
to head out of town.

Chapter Forty-two

Finally, things were going right. With the sun out and highway in front of me, I was headed south. In five miles, I could pick up the Interstate and take that to some preservation land where nobody would be building condos, at least not during this raccoon's lifetime.

Any other day, I'd have taken the local roads all the way. It would have been a nicer drive, but there were too many tourists clogging up our byways. As it was, I'd have to wade through leaf peepers from here to the entrance. Well, once I was there, we'd be home free. The preservation land was twenty miles from Beauville, far enough to keep the raccoon out of trouble. Then, once I set this little fellow free, I'd go get my first rabies shot. I had a good feeling about this animal, but there wouldn't be any harm in being careful, and four shots was a small price to pay to continue being able to live, breathe, and drive on a day like this. After that, I thought, maybe I'd celebrate. Treat myself to a late lunch. Order two burgers, maybe, and bring one home for Wallis.

Burgers, or maybe a steak. My mouth was watering as I slide past another SUV and back into the lane. I was nearing the turnoff for Evergreen Hills and so I kept my eyes open for Jerry's truck, but all I saw were more SUVs, most packed with kids, like nature was the latest version of a Disney thrill ride.

I shouldn't complain. As I passed another slowpoke, I thought of the alternatives. At least they appreciated what we had. At least they'd be spending some of that city money here. My own mother had no patience for sightseeing. She was working too hard, once my father left. Though I did remember her, some evenings, sitting on our covered back porch and staring down the mountain. At the time, I'd thought she was just staring into space. Half the time, I took the opportunity to sneak out—often with her car keys. No, we didn't have much use for scenery when I was growing up. Family time, either, come to think of it.

I wasn't sightseeing today, either, I told myself as I sliced by another dawdler. And if I was hungry, I couldn't imagine what the raccoon was going through. He'd been scratching at the corner of his carrier when I first put him in, but I hadn't heard anything in a while, so I sneaked the blanket back. Two black eyes blinked up at me, and I nodded. Two miles to go till the interstate, up over one more rise, then a quick shot to that park.

"Oh, hell." I'd looked up and seen it. A gumball rotating in my rearview mirror. The removable kind, placed on an unmarked car that was right now signaling for me to pull over. Too much passing, too little concern for the moneyed visitors to our fair burg. Shit.

I pulled over, but kept the engine running. For all the day's beauty, it was cold. And even if I could deal, I didn't want the terrified animal beside me to suffer. I rolled down my window and smiled as the cop approached. The smile wasn't hard to manage. The cop was Jim Creighton.

"Hi, Jim." I looked up at him. "How fast was I going?"

"Pru, I thought it was you." I didn't respond. How many baby blue almost fully restored 1974 GTOs are on the road? In western Massachusetts? "Look, it wasn't your speeding."

That surprised me, and my face must have showed it.

"It was your driving. You can't keep weaving around other cars like that."

"Even when they're leaf peepers?" I smiled. Creighton often finds my smile fetching.

"Even then." Today he didn't. "Look, I know you're a good driver, but you're not alone on the road. You drive like that, you could make one of them panic. You could even make a mistake yourself."

I felt, rather than heard, a rustle in the carrier on the seat beside me. I needed to end this. "You're right, Jim. I was being careless."

"That's one word for it." He leaned on my car's roof and looked down the road. I breathed easier. But he didn't leave, not yet. "I also wanted to talk to you about this morning. What were you doing at Evergreen Hills, Pru?"

"I told you, Jim." I didn't want to bring up the raccoon. Not with the carrier beside me. "I was helping Albert, that's all."

"Yeah, well, we've got people asking questions. Like, was someone tipped off?"

That was interesting. "Why, what did you find?"

"Nothing, Pru." He was squinting into the afternoon sun. The lines around his eyes made him look sexy and intense. "Nothing, and I'm having problems finding out about other properties. The place is run by one of those blind trusts, and once the lawyers start getting involved, forget about it."

"Tell me about it." I thought about the letter. If there were repercussions for what I was about to do, I wouldn't be the only one taking the heat. "You wouldn't know who is really behind it all, would you?"

"Why?" He turned those eyes on me, and then past me to the carrier. "Hey, what is that, Pru? What do you have under that blanket?"

"You don't want to know, Jim." I braced. "Trust me."

"Pru, as an officer of the law—"

He didn't get a chance. My engine was warm and running, and I slipped her into gear. He jumped back—reflexes taking precedence over training—and I took off, rolling up my window as I drove.

"Please, Jim, don't do this." There'd been a lull in the traffic, and I took advantage of it to accelerate, keeping a half an eye on my rearview. "Damn." His car appeared behind me, gumdrop revolving—and getting bigger.

"Sorry, Creighton." I leaned back in my seat and we took off. The point of a car like this is its power, and I felt like I was riding a thoroughbred, the way she responded. I slammed into third, then fourth, and we ate up the road.

Only cop cars tend to be pretty good as well. Jim's might look like some bland K model, but whatever it had under the hood was in top shape—and less than forty years old. Even as I let my foot down, I saw Creighton gaining on me. I could see his face in flashes, between reflections of sky and trees. I didn't take the time to study it. I could imagine it well enough.

"Hell." The carrier beside me rustled, the raccoon responding to the acceleration if not the roar of the engine. And then I saw it: as I crested the ridge, a series of minivans, four of them, all trudging down the hill in front of me. Looked like a convoy, and none of them going more than thirty miles an hour. In the opposite lane, a logging truck, heading south with lumber. It was laboring up its side of the hill, the driver distracted, shifting to make the climb.

"Hang on." It wasn't a rational decision. I didn't decide. I simply pressed, and my car responded, bounding ahead. With inches to spare, I swung in front of that lumber truck and back into my lane ahead of the tailing van, slipping into just enough space so as not to scratch anyone. The lumber truck was in my rearview now, and I leapfrogged again. Another minivan gone. Heading downhill now, I could feel them all gaining speed. This was what Creighton had meant—I could drive this way, fast, reckless. These city folk? It wasn't safe for them. I checked my mirror. Now that the logger was safely gone, Creighton was there again, behind the trailing tourist. Time to make my move.

I looked ahead and saw them: another knot of cars coming my way. Traffic or families traveling together, it didn't matter. Four cars, no five, all charging up the ridge as we came down. There were two more minivans in front of me, then open road. The approaching convoy was an eighth of a mile away. Less. Creighton was signaling to pass.

So I just did it. Gunning the gas, I slipped into the middle of the two-lane road. One van passed, a brief glimpse of a white face, open-mouthed. The cars were coming on. I pressed harder. Prayed. Slipped in front of the remaining van in time to feel the air from the lead car. Another shocked face, wide-eyed with panic, but the road was mine. I laughed out loud as the highway disappeared before me. That made me breathe again, and I realized I hadn't been. Sure, I'd have Creighton to deal with at some point. He'd have every right to be furious. For now, I had an open road. I'd reached the turnoff for the interstate with nobody in sight.

"Hang on a little longer, Rocky," I said to the bundle beside me. "You're going home."

Chapter Forty-three

The Beauville Area State Reservation Land is not much of a park. No restrooms, no picnic area, and not much of a lot, it spreads from the interstate exit to the county line. As I turned down a service road, I remembered when I'd first discovered it. A little too far out of town for drinking, my gang rarely came out here. I'd found it on my own, one evening, when my mother had come home in a rage. I'd bought the Pacer by then, not much of a car but it was mine, and I took off, just looking for peace. I'd turned down this very road, not sure what lay at the other end. Just ahead, I'd found a slight widening of the dirt road—a turnaround for the staties who patrolled the area. That's where I was heading now.

I took a moment for myself, once I'd parked. The air was different here, moist and full. It was funny, I thought, how quickly I'd become a country girl, losing my urbanite's tolerance for the smoke and the noise. Well, I'd lost my tolerance to a lot of city things. Back when I'd first developed my so-called gift, I couldn't take the close quarters: rats, pigeons, the inane inbred pets of all my neighbors. It had been too much for me. Out here was hardly quiet, but the din was softer, falling into patterns that had formed themselves millennia before we interposed.

"I'm here! I'm here! I'm here!" A wren, unseen, called.

"Hide it! There!" A busy squirrel secreted another acorn away.

I stood still for a moment, taking it all in. Then I opened the passenger-side door and took out the carrier. Inside, the raccoon scrambled around, aroused by the motion and, probably, the wealth of scent. When I pulled the blanket off, he blinked around. Late afternoon would still be early for him, but here, under the shade of trees, the muted light wasn't too harsh.

I waited a minute. I wanted to let the little fellow process, maybe figure out from the smells and sounds around him where to go or what to do next. It was, I confess, a self-congratulatory moment. A validation. Maybe I hadn't gotten to the bottom of Polly Larkin's death. Maybe I'd never understand what Randolph the parrot was squawking about. But I could do this, at least. I felt good.

When I bent down to the carrier, I wasn't expecting the look I got in return. I'd thought the raccoon would be staring into the trees, eager to run out. Instead, I faced down two button-black eyes that seemed to burn with intent.

"What?" I asked. It was an automatic response. This animal had never really spoken to me before.

"*Watch out.*" The message came loud and clear. "*Don't trust.*"

"Well, you can this time, little fellow." I sighed, remembering my past foolishness, and stepped back. I'd rigged a shoelace on the carrier top and, now that I'd unlatched it, I managed to pull it open from several feet away. Just because I was due for a cycle of rabies shots didn't mean I wanted to get bit a second time.

"*What?*" A flood of some emotion that could only be described as curiosity washed over me as the raccoon ventured out, sniffing the air furiously. I watched, a little intrigued myself. I'd have thought the animal would bolt, desperate to escape after so many days of confinement. He was being careful, though, checking out his surroundings before he leaped.

"*Don't trust…careful.*" Well, that made sense. New place, new rules. New rivals, probably, though a young male, out on his own for the first time, would have to battle for his turf anywhere.

"*Be alert!*" New alpha predators, as well, and for a moment I doubted myself. Was it really fair to remove this animal from everything he had ever known? There were reasons for the rules about transporting wildlife. Even beyond the possibility that I was spreading a fatal disease, I might be condemning this raccoon to a short, miserable life. There were many threats to a small animal; humans were only one variety.

"*No!*" The voice in my head was so loud, I turned. The raccoon was out of the crate and facing me, whiskers twitching. He must be reacting to my thoughts, I realized. To the memory of Albert and his trap. Maybe he'd even picked up the idea of poison from me.

"It's okay now." I spoke softly, doing my best to think calming thoughts as I did so. "You'll be okay. Just find your way."

"*Don't trust. Be careful.*" I had the damnedest impression that the raccoon was talking to me, shaking his head ever so slightly. "*Stay alive!*" And with that he turned and lumbered off.

I watched him go, his woodland coloring fading swiftly into the fallen leaves and shadows. Even after I lost track of the slight movement, I stared after him as the dusk deepened. It must be because of Wallis, I told myself when, finally, I bent to retrieve the carrier. At some level, I expected every animal to want to converse. Even Growler showed me that wasn't true often enough. He'd talk, but I was a poor substitute for the smells and signs of his own kind.

Swinging the empty carrier into the car, I was reminded again of the price of folly. Last time I'd tried to communicate with that raccoon, he'd bit me. Now, walking around to the driver's side, I flexed my bandaged hand. Maybe it was just as well. I'd relearned a lesson I shouldn't have forgotten. And if I could get over to Berkshire General, I wouldn't pay too steep a fee for my foolishness.

Backing out of the turnaround, I paused for one last look at the darkening woods. This place had been my refuge, back in the day, and then it hit me. I'd brought that poor lost raccoon here for the same reason. Peace. A little privacy. A chance to be oneself.

I could imagine what Wallis would make of that and heard the conclusion as clearly as my own thoughts. Didn't matter how much I learned, she'd say. At heart, I was as sentimental as any human. At least I wasn't a prey animal, I answered back as I pulled onto the road. That kind of weakness could get you killed.

Chapter Forty-four

Sunday morning, I woke with a start. The excitement of the day before had kept me going, and I'd crashed like a dead thing, barely making it home from the preservation land. I needed to start those shots today, however. It had been three days: enough was enough. But my belly was growling louder than my engine, and so halfway to Berkshire General, I pulled off at the Blue Diner, a greasy spoon that had been around since before I left.

"Eggs over easy, home fries." I gave my order as I was sliding into my seat. "Coffee, black." Once that was done, I checked my phone. Three calls—all from Creighton. Well, that wasn't a surprise. I could only hope there wasn't also a warrant out for my arrest.

"Pru." He sounded pissed. "That was not cool. Call me."

The waitress brought my coffee, and I took a long hit before I clicked through to the next one. "Damn it all, Pru. Where are you?" I nodded. She topped me off.

"Pru, don't think that just because we—" That was it. I had the distinct feeling that whatever he'd been about to say might not happen again soon. Might not happen at all.

I should have called him then. I knew it. All I really needed to do was come up with a story that wouldn't cost Albert his job—or land me in jail. But while I was thinking one up, my breakfast came.

By the time I had finished the last fry, the urge to confess had gone. Besides, I had more pressing concerns. Let me just get my first rabies shot and I'd call Creighton back. Once the series was started, he could throw me in jail, even, as long as he agreed to look in on Wallis.

My tabby was on my mind as I drove over to Berkshire General. I knew she'd think I was crazy for what I had done. An animal had lacked enough common sense to avoid a trap, and here I was, putting myself out on a limb for him. An animal who had bit me, no less. She might accuse me of being soft. Correction, she *would* accuse me. But I had to keep in mind that Wallis saw things in black and white. Some animals were predators, others prey. Who was what might change depending on the circumstance, but within any particular scenario, the roles were clear.

She never had to deal with some of the gems I met. Jane Larkin, for example. My newest client seemed at first glance like prey—easy pickings for anyone who wanted to take her down. But not only had she resisted her brother Marc, she'd pretty much pawned her mother's parrot off on me. Maybe Wallis would call that a case of protective coloration, I wasn't sure. Or what about Tracy Horlick? That woman was a predator, for sure. She needed me, however. Needed her daily fix of gossip, if not dog walking. I amended my classification: some animals were predators. Some were prey. Others were scavengers. I thought of old lady Horlick as a vulture, the saggy skin on her neck would fit.

Even Rose Danziger might be more complicated than she first appeared. As I got closer to the hospital, I found myself mulling over what I knew of the blind old lady. She was prickly, that was for sure, and I liked that about her. Was that the only reason Marc Larkin talked dirt about her? Actually, as I thought about that one, I figured it probably was.

I'd go visit, I decided as I pulled into Berkshire General. Get my first shot and then go look for her. Hell, the hospital already had me listed as her niece. I might as well take advantage of that.

"Name and nature of your emergency?" The attendant behind the glass didn't even look up.

"Pru Marlowe, animal bite." I figured I'd save the rabies part for when I saw an actual doctor.

"Have a seat. The triage nurse will see you soon." Funny, he didn't even check to see if maybe I was bleeding out. Then again, the fact that I'd managed to make it up to the window by myself might have been the first stage of triage. Looking around the half-empty room, I figured the wait couldn't be that long. Two rough-looking types glared at each other in a corner, mud and what could be dried blood on their denim and work boots. I figured they were the survivors of a Saturday night bar fight, though neither looked too cut up. A few seats away, a mother was rocking a toddler. The kid was silent, which I appreciated until I started to wonder what that meant. The remaining waiters looked like a couple of tourists, the color-coordinated L.L. Bean outfits were the giveaway, who seemed to be in the midst of their own little drama. He was pacing; she was hunched over in her seat. Had he punched her, or had a bout of stomach flu disrupted his vacation plans? I really hoped I wouldn't be here long enough to find out.

"Irma Wallace?" A stout woman with hair the color of steel wool stood in a doorway. "Come with me please."

Good, the triage nurse. I counted the cases. I'd be out of here in no time.

"It's Wallitz," the mother said. "Irma and Troy Wallitz." I saw a teary face look up from her shoulder as she walked past. At least the kid was conscious.

In the quiet that followed, I considered reading a magazine. I don't often get to see *Nursing Today*, after all. Or *BP: Happy, Whole, and Bipolar*. Instead, I pulled out my phone. Now that the raccoon and I were both, presumably, on the verge of being safe, there was no reason not to tell Creighton everything. He already knew about some of my idiosyncrasies. Besides, I'm bad at lying. I always forget what my story was.

I flipped my phone open.

"No cell phone use in the waiting area." I glanced around. The attendant, or whatever he was, hadn't even looked up. I turned toward the wall.

"If you're going to use your phone, you have to leave the waiting area." There was a peevishness in his tone that made me look back. He still hadn't raised his head, so I walked over, phone in hand.

"Can you tell me how long it'll be?"

"Excuse me?" He had a Sudoku game book open before him. Obviously, it was fascinating.

"My wait." I held the phone up like an explanation, just in case he did have eyes on the top of his head. "I'm wondering if it makes sense to cancel an appointment."

"Average wait time is determined by a variety of factors, including time of day. Priority is given to urgent care patients and those with life-threatening injuries."

I was about to argue, to ask what exactly the difference between those two classifications were, when the ambulance pulled up. Lights swirling, the wail of its alarm was enough to make even the window boy look. Not that the EMTs needed him. As we watched, the ambulance backed up out of sight, and seconds later, we could hear it. Technicians, calling to each other. Somewhere behind the gatekeeper, a door had opened and the pop and rattle of a gurney, maybe two, rolling down a hall. Behind the attendant, I caught a flash of blue as a woman in scrubs ran by.

"It might be a while," the attendant said to me, nodding toward my phone.

"Got it," I turned to go. "Don't take me off your list though." I said as he went back to his puzzle. "I'm just going to make one phone call. One call."

He nodded, or maybe that was just a reaction to his puzzle, and I stepped outside. From here, I could see the ambulance, a big white van with a red stripe down the side. The siren had been turned off and the doors closed, but the engine was still ticking as it cooled. Someone had driven fast. An emergency call, a real one.

To hell with Creighton, I thought. I was here, and clearly I was going to be here a while. I went in search of Rose Danziger.

Chapter Forty-five

"I'm sorry, but we don't have a Rose Danziger on our patient list." The blue-haired matron at Patient Information adjusted her half glasses and scanned the computer screen.

"That's impossible. She was brought here yesterday—early in the morning." I tried to peer over her shoulder and was rewarded by a stern look.

"Well, maybe she hasn't been registered yet. One moment please." The matron pulled a clipboard toward her and ran her finger down a page. "No, I'm sorry."

I opened my mouth to argue—blue hair doesn't scare me— when I heard a voice behind me.

"Pru Marlowe." It was Creighton, in the flesh. With his hands on his hips and a scowl on his face, my sometime beau looked hot. Angry, but hot. "I assume your phone's broken?"

"I was just going to call you." I held up the offending device as evidence. Somehow, I'd never put it away. "You could've come by, you know."

"I—No." He shook his head. I could tell he was weighing his words. "Last night turned crazy, Pru. There have been some developments. And now we've had a fire, of sorts, over at Evergreen Hills."

"Of sorts?" That last message. He hadn't hung up; he'd had a call. "What happened?"

He shook his head. It looked like it was bothering him. "I let most of the team go for the night. We had a guard set up but…. People got hurt. Two of the weekenders were there."

The ambulance. "They okay?"

"Smoke." He shrugged, and as if in response, I heard a discreet, and clearly fake, cough.

"I've found it." I'd forgotten about the patient services matron. I turned back to her as she blinked up to me. "R. Danziger, with a 'D.'" She looked at me as if it were my fault. "She's was released this morning to the LiveWell rehab unit. That's over by—"

"Thanks, I know where it is." I looked over at Creighton. Shrugged. "I was about to call you. I multitask."

He waved off my explanation. "I'm going with you."

"Excuse me?" I'd already figured that I wasn't going to see the ER doctor anytime soon. But, still…

"By coincidence, I'm going to LiveWell, too."

There was a little too much emphasis on the beginning of that sentence. An emphasis that changed my priorities. "Am I under arrest, Jim?"

He snorted, the first sign of humor I'd seen in a while. "You should be. God knows, Pru, if you were anyone else. Hell, if *I* were anyone else."

"I pride myself on being a bad influence." I liked the humor. I was also relieved.

"Don't get too cocky, Pru, I have to think about it. As it happens, I do have to follow up with something over at LiveWell. Shall I drive?"

"Jim, I can't leave my car here." He knew my GTO. He knew it was my baby. "Besides, I'd be stranded. You'd have to drive me back. Or ferry me around."

He nodded, but he wasn't happy. "Okay, but you follow behind me. You don't drop back. You don't peel off. Pull any funny stuff, and I swear, Pru…"

"Gotcha." We'd already given the information lady enough of an earful to keep her in gossip for days. With a brief pang of regret—maybe I'd only have had another hour to wait—I followed Creighton out the ambulance entrance and let him drive me to my car.

This hadn't been my original plan, but I needed to go back to LiveWell at some point, anyway. I had to do something with Randolph. I thought about the options as Creighton drove out of town, doing a steady forty, even as we pulled onto the highway. It was annoying, driving this slow, but it had its charms. I loved watching the tourists brake as they recognized the unmarked car for what it was.

Randolph...Depending on how long Rose was going to be in rehab, I probably needed to find another place for him. Polly's unit was out of the question. Even if Jane didn't have avicidal leanings, the dust and commotion of packing weren't good for him. I could take the parrot back to my place, I figured. That is, if we ever got to LiveWell. Well, I had wanted to check in on Rose. Whatever else was going on, I liked the tough old bird.

Buster! I nearly slammed on the brakes. I had meant to collect the service dog as soon as I'd got my first shot. I couldn't leave her alone in the empty shelter. Besides, Rose would want to see her dog.

Okay, "see" wasn't the right word, but I still thought a visit from the loyal mixed-breed might do her good. If only I could get out of this slow-motion parade. I reached for my phone and then dropped it. What was I thinking? Creighton wouldn't answer, not even while driving like that blue-haired matron we'd left twenty minutes before.

"Creighton!" I called his name and waved, in the hope that he might be looking in his rearview. I flashed my lights, and then honked—ever so briefly—trying to catch his eye. Either he was ignoring me, or he had a lot else on his mind, because we were nearing the turnoff for Beauville before I made my last attempt.

I'd had my lights on for a good quarter mile, my blinker, too. Finally, I simply pulled over to the side of the road. Let him think I had engine trouble, I didn't care. I needed to stop.

He must have been aware of me at some level, because after about thirty seconds on the shoulder of the road, I saw dust and taillights. He was backing down the shoulder. He had his sunglasses on as he walked over to my car. They didn't make him look friendly, and I had to fight the urge to reach for my license and registration.

"I said, no bullshit, Pru."

"Rose's dog." I wanted to be sweet and to the point. "I left Rose's seeing-eye dog at the shelter overnight. She hasn't been fed or walked, and I want to bring her back to Rose."

A sigh, while he looked down the road. Already the tourists were speeding up. "You could have gone and gotten it after."

"I know. But then I'd have to make two trips, and we're right near the turnoff." I tried to make out his eyes behind those dark lenses. "Please, Jim?"

He nodded. He wasn't going to say yes. "Remember, I know where you live."

I couldn't help but smile at that. "I was hoping you'd recall that, one of these days."

He slapped the roof of my car and walked off. I waited till he was a good half mile down the road before I tore off. It's not good for my engine to drive that slow.

Chapter Forty-six

"There you are." Much to my surprise, the shelter had been unlocked and Albert was sitting at his desk when I walked in. "I was beginning to think I'd have to take that dog for a walk."

"Not to worry, Al." I eyeballed his desk, looking for Frank. "I said I'd be back. I thought I'd look in anyway," I dangled my own key, "seeing as it's Sunday."

Albert blushed. Not a pretty sight. "I had some paperwork to catch up on," he said. The half-finished fishing lure in front of him told a different story, but I smiled and nodded as he hit the release for the door. As I reached for it, I saw him slip a peanut into his open desk drawer. Good, I hated to think the little ferret had gotten in trouble doing me a solid.

Buster was lying on the floor when I approached, and I kicked myself for not having thought to give her a blanket. She rose silently as I came close, though, without any rancor. "*Walk?*"

I nodded and unlatched the door. She headed for the side exit, toward the dog run, and I let her lead me there. She needed to go, but as I watched her sniff at the ground where I'd set the raccoon's carrier, I thought something else might be at work, too.

"*Out!*" It was a quiet bark, much softer than the frenzied noise she had made back at Rose's.

"You want to go? We should go through the building." I started to turn, but Buster held firm.

"*Out!*" Another bark, almost questioning.

"Yes, the raccoon went out this way." I wasn't entirely sure what I was responding to. The question in my head was so vague. "The raccoon went back to the woods. Is that what you wanted to know?"

Buster didn't bark again, and after a moment's silence, she turned with me and led the way back into the shelter. She was, however, wagging her tail.

"So, we're off, Albert." I waited. Could it really be that he hadn't noticed that the raccoon was gone?

"Okay." He was closing his tackle box, making ready to follow me out. "Oh, hey, Pru?"

"Yeah?" I'd almost made it to the door.

"That raccoon—You'll help me with it?" So he hadn't gone into the back.

"Yeah, Al. First thing tomorrow."

"Great," he picked a fishing rod off the floor. With any luck, in a day or two, he'd forget that the shelter had ever housed a raccoon. "Thanks." As he stood, I saw a quivering nose poke out of the desk drawer. Frank.

"Hey, Frank." I needed to get moving, but it seemed rude not to acknowledge the alpha male in the room. Albert looked down at the ferret, who had surfaced holding a peanut.

"Mmm...salty!" Frank bit into the nut. I turned to leave. *"Be careful out there."* Frank's voice reached me, along with an intense sensation of sweet and salt. *"He was right, you know."* Frank was eating, but his attention was focused on me. *"About trusting."* Another nibble, the flavor overwhelming. *"Trust leads to traps."*

I didn't know what Frank was referring to exactly, though it did strike me as odd that I was voluntarily doing what a police officer had wanted me to do. I've never been one for committed relationships. They last as long as they last. Maybe it was being back here. In a small town like Beauville, the pickings were slim. Besides, I still enjoyed Creighton, or would if he'd stop acting like a cop. Then again, maybe he'd taken the ferret's advice. I hadn't seen him in a few nights, so maybe he'd moved on like some woodland creature: silent and smooth.

Buster sat on the passenger seat beside me, appraising me with her dark doggy eyes. "Do you think I'm a fool, Buster?" Nothing. "Come on, just between us girls."

She turned and looked ahead. I'd rolled the window down, but unlike every dog I've ever known, she hadn't pushed her nose through it. Instead, she simply stared at the road. Buster didn't say much, but I was beginning to sense that there was more going on than rigorous training. She knew she was going to see Rose, and she couldn't wait.

Buster's impatience finally took on a sound as I pulled into the LiveWell parking lot. A soft whine, almost as if she were trying to calm herself, started as soon as I'd parked and gained in intensity as I let her lead me to the big double doors.

"Hi, Nancy." Buster wanted to keep moving, to go to the elevators. I could sense the urgency. She felt me stop, though, and waited. Training dies hard. "How do I get to the rehab unit?" I nodded down to the dog. "I thought a visitor might do Rose some good."

"We call it LiveWell Transitions," said the receptionist. Well, it was her job. "And you can go down the hallway to administration. Follow the hall past the offices, all the way to the fire door. Once you're through there, you're in the hospital wing." She caught herself. "The Transitions wing."

I smiled. "Got it."

"Or you could just walk around the outside of the building." She shrugged. "It's shorter, and it's a nice day."

"Indeed it is." I could sense Buster's reluctance, but she turned with me toward the door.

"Tell Rose 'hi' from me, will you?" Nancy said, a little softly, stopping me as I began to walk away. "Tell her I hope she feels better soon. I know it must be hard, but, well. Just tell her we're rooting for her."

I nodded. Conventional wisdom must have decided about the nature of Rose's "accident," and maybe there was some sense to it. The brightly lit lobby, the pastel logos aside, this was still an old-age home. I could walk in and out of this place under my own power. Maybe Rose had chosen to do the same.

Chapter Forty-seven

No matter what euphemism they used for LiveWell House proper, this part of the complex was clearly for the sick or the frail old. There was no sign of Creighton, here, but he knew this was where I'd be. And so I'd checked in at the nurse's station and was directed down a hall where monitors blinked and IV frames stood waiting, as if on break, outside the doors.

"Miss? Oh, Miss!" I heard a voice call after me. Buster, of course. I should have donned my own dark glasses, but now I turned with a big, fake smile.

"Yes?"

"The dog." The nurse who'd signed me in was standing. Pointing. Buster ignored her.

"She's a service dog. I need her." I tightened my grip on Buster's handle, as if I'd fall into a seizure without her. Or start crying. Whatever, it worked. She sat back down.

And Buster barked. *"Help! Help!"* Loud, ringing barks.

"Quiet." I stepped in front of the dog, where she could see me, and signaled, palm down, for her to stop.

"Oh, this won't do, Miss." The nurse was standing again. I looked behind me. A closed door.

"We'll be quick." Rose's room was right next door, and so I hustled Buster over to it before the nurse could object further. "Thank you!"

"What was that about?" I turned toward the dog. We were in some kind of anteroom, curtains separating us from the beds.

Buster lifted her big, sad eyes to mine and moaned softly. An answering moan from the other side of the curtain.

"Rose?" Buster strained forward, tail wagging.

"Who's there?" A voice so weak, I could barely hear it. Buster recognized it, though, and I pulled back the curtain to see Rose. Without her glasses, she looked shrunken and pale.

"It's me, Pru Marlowe. And I brought Buster." As if on cue, the dog put her big front paws up on the side of the bed and shoved her face toward Rose, licking the pale cheeks. I reached for her harness, to pull her back. But Rose was laughing.

"That's my good girl! I thought I'd heard you out there!" Whether it was the company or the miracle of doggy saliva, Rose's color seemed to come back, and I pulled up a chair to enjoy the visit.

"She barked as soon as she could sense you," I said. It wasn't strictly speaking true: the dog had seemed to bark at the closed room next door, but I wasn't under oath.

"So I heard!" Rose was smiling, but she hadn't moved much otherwise, her head lay still on the pillow. "And Pru, how nice of you to bring her."

"We were worried." I felt I spoke for both of us. And then, because I couldn't help it. "What happened?"

A slight shake of the head and a frown that furrowed her brow even further. "They say I took a dose, a double dose. I don't know."

"You don't remember?" I didn't know what she'd taken, or what lingering effects it might have. Buster, meanwhile, had sunk to the floor. I could feel her tail thumping out its happiness at the reunion.

Another shake, almost imperceptible. "I felt so out of it. It's a time-release, they say. I'm supposed to wait for it to work. I know that."

This didn't sound like a suicide attempt to me. "Were you in a great deal of pain?"

"No." That frown again. "At least, I don't think so. That's what I don't understand. I don't think I asked for all those pills—"

"And who have we here?" It was Wachtell, pulling back the curtain with a grin. Close behind him was that nurse. "Ms. Marlowe. How nice of you to visit."

He reached across the bed, where a blood-pressure cuff waited. That movement, though, or maybe the shadow, sparked something. Suddenly Buster was on her feet, barking. "*Help! Help! Help!*" It was her alarm bark. "*Help!*"

The nurse started and looked up at Wachtell, as if expecting him to do something.

It was up to me. "Buster, silent!" With my left hand, I gestured for quiet, with my right, I pushed her hindquarters to make her sit. She did, whining softly, and the nurse proceeded to take Rose's blood pressure.

"Ow." Rose complained as the cuff tightened. Beside me, Buster strained to respond.

"*He was right, you know. He was right.*" The external barking may have died down, but suddenly and for the first time, Buster was besieging me with thoughts.

"*It's okay.*" I reached down, hoping both to keep the large dog in her place and to convey some sense that this was normal. Despite her soft protestation, Rose wasn't really being hurt.

"Excuse me?" Wachtell had said something, and I'd missed it. Was the doctor "he"? Was it Creighton?

"I said, you'll have to take that animal out of here." Wachtell had his stern doctor face on. Clearly, I was annoying him.

"Buster is a service dog." I didn't see why I had to point out the obvious. "She's Rose's dog."

"I understand." Wachtell was writing on a chart as the nurse unwrapped the cuff. "But Rose doesn't need it right now, and clearly the animal is reacting badly to the situation. We have other patients here."

"But—"

"You've brought it here for a visit, and that was very thoughtful of you." He replaced the chart and nodded to the nurse. "We will let you know when Rose is ready to make use of her service animal again. Now, if you'll please…" He motioned toward the door, and I stepped toward it. Buster was reluctant to leave. I could feel her straining back toward Rose's bed, but there wasn't much else I could do. And then Wachtell drew the curtain behind him, separating us from Rose. I could feel his eyes on us as we walked back down the hall.

Chapter Forty-eight

"I know, Buster, I don't like him either." We were taking the outside route back. We both needed some fresh air after that exchange. "But she's going to be okay."

Even as I said it, I was wondering. Rose had faded a lot since I'd first met her, less than a week before. That day, she'd been bright: funny and so sharp I wasn't sure what she was doing in a place like LiveWell. Since then, every time I'd seen her, she'd been tired, half asleep or more, and increasingly out of it. Today, she'd seemed so confused she hadn't been able to tell me what had happened. Age was a bitch, there was no doubt about that. But I couldn't discount the role of the drugs. Maybe she did need them more than she admitted. Maybe she'd hadn't wanted to talk about her pain. Still, I wondered. I knew from my mother that at some point, balance isn't possible—that one begins to sacrifice awareness, even personality, in the quest to dull the sharp edges. But sometimes people—practitioners—are careless. There were so many links in the human chain: the pharmacist, the aides. Maybe Wachtell did overprescribe. Maybe Genie had been less than careful. Maybe—Buster began to whine again, even as I formed the thought—Rose had had enough.

"You don't think that, do you, girl?" I reached down to stroke that dark head. We both needed the comfort. As I did, I got a flash of the raccoon. Of course, I was using my right hand. "Yeah, you're right, Buster. I'll go back this afternoon, once everything is straightened out, and start the shots."

For now, however, I had animals to deal with. There was still no sign of Creighton as I came back through the LiveWell lobby, and Nancy had stepped away. A little placard, with that knockoff logo, was propped up. "LiveWell! We'll be right with you," it said. "Please take a seat."

I ignored it, letting Buster lead me to the elevator instead. As we waited, I tried to figure out what to do. I didn't think I could leave Buster here again, and I didn't want to bring her back to the shelter. For starters, Albert might not have left yet, and there was only so long I could keep him in the dark about the raccoon. Besides, that sterile back room was no place for an animal.

I think I had a half a thought about asking Jane. After all, I'd cared for her parrot. But as we walked down the hall, I could hear the yelling.

"You *lost* it?" Jane, as angry as I'd ever heard her. "All of it? I—I can't believe you."

"Come on, Sis. It wasn't like that." Marc must have finally been forced to reveal the truth. I wondered if my bill would be paid. "It's just temporary. Just wait." I wasn't going to hold my breath.

"Forget that idea." I also wasn't going to interrupt. As if of one mind, Buster and I both ducked into Rose's unit. I closed the door behind us before I even turned on the light.

"Hello? Hello?" The voice sounded so much like Rose that I caught my breath. "Pretty bird?"

Randolph! I turned on the light to see the parrot hopping around his cage. Suddenly he stopped, tilting his head to stare at me. That one eye seemed to take me in. To see me, and once again, I felt that there was a consciousness behind it—if only I could reach it.

"You!," the parrot squawked, and I waited. That "hello" and that "pretty bird" had been encouraging.

"Hello?" I tried.

"You!" Another wordless sound, and that was it. I waited, once again, to feel something—anything—and got nothing.

At least the verbal abuse seemed to have abated. That was the progress I was being paid for.

"Come on, Randolph." I reached for the cage cover. Progress or no, I didn't need the bird sounding off as we marched through LiveWell. "Let's go."

Either the fight across the hall had been resolved, or both the combatants were exhausted. The hallway was quiet as we made our way, me on tiptoe, toward the elevator. Dealing with Wallis, I'd decided, would be easier than getting more involved with the Larkins, and I counted myself lucky to be moving out of their reach.

"No, no. No!" I'd counted too soon. Jane's voice was shrill. Marc's response—I could hear his baritone, low and inaudible—did not seem to be having any effect. "The insurance company always investigates."

"Sqwah!" As if in response, Randolph came awake. I could feel him moving about in his cage, and I hurried toward the elevator before he could alert Jane and Marc to our presence. "Hand's off! Stop that! That's mine, you bastard!"

Thankfully, the elevator opened seconds later, and I collapsed in, almost pulling Buster behind me. Then I started laughing, and the laughter came so hard I couldn't control it, collapsing against the back of the elevator, which was blessedly empty. Randolph's voice had been so close to Jane's, his sentiments so seemingly similar. As the fit of hysteria passed, I wiped my eyes to see Buster looking up at me, those dark eyes sad and quizzical.

"Sorry, Buster." I smiled down at the dog. "You're right. There's nothing funny about any of this." In retrospect, it seemed clear. The two voices sounded so similar because Randolph had copied Jane's mother. And the content?

"Hey, Nancy." The receptionist was back at her post, and she turned as I came forward with the two animals. "I was wondering, you keep track of all the visitors, right?" I nodded toward the big ledger on her desk.

"I try to." She saw me looking and pulled the ledger closer. "All the aides know to, when they're covering."

"I was wondering. The night that Polly Larkin died. Her son wasn't visiting then, was he?" It was a horrible thought, but one I couldn't shrink from.

The receptionist was shaking her head. "No, no way. I didn't even meet him until after she'd died. His sister was the one who kept coming around."

"Was she there that night?" This time, Nancy flipped back a few pages.

"That was the second, right? No." She ran her finger down the page. I could see several entries. "She'd been here earlier in the day. In the morning. It was a Thursday. She went to the support group on Thursday evenings."

"Every Thursday?"

Nancy nodded. "It's over at the church," she said. "They have cake."

Well, at least she got out, I thought but didn't say. We all have our vices. Inside his cage, Randolph muttered. "You!" Nancy looked up. "You!" It was time to get these animals home.

"The parrot." I said, unnecessarily, and headed for the door. "What are you doing?" It was Rose's voice, so close that Buster went on alert, staring at the cage—and then at me.

I had a bad feeling. "Nancy, was Marc Larkin here yesterday?"

She laughed. "He's a businessman. He's not here *that* often."

I nodded and wondered, not for the first time, what exactly his business was.

Chapter Forty-nine

I hadn't seen Creighton—and I didn't see his car in the lot as I loaded Randolph's cage into my vestigial backseat and motioned for Buster to jump in the front. That was fine. He knew where I lived, as he'd put it. If he needed to catch up with me, or wanted to, he could.

Whether I wanted him to was another question, one I found myself mulling over as we drove. There was a lot to like. Not just what Wallis would call the basics, referring to her own legendary and now far distant past. No, I thought as I pulled onto the highway, there was something more than mere physical attraction between us. Creighton came as close as anyone in knowing about my particular skill. Usually, he knew enough not to ask, too, which considering how crazy any normal person would peg me as was a blessing.

He was a cop, however. True blue. I wasn't sure what he'd wanted to talk to me about at the hospital, but I knew it had to do with Evergreen Hills. I'd told him the truth about why I'd been there, more or less. And now that the raccoon was, I hoped, cleanly away, I could even go into some detail—tell him about sheltering the animal, wanting to save its life. He'd known there was something else going on than a simple animal rescue. And without the real story, his mind had gone first to Mack and then moved on to my earlier connection with Jerry Gaffney and his unsavory clan. Maybe he even knew about Marc Larkin, and his shady attempts to keep the ill-fated condo development afloat.

Maybe he had his own extranormal senses. Cop sense, which tells you when somebody is holding out even the tiniest bit of the truth.

Well, I could tell him a thing or two, I thought as I drove. The clouds were rolling in again, and the roads were clearing. All the SUVs were being loaded up at the quaint inns; the children being sedated for the drive home. I wondered if Jane and Marc were still fighting, and how that particular dispute would end. It had sounded like Marc had been promising to repay what he'd borrowed—stole, would have been my word—from Polly Larkin's accounts. I wondered how. That fire at Evergreen Hills? Was that the insurance Jane had been asking about, or was there something more?

When I saw it, I thought it was a hallucination. Too much thinking while driving, or maybe a trick of the light in the trees. But I took my foot off the gas and as my baby slowed, I recognized the colors. Not colors found in the foliage, not around here. It was the turnoff. Jerry's truck was making its way, and I could see its bright siding through the trunks of roadside trees. The timing was just too perfect.

"Hang on, kids." I whipped my car around, pulling a U-turn across the double yellow. I didn't know what was up with Jerry Gaffney, but he had the answers to some of the questions I'd been asking. I was going to get them from him now.

Randolph squawked at the first bump and cursed at the second. I had to slow almost immediately once I'd pulled into the cut out. It was a road, of sorts, but more pothole than pavement, and my GTO didn't have the suspension of the truck that had gone before me.

"Sorry, guys," I said to my animal passengers as the road narrowed. Jerry's truck had disappeared among the trees ahead, and I was beginning to doubt my decision. If this track was just a shortcut to a state road, I was wasting my time. Hell, even if I cornered the condo manager at his favorite fishing hole, I really had no way to force him to talk. I'd just been so sick of running around in circles. Now, maybe I was driving in one.

Between the clouds and the shadow, I should have turned my lights on. I could barely see the road, and if anyone were coming my way, I'd be in trouble. I didn't, though. Call it part of my second sense. And when the track opened out to a clearing, I stopped worrying about a collision and congratulated myself instead on managing to arrive unannounced.

It was a worksite, at least that was my first guess, and I remembered my earlier thoughts that perhaps Evergreen Hills had been intended as only the first of several condo developments. The trees had been felled and the brush cleared in an area big enough for another building or two the size of those at Evergreen Hills. For a moment, I flashed back to the condo. This area didn't have the view, but a good landscaper could remedy that, taking down some more trees to let in the sun and put in some gardens, maybe a fish pond.

The money must have run out awhile ago, though. The ground was still bare and beaten down, but the cutting looked old, dry and dead. The only sign of construction were a couple of sheds, the kind of corrugated metal ones that crews use to store tools. The door to one was open. Parked next to it was Jerry's truck and another small pickup, beat-up blue and muddy. Neither Jerry nor the owner of the other truck could be seen.

I parked by the edge of the clearing and got out. As an afterthought, almost, I let Buster out, too. Having a large dog by one's side is never bad for a discussion. She was quiet, which I found reassuring, and seemed to be taking in the surroundings, sniffing the air, those large ears alert.

"Come on," I murmured, as much for my own benefit as for hers. Together we walked toward the shed.

"Hello?" I called out. I didn't know what Jerry Gaffney got up to in his private time. Outside of Evergreen Hills and its connection to the animals in my care, I really didn't want to. "Anyone there?"

I didn't think they'd heard me, and I moved a few steps closer. In the middle of the clearing, a ray of sun broke through, but the shed was in shadow, its open door a gaping hole. Then suddenly a man was in it. Jerry's cousin, Joey, carrying a crate of some kind, his arms crossed around it protectively.

"Hey, Joey." I nodded. Buster picked up on my cues and stood at the alert.

Jerry appeared next, emerging from the shed to step in front of his cousin, as if shielding him. "Pru, what are you doing here?"

"I saw your truck." I decided to play it straight. "I had some questions."

"Yeah?" He crossed his arms. Meanwhile, behind him, his cousin lugged the box over to Jerry's truck. "You finish up," Jerry called back to his cousin, as he set the box in the truck bed. "I'll deal with this."

"So, is this official Evergreen Hills business?" I nodded toward the truck. "Does the board know about this?" I was fishing. I had some ideas, but barely enough to chum the waters. "Is this the payoff for torching the condos?"

Jerry laughed. I'd guessed wrong. "Get out of here, Pru. I wouldn't want you to get hurt."

I stood my ground. "You know me, Jerry. I don't scare easy, and I'm always up for something interesting."

He smiled at that. "Not anymore, Pru. You've changed. And this isn't fun. This is business." As he spoke, his cousin emerged with another carton. It must have been heavy, because Joey had to prop it on the edge of the truck bed for a moment before shoving it in. It was only there for a moment, but it was long enough for me to see a label on the box. A logo, in cream and brown.

"That's from LiveWell." I said it before I could think. I'd thought this had to do with Evergreen Hills, with the condos.

"You shouldn't have seen that." Jerry's voice was low, but threatening. He nodded to his cousin and they both started to walk in different directions. They were going to circle me, I saw. Separate me from my car. I took a step backward, trying to judge the distance. Wondering if it were already too late.

"Buster," I said, pulling slightly at her harness. "Now would be a good time to start acting like a guard dog." She remained silent, but as I stepped back, she took a few steps with me, both of us acutely aware of the two men now flanking us. And then of a different noise: tires on gravel. Another car was approaching.

I'm not the damsel in distress type, but as I turned around I felt a flood of relief rushing through me. Now was the perfect time for Creighton—even a pissed-off Creighton—to have tracked me down. Only it wasn't. The vehicle that pulled into the clearing, next to mine wasn't his dull dark cruiser. It was flashier. Bigger. An oversize SUV in menacing black with chrome bumpers as high as my head and wheels to match. I registered the MD plate as the door opened, and George Wachtell stepped out.

"Well, well, well," he said, smiling. He had changed his medical whites for a sports coat, his raw silk tie looking particularly out of place in this rough setting. "If it isn't the officious Pru Marlowe." The effect was creepy, like a comic-book villain. "Lost in the woods."

Whatever comeback I could have mustered didn't have a chance. It was Buster who responded, barking like mad. *"Help! Help! Help!"* Her bark rang out, loud enough in the clearing. *"Help! Help!"* I doubted it would reach beyond the trees, though, Wouldn't summon—

My own stupidity hit me. *"Help! Help! Help!"* This wasn't a call for aid; it was how Buster knew the doctor. People called for him in that way—they called for help, and the doctor was there. It might even be what some had called out, as he came too near. "Wachtell" would mean nothing to a dog. "Help," however, meant "doctor." I didn't have time to muse on my ability to misinterpret. I needed to get out of here.

"Good to see you, too. Doctor." I stepped toward him, and also toward my own car, and saw him nod to Jerry. "I should've known."

The over-prescribed painkillers. The flood of illicit drugs— newer and more powerful. More valuable on the black market. An investment that was underwater.

"You were keeping Evergreen Hills afloat by selling drugs." I said. "Drugs you prescribed, including that pricey new synthetic. Only you were ordering more than you gave out and you still didn't have enough. So you stole from your patients at LiveWell. They were helpless. Nobody ever believed them."

Except Genie. She'd told me the doctor was a bad guy. I'd put it up to his racism, the power he lorded over her. The raccoon had told me: *"Don't trust."* Particularly don't trust those in authority. Frank had confirmed it: *"He's right,"* the little ferret had said, picking up the raccoon's warning. Even Buster, when my bitten hand had held her down, had added her voice. *"He's right,"* she had said to me. Trust the wild thing, she had meant. That raccoon had better instincts than I had.

"Do your colleagues here know about the real victims?" I looked at the cousins. "That you killed an old lady, and tried to kill another?"

"Shut up." That was it—the phrasing, the intonation in two short words—just as I'd heard Randolph repeat so often. The good doctor wasn't always so polite. But while I was processing this, thinking about how he must have told old Polly off when she complained, when she caught him raiding her stash, he was moving on.

"Jerry?" Wachtell had turned to his colleagues, and Jerry started to walk toward me again. But a barking dog is a wonderful companion, sometimes, and if Jerry was too stupid to be afraid, Joey wasn't. The younger Gaffney held back, and I saw my opening. I raced to the car, diving in on the passenger side. As Buster dove in behind me, I started the engine. Jerry was at the car door by then, grabbing at the handle, reaching for the keys, when Buster grabbed his hand in her powerful jaw.

"Shit!" Jerry jumped back, and Buster let go. I slammed the door, manhandled my car into gear, and took off—backward—down the trail.

"Gaffney!" I heard Wachtell over the sounds of tires and stones. He must be used to obedience. My last sight of Jerry, however, was of him holding his wrist tight against his body, and Joey backing away. Then the road turned and I had to watch it, peering around Randolph's cage behind me as I weaved around potholes as fast as I dared, trying to remember if there would be any place to turn around. How far it was back to the highway.

Clunk! Under the trees it was too dark to see, and I'd hit something—a rock, a log. I kept going. *Thunk!* That one shook the frame. This wasn't like the other day, with a smooth road that let my baby ride. This was a trail, unpaved and deep in shadows. And Wachtell wasn't like Creighton. Whatever else I might think of Beauville's finest, he'd play by the rules. And then a sudden flood of light hit me, highlighting every tree, and I glanced behind me. The doctor's SUV was barreling down on me, eating up the rough road without a pause.

I turned back to the road. I needed to concentrate. Those lights were doing me a favor, allowing me to accelerate around the biggest holes. It didn't matter. He was gaining. I didn't want to think of how high that silver bumper was. How his SUV outweighed my car.

"She must have been drunk." I could hear him now. *"She'd been acting erratic. She had no reason to go off-road in that old car of hers."*

I put it from my mind. I hit a rock, and Randolph squawked. Buster had started barking again and in a moment, I knew why. A jolt—too big to be a rock—knocked me back. Another. The lights were getting brighter. Blinding. I could hear Wachtell revving his engine, preparing to ram me again. Something smacked the hood—another stone—ricocheted off a tree. Or, no, gunshot? A bang, as loud as an explosion, and the car jolted, nearly out of control. I gripped the wheel, as desperate as any wild thing ever caught in a trap. I hit the gas.

Chapter Fifty

If there were any tourists on the highway, we'd all have been dead. My bumper hit the pavement with a bang, and we bounced high enough to set Randolph squawking. But the suspension and the tires held up, and once we were off the dirt, I could feel my baby digging in. We squealed backward, nearly skidding as I turned us wide, across both lanes. Then, without looking behind me, I jerked into gear and we tore down the road—away from the turnoff and that crazy doctor. I knew I left rubber behind, but on the open road that SUV was no match for my GTO and after a few minutes I even started breathing again.

"Everyone okay?" I reached over, to feel Buster panting beside me. She'd dug her claws in to stay on the seat. I knew the upholstery would show the marks. I didn't care. "Randolph?"

"Bastard! Hand's off! Mine! Mine! Mine!" A little fluttering, but I figured that was good. The parrot was okay. "What are you doing? Stop that! Hand's off!"

"I got it, Randolph." I was still driving, fast, but I had the breath to think now. To talk. "Wachtell killed Polly. Tried to kill Rose, too, though I don't know why—"

I stopped. I did know. I should have. Wallis had told me. She'd said Randolph had felt guilty, or at least, that's what I'd heard. How often had she told me—had I told myself—that animals don't experience emotions as we did? Randolph hadn't felt guilt, per se. He'd felt *responsible*. Maybe with reason. In

Rose's empty apartment, I had asked Buster and Randolph what had happened. They'd done their best to tell me. Randolph had gone into his routine, mimicking Polly's protests. Saying, as he'd said so often in my presence: "That's mine! Hands off!" Parrots learn best by repetition, and I wondered if this had happened more than once. After all, who would believe an old lady if she accused her doctor? And if the old lady had been increasingly sedated, maybe she wouldn't even have remembered what had happened. What she'd said.

But Randolph had. And Randolph had taken up the responsibility of calling out the thief. And Randolph had then seen what had happened—at least in part because he kept repeating the damning words. Maybe that was what switched him to his quiet mode, saying "hello" and "pretty bird" like it was all he knew.

I thought about that one, as I drove, about what had happened to Rose. The road was clear behind me, no headlights in sight. I knew what Wachtell was capable of, however. I could guess what had happened to Rose. Randolph had tried to tell her, but then Wachtell had come in. Then it was all "hello" and "pretty bird" again. At least until Jane had shown up: Jane, who should have known better. Afterward, when I had asked, the parrot had returned to the innocuous words, but they had come to mean something more. "Hello" and "pretty bird" were Randall's way of saying Wachtell, just as "help" had been Buster's.

Buster had been doing her best to tell me, too—and to help Randolph. I still didn't know what had happened to Randolph back in Polly's apartment, but I could bet. Easy enough to sicken a bird: a spray of cleaning solution. A ground-up pill in his water. Or maybe it had been coincidence: stress or the dust raised by Jane's cleaning. Either way, I bet it had given Wachtell the idea that he could try again, once Randolph was alone in Rose's apartment.

◇◇◇

What he hadn't known—what he hadn't counted on—was Buster being there with the parrot. Her continued barking had not only been her way of trying to communicate—what

I heard as *"Help! Help!"* was really her way of saying *"Doctor! It's the doctor!"*—it had kept Wachtell from offing the parrot. It had also resulted in the frenzied call for Buster to be taken out of there. I was suddenly very glad Genie had called me, and that I'd been there to take her. Glad as well that I'd returned on Sunday. Wachtell might not have been on duty, but I'd bet he'd have found a reason to stop by Rose's room. To stop Randolph. I didn't trust that doctor, no way.

I'd have a hard time proving any of this. Officially, Wachtell hadn't been there. Nancy, clearly, had been under orders to say he wasn't on duty. But I already knew how the doctor lurked around LiveWell. What had he said? He hadn't wanted the residents to think he made housecalls. That was a good story, for Nancy and for any nosy civilians. The residents, though, they learned he had very different reasons for covering his tracks. Some of them even survived.

Rose had known. I'd let other concerns take priority. Rose, though, she had the time to think about this. She was mourning her friend, and she knew something about Polly and how LiveWell was run. And so when Randolph had replayed Polly's death scene, Rose had understood.

Had she confronted Wachtell? That seemed unlikely; the old woman was too smart for that. But he'd heard. He'd probably eavesdropped on the pair. And he'd begun drugging her too. He'd probably overdosed her, that night, and I'd have been willing to bet that the rumors of her depression came from him, as well. I remembered his words, his smirk. His self-righteous attitude, as I drove through the lengthening shadows. "Patients confide in me," he'd said. Yeah, right.

Chapter Fifty-one

After about a half hour of driving all over town, I was pretty sure nobody was following me. For all that it was still light out, I felt myself nodding. It was time to get off the road. My long day yesterday, the excitement today: all of it had drained me and the adrenaline was wearing off.

I wasn't sure how to explain any of this. I wasn't sure if I could. All I knew was that I needed to get home, to spend some time with Wallis, and to keep these animals safe. About ten miles out of town, I swung my last crazy U and headed home.

When I turned into my drive and saw that big black SUV, I panicked. Wachtell—Wallis. The doctor must have found out where I lived. I left the engine running and tore up the drive. "Wallis!" I called. If that bastard had come to my house…If he'd hurt my cat…

"Relax, Pru." Creighton stepped out from the shadows and grabbed me, nearly spinning me around. "It's okay. Everything's okay."

"Wallis." I pushed against him. "Wachtell."

"I know. He's a bad egg." Creighton held me. "But we have him. It's okay. It's all okay now."

Gently, his hands on my shoulders, he turned me. There, off in the bushes, I saw Creighton's car. Beside it, a cruiser. And leaning on the cruiser, legs spread, was Wachtell. A uniform was patting him down, big hands moving roughly over those expensive clothes. As I watched, he kicked one of the doctor's fancy loafers, spreading his legs farther apart. Wachtell grunted as he fell against the hood. From the bruise on his cheek, I didn't think it was the first time. Stupid fool, so self important. He must have resisted, and I was glad.

The wave of satisfaction receded as I remembered why he was here, and Creighton couldn't hold me then. I tore away and raced to my front door. Somehow the keys didn't work and I kept dropping them. It was Creighton, finally, who took them from my hand. He opened the door and stepped back, and I fell on my knees to embrace the tabby who waited there.

"*Took you long enough,*" she said, the purr already starting. "*And I gather you've brought a dog?*"

◇◇◇

With Wallis' consent, I brought both Buster and Randolph up to my old bedroom, and closed them in. Buster had been quiet, acknowledging my tabby's turf, and she had watched from the top of the banister, tail twitching and alert. I left her there, on guard, and went downstairs to get the rest of the story from Creighton.

"So you knew it was Wachtell?" I looked at him, his words sinking in. "Behind the drugs?"

"Believe it or not, Pru, I do know my job," he said, a hint of a smile on his face. "We've been tracking the money. He set up a shell company, and it took us until today to find out who was behind it. But we did, and it's Wachtell. We thought so, from the nature of the drugs, but we weren't sure until today—until I could look at the records at LiveWell, at what he'd ordered and prescribed. It explains a lot. There's been cash poured in, and then this morning, when someone tried to torch the place. It all fits."

"There's a shed, you know." The memory almost hurt. "Two sheds, in a clearing off the highway."

He nodded. "You said. You may have to point it out on a map. The staties are being very difficult about their helicopter."

I nodded. I'd given him the details. For me, it was all fading into a blur. After the shock of seeing him here, seeing the cruiser, the last jolt of my adrenaline had been used up. I was wired. Tense. Exhausted, but as I lay against him on the sofa, his warmth was beginning to relax me. "I didn't expect you here. It's been a while."

"I've been busy." He took my hand, looked at it. "You've been, too."

I nodded. The bandage was half off and filthy. I'd not had the energy to change it. "This is why I was at the ER, actually. I need to start a series of rabies shots."

He looked alarmed. "Should I run you back now?"

"No." I smiled. "It can wait. It can all wait until morning."

Chapter Fifty-two

The shot wasn't as bad as I remembered, or maybe it was simply that so much else had happened that I was too tired to fight it much. Either way, it had gotten done without too much fuss. That is, unless you count being driven to the hospital with a police escort fuss.

"You didn't need to do this, Jim." I'd protested over coffee.

"I have a vested interest in you staying alive," he'd replied.

"*Huh.*" Wallis, who joined us at breakfast, had snorted. "*A bird, a dog, and now him, too?*"

"Wallis..." I'd forgotten. Creighton looked at me, looked at the cat.

"I'm going to get dressed, and then we're going to the hospital."

I nodded, my eyes still on my tabby.

"*Well,* that *was smart,*" she said, licking her chops. I'd given her a can, to show Creighton that she was "just a pet." She didn't appreciate it.

"*No, it was all right. For a change.*" She sat to wash. "*It's you I'm worried about.*"

"Me?" I kept my voice low, although I had a feeling that Creighton was giving us time.

"*You.*" She ran her white paw over her ear. "*You're getting quite...domesticated.*"

"Ha." I was too tired to make more than a halfhearted objection. "You wish."

The look she gave me as she left the room said volumes, I was sure. Only this time, I couldn't interpret them all.

"You ready?" Creighton was waiting for me when I got out of the doctor's office.

"Yeah," I said. "It hurt." I was rubbing my arm, just to stress the point. "And I've got to come back for three more." At least my hand, neatly bandaged once again, was healing. Odds were, I wasn't going to die anytime soon. At least not from this series of mishaps.

"Good." He led the way. "Maybe that will keep you out of trouble."

"Hey, I solved a murder for you." I'd laid out my theory about Polly the night before. It didn't sound quite as good without all the extras from Buster and Wallis. He'd nodded, though. The drugs were the ones he'd prescribed to Polly and to Rose, powerful new synthetic opiates—worth their weight on the black market. It was circumstantial, but it made sense. "Maybe an attempted murder, too."

"And we're looking into it." He glanced at me as he unlocked the cruiser. "But, Pru, we would have had this guy without you getting involved. Had him and his ring of troublemakers, too." He meant the Gaffneys.

He started driving, staring straight ahead. "I won't have you getting hurt, Pru."

"Come on." I raised my hand as if this was what he was talking about. "This is what I do."

He didn't say anything after that, just drove me home. When he came back later, though, he brought pizza. I took that as an apology. I even let him stay the night again. This time, Wallis refrained from comment.

Chapter Fifty-three

Buster remained with us until Rose was released a week later. I like to think it helped the old lady's recovery to know the dog was in good hands. Besides, it was good for me to work with Buster. I'd finally cornered Doc Sharpe, and he'd admitted to—in his words—"feeling his age." He needed help, more than Pammy could deliver, and we were talking about me taking some shifts, finishing up my degree. Training service dogs is a specialty, and not one I'd ever planned on. I was never one to look a gift horse—or dog—in the mouth, though, and knowing that I might soon become more employable seemed to relax Doc Sharpe a bit.

It certainly amused Wallis. What Buster thought was harder to tell. With me, she was all business. When I brought her back to Rose, though, it took all her service dog training not to leap on her mistress and lick her face again, as she had in the hospital. Rose did look great. "It's the rehab," she said to me. "Those young hunks really made me work my ass off."

I laughed. The fact that she was no longer being drugged probably helped, but the glance Genie gave me, over the old woman's head, reassured me that Rose was in good hands.

Randolph stayed with us a little longer. Jane had been shocked—almost overwhelmed, she'd told me—by the news that an investigation was being opened into her mother's death. But she'd been aware enough to parlay that shock into additional time with her mother's apartment—at no extra cost.

I wasn't as foolish—or as culpable. I told her I could keep her mother's beloved pet for a while longer, at my regular rate. I stressed that last bit, and she made some noises. I let her. In truth, he wasn't any bother, and I had stopped worrying after the first time I found Wallis in his bedroom.

"We've come to terms," my tabby had told me, when I'd opened the door to find her on the dresser, staring at the big bird. *"He's seen quite a lot, you know."*

"Really?" Wallis didn't respond to that, so I looked to the parrot. He'd stopped pulling out his feathers by them, and his plumage was filling in, gray and smooth.

"Ignorant slut!" Randolph replied. *"Took you long enough."* My double take sent him squawking, in an uncanny facsimile of Rose's cawing laugh. Even Wallis seemed to smile, her whiskers going wide and flat. Shaking my head, I left them there. To talk. I know when I've been outwitted.

I was beginning to wonder if this would be a permanent situation when Jane called back.

"I don't know how Marc got dragged into all of this, I really don't." I'd heard he'd been subpoenaed. I hadn't heard he'd been charged. "This is another blow to the family." Jane sounded breathless.

"Uh huh." I didn't believe it. I remembered them arguing. I knew she'd come out ahead.

"So much of the money is gone." She was leading up to something. "He's had to take some awful job, and he'll be paying restitution for years out of his paycheck, though I don't know why…"

I geared up for a fight. I'd done the family a service, and I was getting paid.

"Anyway," she seemed to be winding up. "Because they're such a good deal now, I *am* buying one of those condos, now that they're all fixed up again. Thank goodness, Mother left me some money that he couldn't touch."

"Ah." I didn't see her point, but I grabbed a pen and started tallying my bill.

"So, once I move, I'll be able to take Randolph back."

"He still curses sometimes, you know." I didn't know why I was telling her that. "You don't have to."

"Mother would want us together." She sounded firm. "But I trust you'll give me a discount."

◇◇◇

By November, Wallis and I were alone again. Once I was back to my old self, Creighton had enough sense to give me space when I needed it—and company when it suited. Despite what Wallis had said, I wasn't going to push for more. I liked my freedom, even if it meant quiet evenings by the fire, with my bourbon and a book.

"You're getting old. You know that?" It was snowing out, the first snow of the year. Wallis' eyes glittered in the firelight. Her fur looked glossy and sleek. *"You miss that parrot."*

"You should talk." I'd put the book aside ages ago. The play of flames was enough. "You made friends with him."

"He'd seen some things." Wallis shrugged and settled down into her Sphinx pose. *"Death. Murder."*

"That interests you?" I turned toward her, saw the fire reflected in her eyes. A miniature tiger in my house.

"Oh, please, Pru." She shuffled again slightly, getting comfortable. *"Like you're any different."*

I couldn't argue, and just then the fire sparked, cracking a log. Neither of us jumped, not after this much time. Instead, we sat and watched the flames together, feeling the room grow warm.

"It's the hunt." I felt the words, rather than heard them. *"Neither of us ready to give up the hunt."*

"You may be right," I said, and she purred.

Acknowledgments

Writing is always an adventure, but this book more so than usual: birds are new to me, and I found them as enticing as Wallis does. Several folks helped me out, but thanks most to Michelle Jaeger, who first turned me on to the work Dr. Irene Pepperberg did with Alex the parrot. I stretched some facts for plot purposes, but I hope I stayed true to what is known about these amazing birds. As always, any outright mistakes are mine alone. Randolph may have some superficial resemblance to the African gray at Ritual Arts in Allston, Massachusetts, but his behavioral problems are entirely his own. The usual crew helped me through the writing and revision process: Chris Mesarch, Brett Milano, Lisa Susser, Karen Schlosberg, Naomi Yang, and Jon Garelick, while—as always—my fellow writers Caroline Leavitt and Vicki Constantine Croke, cheered me on. Thanks as well to editor Annette Rogers for letting Pru be Pru (and Wallis be Wallis) and to agent Colleen Mohyde of the Doe Coover Agency for her faith. Love to Sophie Garelick, Frank Garelick, and Lisa Jones. And, always, to Jon, for helping me realize my dreams. Purrs out, sweetie.

To receive a free catalog of Poisoned Pen Press titles, please contact us in one of the following ways:

Phone: 1-800-421-3976
Facsimile: 1-480-949-1707
Email: info@poisonedpenpress.com
Website: www.poisonedpenpress.com

Poisoned Pen Press
6962 E. First Ave. Ste 103
Scottsdale, AZ 85251